The Vagabond Healer

James R. Olson

Erian Press
Pittsburg, TX

The Vagabond Healer

Previously published by Publish America
under ISBN: 978-1-4241-6938-0

ISBN: 978-0-9800716-8-9 (pbk)

Printed in the United States of America

Dedicated to Frances, Eric, Andy,
and everyone who believes, or wants to believe in angels,
the beauty of friendship, and the magic of love

One

Memory is a capricious thing. There are periods of my life I can barely recall and others that are crystal clear. I vividly remember the evening John Hampton and I got caught stealing watermelons from Old Man Jacob's field. Yet try as I might I can't recall anything else from that long ago day. Of course that could be old age, but I suspect it's a deception of mind.

Some days are sharply focused in their entirety, as if they happened only yesterday. After all these years I still remember every detail from my wedding day, including how nervous I was. Every moment of the day we learned Mary had terminal cancer will be embedded in my heart forever.

That's where memory becomes tricky. I had believed the really important moments of life are the ones I would remember in the greatest detail. But it just doesn't work that way. The mind seems to pick and chose and we never know for certain which days will remain and which will fade. I remember very little about the day we learned Albert had been killed in Vietnam—only the pain, which has never lessened.

Before the vagaries of old age begin to cloud the memories I feel compelled to tell Eddy's story as it actually happened.

Of course, I didn't know it at the time, but Thursday, April twenty-fourth, was going to be one of those special days the mind treasured and kept forever. A mixture of sadness and joy still touches the memory. If I were able to go back in time I doubt whether I would want to change a single moment of those magical events. Perhaps the joy and sorrow were meant to be just as they happened.

At the time a lot of people read about the happenings in the newspapers because there had been a great deal of sensational coverage. However, very few people ever heard the entire story. But I know all the details and still remember every moment of those weeks that Spring.

* * *

It was unseasonably warm, one of those rare days we look forward to all winter, with thoughts turning toward a fishing pole and napping beside some meandering stream. By mid-afternoon the temperature had passed seventy degrees and the sun warmed right through my shirt and into my bones. In our part of the country, we generally don't enjoy such pleasant temperatures until late May or early June.

Thursday is the slowest day of the week, so after the brief morning commuter rush I occupied myself with mundane chores. I opened both service bays to allow the warm, fresh air to penetrate into the cold dank corners. The temperature change sweated the concrete floors until they looked as if it had rained.

I swept the service area, but the moisture had muddied the soil so the broom marks caused the floor to appear dirtier than before. I debated whether I should mop the area or wash it down with the hose, but decided I didn't have enough energy. Suffering from a case of spring fever, I was willing to let chores slide for the rest of the day. I hauled a folding chair outside and sat in the sun, enjoying my laziness, half wishing no one would stop for gas.

The plastic sign above the pumps, reflecting the bright sun, looked shabby from an accumulation of winter debris. A streak of mud caused the word service, in 'Johnson's Premium Service'', to look like SER   ICE. Without any real interest I wondered how a blob of mud had gotten up there. I made a mental note to clean it next week, when I was feeling more ambitious.

From where I was sitting, I could look east down the road, toward the Cranston city limits sign and the expressway that lay out of sight beyond the curve and over the hill. The State had constructed the freeway two years earlier, bypassing Cranston by three miles, making old Highway 16 obsolete. Consequently there was no longer much transient traffic through town. Before the expressway I had been so busy I had to hire help to keep up with the customers, but no more. Now I got a few hunters and fishermen who were passing through because of the woods and lakes in the area. Periodically tourists were drawn off the freeway by the State erected signs proclaiming fuel and food. But mostly business was limited to local folks, and there weren't many of them.

Cranston had never been much of a town, but I had lived here all my life, and had no desire to reside elsewhere. We had to drive to the county seat in Elliott for shopping and doctors and such, and with the expressway bypassing us, Cranston wasn't likely to attract additional businesses or people. But the residents were friendly and I enjoyed the slow paced life. I had outgrown the expectation of making a million dollars and retiring to some tropical island. As long as I could pay my bills and put away a few dollars for my old age I felt satisfied

Before Albert had gone to Vietnam, I had considered purchasing the abandoned property across the road and expanding with a motel and restaurant. The idea of Johnson and Son, Inc. had always given me a warm, fuzzy feeling. That dream had died with Albert, long before the State bypassed Cranston. Now any new enterprise would be an exercise in futility.

Along about three o'clock I was getting drowsy, so I walked around a bit to stretch my legs and get the blood flowing. About a mile east I noticed a man walking toward Cranston along the old highway. I watched him for a few minutes, wondering if he'd had car trouble. I didn't offer a wrecker service, but if the man needed help, I could phone Bud Lawler in Elliott, who provided a towing service out this way.

As he came closer I could see he was a young man wearing a backpack, striding along with the gait of a practiced walker. A medium sized, longhaired, brown and white dog ranged back and forth along the ditch, nose to the ground, never lagging far from the youngster. After a moment's consideration, I decided the man was probably a hitchhiker who walked more than he rode. Most folks wouldn't offer a ride to a man with a dog.

I resumed my seat by the office door and waited. I have to admit I was a bit curious why he was hiking down old Highway 16. The three mile walk from the expressway was a long detour unless he was headed toward the camping areas north of town. Since my station was the only business in the area I figured he'd stop to use the rest room and I could satisfy my curiosity.

The young fellow paused beside the premium pump, looking somewhat lost and travel worn. Not dirty or ragged, just tired, like he hadn't gotten a ride for quite a few miles.

"Afternoon. Beautiful day, isn't it?" He slipped off a tattered baseball cap and wiped his forehead on the sleeve of his shirt. The dog sat at the heel position, head cocked in my direction.

"Howdy," I answered, being friendly although he obviously wasn't a customer.

Now that he was closer, I decided he was older than he'd appeared from a distance. More a young man than a boy. Maybe in his early twenties. He was wearing faded jeans, dusty from travel, but not grubby like most hikers. His shirt was a lumberjack plaid flannel; sweat damp where the pack straps pulled back against his shoulders.

He smiled and there was something about the way it lit up his eyes that made me like him right away. He didn't have a remarkable face. Straight nose, wide set eyes, a generous mouth, and a heavy tan from being outdoors a lot, but nothing anyone would call handsome. His light brown hair was long, like he'd been a while between haircuts, but not down to his shoulders and scraggly like some hippie. It was neatly combed and looked clean.

"Don't mean to bother you, but I was wondering if you might have some drinking water for my dog?" he asked.

The dog was obviously a mongrel, sort of a collie and shepherd mix, tending to look more like a collie. The young man hadn't given any signals or commands, but the dog remained patiently sitting at the heel position, a long, pink tongue hanging from the side of his mouth as he panted in the heat. Obviously the dog was well cared for and well trained. He showed wear and tear from travel, but the long coat glistened from frequent brushing.

"I believe I can arrange some water," I said. "Why don't you both step in out of the sun and rest a bit?"

A couple of years earlier I had kept a night watch dog in the station to discourage vandals, but that was pretentious in Cranston. We never had a large enough population to have vandals and the dog proved to be more trouble than he was worth. Certainly he hadn't been as well trained or well behaved as this fellow's animal. After I'd sold the watchdog, I'd kept the water bowl and food dish for no reason I could remember except that I'm a bit of a pack rat and hate to throw out any thing that might be useful some day.

I scrounged around under the workbench until I found the bowl behind some old oil filters. I wiped it with a rag and rinsed it off with the hose before filling it and setting it on the ground just inside the bay.

The dog had followed the hiker into the service bay and stood at his side eyeing the bowl of water. He licked his lips and looked at his master, then back at the water, then back at the youngster.

"It's alright, Mica," the fellow said. "You can have a drink."

The dog gave a soft woof, trotted over to the dish, his tail going a mile a minute, and lit into that water like he hadn't had any liquid for a long time.

"Mind if I help myself to a drink from that hose?" the fellow asked.

"Sure." I handed over the hose, careful not to splash him. He held it so he could take a long drink, sort of like going sideways at a water fountain.

"Thank you, sir," he said. "Hiking in the sun is thirsty work. Can I fill my canteen?"

"Help yourself."

He refilled the water dish for the dog, filled the old style military canteen he carried on his hip, and turned off the hose before handing it back.

"Just passing through?" I asked, feeling curious. "Looks like you've come a fair piece."

"Yeah, we didn't get any rides today." He said it like hiking more than hitching was standard procedure.

"Where are you headed?" I asked. "There isn't much in the direction you're walking."

He shrugged. "No place special. Mica and I are just following the yellow brick road, seeing as much of the country as we can."

That surprised me. He didn't look or act like a bum, but a hitchhiker without a destination was the modern equivalent of a hobo riding the rails.

"Is there any place in town a fellow might work for a meal and a can of dog food?" he asked.

"What kind of work you looking for?" Cranston wasn't a town with many job opportunities.

He shrugged and gave a shy smile. "I've done a lot of different things. I'm willing to do most anything that isn't illegal or immoral."

"Ever done any auto work?" I don't know what possessed me to inquire because my place was the only garage in Cranston, and there wasn't enough business to keep me busy. Almost before the words were out of my mouth, I regretted having asked. But there was something about the way the fellow smiled and the shine in his eyes that compelled me to want to help him.

"I've done minor repairs and pumped gas a few times. I like working with my hands."

He waited patiently while I studied him, trying to make up my mind. I did have Bill Hendley's car in the first bay. Although I'm a pretty good mechanic, I sure as hell hadn't been able to get it running smoothly. More than likely this youngster wouldn't do any better than I had, but it wouldn't hurt to let him give it a try. His hands didn't have the ground in grease look of someone who worked around engines, but he could at least clean the plugs and change the oil.

"Where are you planning to sleep tonight?" I asked, wondering why I cared. Maybe the youngster aroused my parental instincts. "There isn't a hotel or motel anywhere around here."

He smiled a lopsided grin. "I sure don't have enough money for a hotel. Besides, most places don't allow pets. Mica and I usually sleep in the open if it isn't raining."

"Well, tell you what. If you can get that Ford running properly, I'll stake you to a meal and a bed for the night. I've got a spare room at my place, and we do allow pets." I was certain my wife, Mary, would approve of my offer. We didn't have many visitors any more, and if Mary felt strong enough, she would appreciate someone new to talk with.

"My name's Johnson, Sam Johnson." I held out my hand and noticed he hesitated for a moment, like he was reluctant. His grip was firm, but not hard. A tingle went through me as our hands touched, and for no reason I could determine, I suddenly felt warm and happy inside. I can't explain the sensation because it wasn't like anything I'd ever experienced. With a simple handshake there was a sense of bonding, as if we'd looked into each other's hearts and liked what we had seen. I felt happy and at peace, but confused at the same time.

"Thank you Mr. Johnson," he said, smiling like he'd sensed the same phenomenon. "My name's Eddy and this is Mica." At the sound of his name the dog waged his tail and gave a canine grin.

"Call me Sam. Don't much like Mr. Johnson." The bell rang signaling a car at the pumps. It was a welcome interruption because I needed a few minutes to settle my thoughts.

"You go ahead and look at that Ford while I take care of the customer," I said. "Tools are in the cabinet along the back wall." He was taking off his knapsack and rolling up his sleeves when I stepped out of the bay. The dog had chosen a place near the workbench, lying down, head on paws, his eyes never leaving Eddy.

The customer was Sid Jessup with his old Buick, and it took longer than normal to service the car. He wanted a fill, better than fifteen gallons at my slow pumps, and then his oil needed a quart to top off. Sid was the local gossip and sensed a tidbit, because I obviously had a new helper. He kept looking past me at Eddy, and when I didn't volunteer information, his curiosity got the better of him.

"Busy enough to take on a mechanic?" he asked. "Don't believe I've seen that young man around here before"

"He's just a hiker passing through. I'm staking him to a meal for a little work." It always went against my grain to tell Sid anything because I knew he was going to stop at Sal's Diner and spread tales to anyone who would listen. My hiring Eddy for room and board wasn't a secret, but it also wasn't anyone else's business. Once Sid told his story, in a small place like Cranston where nothing ever happened, the gossip would be all over town before supper.

When I finally punched up Sid's sale and stepped back in the service bay I couldn't believe my ears. Bill Hendley's old Ford was purring like a kitten.

"How the hell did you get that old engine running so smooth?" I asked.

"I just made a few adjustments," Eddy said, sounding defensive.

"Damnit, I've been trying to get that car to run properly for two days and couldn't get it to do more than cough and sputter. Now it sounds like a new engine. What the hell did you do?"

Eddy shrugged. "I don't know. I've always been good with my hands."

"Good! Hell, Eddy, I'd say you're more than good. I'd say you've got magic in those hands."

Eddy smiled his shy smile but didn't say anything. I figured he was a natural born mechanic, one of those rare people gifted with the touch. I didn't realize how close I was to the truth, but I was going to find out about his gift before the week was over.

Two

After repairing Hendley's car, Eddy kept busy cleaning up around the service area. I'm not very well organized, and the service bays had a major accumulation of empty filter boxes, dirty rags, and tools left wherever I set them. He even took the hose and washed off the sign so that it sparkled in the sun. If I had some glass cleaner he probably would have washed all the station's windows.

I sat in the office, pretending to do neglected paperwork, and watched Eddy as he looked for things to do. He seemed like a happy youngster, humming and softly singing snatches of song. He may have had the touch as a mechanic, but he couldn't carry a tune any better than me.

Mica managed to keep from under foot without any commands, remaining at Eddy's side wherever his master went. I don't believe I ever saw a dog so evidently devoted. It gave me a good feeling just watching the two moving around the service bays. I always figured you could tell a lot about a man by the way he treated his dog.

When the late afternoon commuter rush began he stepped right in and helped. There aren't many stations left that pump gas, check the oil and clean windshields. I suspect that little bit of extra free service kept my few customers coming back.

Around quarter to six, I told Eddy to wash up while I counted the day's receipts. It had been an average day, so there wasn't enough cash on hand to worry about taking the money to the bank in Elliott, a trip I only made once a week unless I was unusually busy.

Before the expressway, I had slaved at the station fifteen hours a day, seven days a week. The virtual elimination of transient traffic had enabled me to reduce my workload.

Cranston had become a bedroom community with most of the residents commuting to jobs in Elliott or surrounding towns. In addition to my service station, there was Bennett's Hardware, Sal's Diner, the Cranston Co-op, the Northern Star Bar, and the Winston Lumber Yard. Total job opportunities maybe numbered twenty. We didn't even have a school, so the kids bussed the fifteen miles into Elliott.

Consequently I opened the station at six-thirty Monday through Saturday to service the commuters heading out of town, and stayed open until six or six-thirty Monday through Friday to catch the same folks returning home. Saturdays I remained open until one or two in the afternoon, so I could handle oil changes and minor repairs. I didn't even bother opening on Sundays. It still amounted to around sixty-five hours a week, but from mid-morning to mid-afternoon during most weekdays it was slow enough for me to run errands or go home for lunch.

By the time I finished my meager bookwork, Eddy had closed and locked the service bays. He waited at the pumps while I turned off the lights.

"Well, are you ready to get something in your belly?" I asked, locking the office and checking to make certain the overhead doors were properly bolted.

"Yes, sir," he said in his soft voice. "I am getting a little hungry."

"Doesn't surprise me. When did you last have something to eat?"

"We had some day old bakery this morning," he said scratching Mica's ears.

"Then the sooner we eat, the better." I could tell there was something else on his mind. "Is anything wrong?" I asked.

He hesitated, pushing the toe of his boot around in the oil next to the pump, like he didn't know quite how to phrase his answer. "Mica and I always sleep together and I don't think he'd understand if I slept inside and him outside."

"I don't recall saying the dog had to sleep outside. Mica is housebroken, isn't he?"

"Yes, sir"

"Then I don't see any reason Mica can't stay in the house. I'm sure Mary won't mind."

"Mary?"

"My wife." I patted Eddy on the shoulder, again experiencing the warm, happy feeling. "Now that we've settled the sleeping arrangements, hop in my truck and we'll see about putting something warm under our belts."

I lived less than a mile from the station, on Oak Street, a two-block gravel road. When we pulled into the long driveway, I was grateful for the early sunset, so Eddy couldn't see the small, two story frame building. During the last year I hadn't taken my usual pride in keeping up the place. The house needed a coat of paint and general repairs. My half-acre yard was littered with fall and winter debris, and the gravel driveway was developing potholes.

I parked in the driveway outside the detached garage. While Eddy and I walked toward the screened in back porch, Mica did a quick survey of the back yard, raising his leg against the old apple tree.

"Have a seat while I check on Mary," I said, pointing at the kitchen table. "Want a beer while you're waiting?"

"No, thank you." Eddy sat at the table, and Mica dropped to the floor at his feet. I could see he was curious, but I didn't offer to explain why Mary wasn't in the kitchen to greet us. He would learn the whole story soon enough and I didn't see any point in bringing it up.

"Okay. I'll only be a minute. Then I'll fix us something to eat."

I felt a deep sadness every evening when I saw Mary. In my mind she was still the vibrant woman who had shared so many years with me. It was always a shock to see her as she had become. The sickness had turned her skin a pasty, grayish white, making even her lips pale slashes. The only color was the bright blue eyes that seemed larger than normal in her gaunt face. The cancer had eaten her flesh and strength until she weighed maybe eighty pounds. Although she never complained, pain lines radiating around those exquisite eyes were evidence of her constant suffering. Even in her wasted condition I thought she was the most beautiful woman I'd ever known.

Mary was dying and we both knew it, but we never mentioned it aloud. I suspect Mary kept her fears to herself because she wanted to spare me her suffering. I remained silent because even the thought of losing her ripped at my heart.

Doctor Calvin had suggested radiation and chemotherapy, but he admitted the treatments were not going to cure Mary, only delay the inevitable. It had been Mary's decision not to suffer the side effects of therapy without the possibility of even a meaningful remission. I would have grasped at any treatment, no matter how tenuous the hope but I understood Mary's choice and couldn't deny her anything. It had also been her wish to finish life at home rather than in a cold sterile hospital.

The county helped with the expense of having a visiting nurse come to the house daily to monitor the pain medications and attend to Mary's other needs.

Alma Smith, a neighbor, and Mary's lifelong friend, volunteered to stay with Mary every morning, arriving just before I left for work. The nurse, Connie Childress, showed up at noon to relieve Alma, and stayed with Mary until I got home

Because Mary could no longer negotiate the stairs to the second floor, I had fixed a bed in our unused dining room. I'd installed an extension phone so I could call during the day, and there was a TV at the foot of the bed with a remote control on the nightstand. When I stepped in the room, Connie was sitting in the bedside chair, her purse and medical bag ready in her lap. She was a plain woman with a constant smile and a take charge attitude.

"Hi, Connie," I said. "How's our patient doing today?"

"We had a good day, Sam," she said. "We watched our favorite soap operas all afternoon, and Mary ate a decent lunch. She's napping now. Sorry to run, but my son has a teacher's conference and I simply have to attend this one. After missing the last two, the school is starting to think I'm a lousy parent. See you tomorrow. I'll let myself out."

"Good night, Connie. And thanks."

I could hear Connie talking briefly with Eddy on her way out, but the voices were soft enough I don't believe Mary heard them.

"Is that you, Sam?" Mary's voice was weak, barely louder than a whisper.

"How are you feeling?" I asked, leaning over and kissing her on the forehead. "You look as beautiful as ever."

"I feel somewhat better today," she said. It was her daily little white lie. We both knew Mary wasn't ever going to feel better.

"Are you hungry enough for a bite of supper?" I asked. Mary had little appetite, and when she did eat solid food, she couldn't keep it down.

She smiled and my heart squeezed into a painful lump. Seeing Mary suffer was worse than if I had the cancer. Mary was the only woman I'd ever loved. Many nights I cried myself to sleep. Some of the tears were because of the unfairness of what was happening to her, but most of them were for my own selfish pain. I didn't know how I would survive when she died. God, I loved that woman.

"I'm not hungry right now, Sam. Maybe a little later."

"I've got company for supper," I said. Generally I prepared some Campbell soup for Mary and something more substantial for myself. Then we ate together in the makeshift bedroom and I talked about my day and the people I'd met and anything else that came to mind. If she felt strong enough, Mary would tell me about TV shows and what she and Alma and Connie had discussed. Having company meant we wouldn't share our evening.

"Oh, Sam, you don't know how happy that makes me." Mary smiled and offered her frail hand. She was always pushing for me to do something with my life besides sitting at home. "You don't have company often enough. Who is it?"

"A young fella stopped at the station today looking to work for a meal. Would you believe he fixed Bill Hendley's car—the one I've been having such a hard time getting to run right? I brought him home for supper and told him he could spend the night. I didn't think you'd mind if he used Albert's room. He doesn't have anywhere else to stay.'

"Of course I don't mind." She squeezed my hand, her grip so weak I barely felt the pressure. "You must be starving. Why don't you and your friend have supper while I take a nap? When you're finished eating please bring the young man in so I can meet him."

I kissed her on the forehead and patted her hand. "I'll bring some soup. Shouldn't be too long."

Her smile was tired. "Take your time. I'll have a good nap knowing you have someone to talk with."

When I got back to the kitchen, Eddy had found the left over meatloaf in the refrigerator and was heating it in the microwave.

"Hope you don't mind, Sam. I thought I could fix something while you visited with your wife."

"No, I don't mind." And surprisingly, I didn't. Usually I'd have been a bit peeved with Eddy making himself at home, but it seemed like the youngster belonged in my kitchen. "Mary's taking a nap right now." I grabbed a beer from the refrigerator. "Sure you don't want one?"

"No, sir, I don't drink."

I sat at the table and nursed the beer while Eddy dug out some lettuce and tomato and put together a salad. He was a guest and I should have felt guilty letting him do all the work, but I didn't have the ambition to do it myself.

"Is Mrs. Johnson very sick?" he asked, his tone indicating he really cared.

Usually I didn't talk about Mary's illness because it hurt too damn much. But there was something about Eddy that made me want to empty the pain from my heart. "Yeah, she's very sick. The doctor thinks she might have a couple of months, but she could go at any time." I could feel the tears filling my eyes, so I turned away and began setting the table.

"Maybe the Doctor's wrong," he suggested.

"Every night I pray he's wrong." I took a slug of the beer, waiting for the lump to dissolve in my throat. "I'm not sure there's a God to answer those prayers."

"God is listening to your prayers and He loves her as much as you do." He said it as a fact, with no room for argument. Somehow the sentiment didn't sound strange or pretentious coming from Eddy.

"Maybe," I agreed without conviction.

"Do you have any children?" he asked.

"We had a son, Albert, but he came back from Vietnam in a box. Now there's just Mary and me. Pretty soon it'll just be me. Makes everything seem pointless, doesn't it?"

Eddy reached across the table and laid his hand on mine. The warm feeling seemed to flow through me and the pain suddenly felt more tolerable than it had in a long time.

"Life is never pointless, although we don't always understand why we have to suffer." Eddy sounded like he knew about suffering. Young people usually don't understand pain.

"You're probably right. It's just that sometimes I wonder why this is all happening to us."

"Lots of people don't have as much as you. A man who loves his sick wife like you do, and can share his supper with a stranger has something special."

I snapped out of my self pity. "Sorry, Eddy. I didn't mean to bend your ear. You earned a meal, not a load of my troubles. I don't know why I'm talking so much today."

Eddy shrugged. "A man can sometimes ease the burden by sharing the load."

The timer beeped on the microwave and Eddy jumped up to get the meatloaf. We ate in silence.

"Do you have any dog food, Sam? Or can I give Mica some meatloaf?"

Mica was such a quiet, well behaved dog I'd forgotten about him lying patiently at Eddy's feet. "Sorry I don't have any dog food. Give him the rest of the meatloaf and anything else you can find in the refrigerator. I have to go shopping tomorrow night anyway."

I got another beer while Eddy gave Mica the remaining meatloaf. Then he gathered up the dishes and opened a can of soup. "I'll warm up some Campbell's for your wife."

"Thank you. I don't know what's gotten into me. I just don't have any energy today. Must be the warm weather."

"Maybe you're just tired," Eddy ignored the dishes stacked in the sink and found a clean soup bowl in the cupboard. "Do you mind if I go with you? I'd be honored to meet your wife."

"She'd like that." Mary had been sick too long and missed talking with someone besides Alma, Connie and me. We seldom got visitors anymore. I suspect folks just felt uncomfortable visiting a dying person. I know I'm always at a loss for words around a sick bed.

I went into the room first, carrying the soup, to make certain Mary was awake. "Hi, I brought your supper and a surprise. I'd like to introduce our guest. Mary, this is Eddy."

Eddy stepped up to the bed, took Mary's hand into both of his and lightly stroked the back of her hand. "I'm pleased to meet you, Mrs. Johnson. You're so pretty and fresh looking, it's hard to believe you're feeling poorly." Eddy's smile brightened the room.

Mary looked startled, as if she felt the same warm, happy sensation Eddy had caused in me. I was delighted to see a warm glow color her cheeks and would have sworn Mary blushed. For a moment she looked like the young girl I'd married more than forty years ago.

"Please call me Mary." It sounded as if her voice were stronger. "Sam told me that you helped him at the station today."

"Yes, ma'am. He was kind enough to let me work for my supper and night's lodging."

"I'm so happy you came home with him. Sam doesn't get enough company and it'll be nice for him to have someone to talk with."

Eddy had been a bundle of energy all day, and I was surprised to see a sudden weariness in his face. Where Mary had perked up at his touch, he appeared exhausted. I wondered whether he was coming down with something.

"If you don't mind, I'm feeling a little tired myself," Eddy said. "It's been a long day. I'll let Mica out and then go to bed. I know you and Sam have things to discuss."

"Mica?" Mary asked, sounding confused.

"I forgot to mention Eddy has a dog," I quickly interrupted. "He'll be staying with Eddy. He's a good dog and won't make any noise."

"Why Sam, you know I love dogs. Of course he won't be a bother." She turned her head slightly toward Eddy. "Could I see Mica, please?"

"Sure." Eddy snapped his fingers softly and Mica padded into the room as if he'd been waiting just outside the door.

Without any sort of direction the dog went directly to Mary, sat beside the bed and laid his head on the covers next to her. He gave a little woof and his tail thumped rhythmically on the floor.

Mary moved her hand so she could ruffle the ears. Most days she didn't have the energy for even that much activity, but she did seem to be feeling stronger. "Why, he's a beautiful dog."

"Yes, ma'am, and he seems to like you. Mica doesn't take quickly to most people. He must sense you're a beautiful person."

"Hi, Mica." The dog sighed as Mary stroked his head.

"If you don't mind, I'll take Mica out now." He snapped his fingers again and the dog instantly retreated from the room. "It was a pleasure meeting you, Mary. I'll see you in the morning."

"He seems like a pleasant young man," Mary said when Eddy left. "I'm glad you brought him home." She looked at the bowl of soup I'd set on the nightstand. "You know, I'm feeling a little hungry now."

I fluffed the pillows and helped her sit up. Mary's strength was gone, and normally I had to feed her, pleading with her to take more than a few sips. It was a welcome surprise when she picked up the spoon and began feeding herself. The effects of the cancer were unpredictable, but it had been weeks since she'd had enough strength and energy to do for herself. I knew better than to have false hopes, yet I couldn't help but feel optimistic.

Mary finished the entire bowl of soup, like she really had been hungry and settled back into the pillows with a satisfied sigh.

"Thank you, Sam," she said. "That was good. But I'm tired now. You visit with Eddy while I take a nap."

I took the bowl and kissed her. "I love you, Mary Johnson."

"I know," she said. "And I love you more than I can say."

I left the night light on as I took the empty bowl to the kitchen.

Eddy was sitting at the table, looking like he could barely keep his eyes open. I realized I had forgotten to show him where he was supposed to sleep, so I led the way upstairs.

It had been several years since I'd been able to set foot in Albert's room. When Mary had been stronger, she had kept fresh linens on the bed and maintained the room pretty much as it had been when Albert had left for boot camp. I guess I'd never completely adjusted to the loss of my only son, and a sense of pain and emptiness haunted me whenever I entered his bedroom. The thought crossed my mind that if Albert's ghost still haunted me after all these years, how many ghosts would I have to deal with when Mary was gone?

I quickly pointed out the bathroom, left Eddy to settle for the night and returned to the kitchen. I considered washing the accumulation of dishes, but just didn't have the ambition. It hadn't been a particularly busy day, but I felt exceptionally tired, in a pleasant way. It had been one of those rare, feel good days. Nothing had changed. Although she had seemed stronger this evening, Mary was still dying and I was still facing a bleak future. Yet, for some reason I didn't understand, I felt happier and more content than I had since Mary had taken sick.

Three

It seemed my head had barely hit the pillow when soft music filtered into my dream, gently pulling me awake. It was pitch black in the room and I was momentarily disorientated until my sleep-drugged mind recognized the summons of the clock radio. I rolled over and read the clock's digital display—five past five. Although that was the time I was supposed to awaken, for a moment my laziness kindled feelings of guilt, as if I had been unfaithful in some way. During the weeks since Mary had come home from the hospital, I had never slept straight through an entire night. Usually I dozed on the edge of consciousness, alert for any sounds indicating she needed me. At first I had camped on the couch in the living room so I'd be close during the night, but Mary had insisted I needed to sleep in a bed for proper rest. I had agreed because with the door open to our upstairs bedroom, I could still hear if Mary stirred or called out.

After switching off the radio, I became aware of someone moving quietly in the kitchen, and remembered Eddy had stayed with us. Usually I woke to a dead silence and the sounds of another human were comforting.

I showered, shaved, and made the bed before going downstairs to see whether Mary had spent a restful night. The smell of freshly perked coffee was heavy in the air as I descended into the kitchen. I was feeling warm and happy and refreshed, but almost stumbled down the last step when I saw Mary, wearing a flowered housecoat, standing at the counter softly humming to herself, whipping eggs in a large mixing bowl.

I must have looked like an idiot, standing there with my mouth open. My knees suddenly came unhinged and I leaned against the wall to keep from falling. Mary was very thin and moved slowly, but there was fresh color in her cheeks. For a moment I thought I was still in bed, having one of those dreams where you know you're dreaming.

Mary smiled as if being in the kitchen was perfectly normal. "Good morning, Sam. Coffee is ready. The scrambled eggs will be done in a minute." Her voice was cheerful and strong, like before the illness.

"Well, don't just stand there with your mouth open," she said in a tone of mock anger. "If you don't get a move on you'll be late for work."

This time her voice jolted me out of the shock and I was across the kitchen in two steps. My arms went protectively around her and I nearly knocked the bowl of eggs off the counter. "Mary, you shouldn't be up. You know the doctor said you need total rest."

"Now, Sam, stop making such a fuss. I feel just fine this morning. You sit down and have your coffee while I fix the eggs." There was a sparkle in her eyes as she gently pushed me away. She had the happy look of someone enjoying a secret. "And mind your manners, Samuel Johnson. We do have company, you know."

I'd been so startled I hadn't noticed Eddy sitting at the table buttering toast smiling like a kid at Christmas. Mica was lying on the floor next to Eddy's chair, his tail sweeping the linoleum as he gave me a canine grin. It was as if all three were sharing the same secret and enjoying my confusion.

I collapsed onto a chair, too stunned to say anything. Eddy poured coffee and pushed the mug toward me. Mary scooped eggs from the frying pan and carried the serving platter to the table. She put a large portion on each of our plates, sat, and began eating.

"Is something wrong with the eggs, Sam?" she asked, her eyes sparkling with a mischievous glint. "You aren't eating."

"I've gotta be dreaming," I said, shaking my head. "This can't be happening." Yesterday Mary had tried a soft boiled egg and couldn't keep it down. Now she was eating scrambled eggs. "You did all this? You got up and fixed breakfast?"

"Well, Eddy made the coffee and toast. I was going to fry up some sausage, but we don't have any. In fact, the pantry is pretty bare. We're going to have to go grocery shopping today."

"But…"

"I know it's hard to believe, Sam." Mary took pity on me, reaching across the table and gripping my hand tenderly. "I don't understand it either. Maybe it's the miracle we've been praying for."

Suddenly I found myself kneeling on the floor, my arms wrapped around her, my face pressed against her bosom. I was crying. Her hands stroked the back of my head.

"There, there, don't cry," she said, like she was comforting a child. "Just because we don't understand is no reason for tears. I slept all night. Didn't wake up once. This morning there was no pain, none at all. I'm weak, but otherwise I feel wonderful, like I did before the cancer."

I lifted my head and looked into her eyes. There was no pain there, just the sparkle of life I had always loved. "God, Mary, I'm stunned. No, I'm happy." I kissed her. Not with passion, but with joy and love.

Mary laughed. A sound I hadn't heard in a long time. "Now Sam, you behave yourself. Remember our company. And you have to eat something before you go to work."

"Work! How the hell can I think about work?" I stood up and began pacing the kitchen. "First, we're going to go to the Doctor and see what this is all about."

"But you have to take care of your customers."

"To hell with the customers. They'll survive."

"I can watch the station for you," Eddy said, like it was the most natural thing in the world.

"I don't know," I said. "I can't think." Work. The station. My customers. None of it seemed important.

"Don't think," Eddy said. "Give me the keys and I'll walk to the station and open up. You can come over after you've taken Mary to the Doctor."

A gentle rapping on the back door interrupted this unbelievable morning. Alma Smith stepped in without waiting for an answer. She froze at the threshold, as astonished as I had been.

"My God, Mary, what are you doing out of bed?"

"I'm eating breakfast," Mary said, giggling like a little girl.

Never in my life had I expected to see Alma Smith speechless, but at that moment she stood in the doorway her mouth open, not making a sound. No one except Alma and I really understood how close to death Mary had been, and now Alma was as shocked as I had been to see the glow of health in her cheeks and the sparkle of life in her eyes.

Suddenly the two friends were embracing and crying together.

"But how?" Alma stammered. She was familiar with cancer and remissions, but this was totally different from anything that had happened before. "I don't understand."

"It's the miracle we've been praying for," Mary said.

As I watched the two women hugging and crying, I felt confused and happy and jealous. Alma had been Mary's only constant and faithful friend during the long ordeal, and she deserved the moment of joy, but I wished she hadn't come this morning. I wasn't ready to share Mary's miracle with anyone.

Eddy put his hand on my shoulder and I instantly felt calmer, and in control.

"Sam, why don't you drive me to the station and show me how to turn everything on?" he suggested.

"Sure, you're right." I didn't know what to do. I wanted to stay with Mary, but I really needed to show Eddy the opening procedures. "What about Mary? I can't just leave her."

Eddy smiled. "Mary will be fine until you get back. Mrs. Smith will be here."

I gave Mary a lingering hug and kiss before Eddy prodded me out the door.

I didn't know anything about Eddy and I wasn't the world's most trusting person, but I felt comfortable turning over the cash box and keys. He could have ripped me off for everything I owned, but I trusted him without knowing why. I have to admit I wasn't thinking very clearly at that moment. Compared with Mary's miracle, I couldn't convince myself any of this was important.

In a daze, I managed to show Eddy where everything was. I got the lights and pumps going, and hurried home, expecting to find Mary back in bed, exhausted. She was still in the kitchen, washing the accumulated dishes while Alma dried them.

"Isn't it wonderful, Sam?" Alma said. "I still can't believe Mary is so much better." Her eyes were red from crying, but she was glowing with excitement.

"I'm beginning to believe in miracles," I said, wrapping my arms around Mary, feeling tears in my own eyes. "All I need now is for Doc Calvin to confirm it."

Mary allowed me to hold her for a moment, retuning my hug, before she pushed me away. "Now, you just behave yourself, Samuel Johnson. I have to take a shower and comb my hair before we can go to Elliott."

"You must be exhausted," Alma said. "Do you want me to help you get ready?"

"I feel fine," Mary said. "It's about time I started doing things for myself."

"I'll give you a call this afternoon." I could tell Alma was reluctant to leave, but she hung the dishtowel on the rack and headed for the door. "I'm so happy for you." She began crying again as she hurriedly left.

"Sam you can make yourself useful while I'm getting dressed," Mary said when Alma was gone. "Call Connie and tell her we don't need her today. Then phone the clinic and let them know we're coming."

When Mary slowly climbed the stairs, I flopped on a kitchen chair unable to believe this entire morning wasn't some sort of cruel dream. Alma and I had both been confused and excited and happy, but Mary was serene, like she knew something we didn't. It wasn't until I heard Mary turn off the upstairs shower that I was able to move.

There was no point calling the clinic because it wouldn't be open yet. I figured we'd go without an appointment. I did reach Connie Childress' answering machine and left a message saying I was taking Mary to Elliott and Connie wouldn't need to come over today.

"I'm either going to have to buy some new clothes or gain a lot of weight," Mary said when she came back into the kitchen wearing a light blue dress that was obviously too large for her. I can't remember Mary ever showering and combing her hair so quickly, but I suspect she was just as anxious as I was to hear what Doc Calvin had to say.

During the drive to Elliott, Mary chatted about the warmth of the sun and the color of the fields and the smell of fresh air. It had been weeks since she had been outdoors. I only spoke occasionally, delighting in the sound of her voice, unwilling to interrupt. It was wonderful listening to her, but in the pit of my stomach I dreaded what we would learn at the Clinic. This recovery—this remission—had to be a fluke. The mass of cancer couldn't simply disappear. I felt grateful for even these few moments, but was already preparing myself for the bursting bubble.

The clinic was open when we arrived, but Doc Calvin hadn't begun office hours and there were no patients in the waiting room. The receptionist smiled at us until I told her we wanted to see Doctor Calvin and didn't have an appointment.

"Doctor Calvin has a full schedule this morning," she explained, turning the pages of the appointment book. "There's an opening next Friday at three."

"This is an emergency," I said. "We have to see Doc Calvin right away."

"I'm sorry. There aren't any openings this morning. If it's an emergency, perhaps you should try the emergency room at the hospital."

Mary had always been able to read me like a book and knew I was about to lose my temper. She laid a restraining hand on my arm, but I was in no mood to be calm. Our visit was too important to be delayed by bureaucratic rules.

"If you don't tell Doctor Calvin we're here, I'm going to go back to his office and tell him personally."

Other patients were beginning to arrive and I think the receptionist was afraid I would cause a scene. "That won't be necessary," she said. "If you'll have a seat, I'll tell Doctor you're here. I'm sure he'll work you in."

"Thank you," Mary said, taking my arm and pulling me over to the waiting room chairs.

John Calvin was a young man, about thirty-five, but he had been treating Mary from the beginning, and she trusted him. Although he and I hadn't always agreed, I knew he was a good physician. He had wanted Mary to stay in the hospital and undergo radiation and chemotherapy, but when his arguments hadn't swayed Mary, he had relented and acceded to her wishes. I believe Doctor Calvin realized it didn't matter where Mary died, and if she would be happier at home, he understood. He knew the treatments and hospital stay would not cure her.

We waited nearly an hour on the hard plastic waiting room chairs. I held Mary's hand, sensing she felt tired, afraid the exhaustion wasn't from the unaccustomed activity, but because the cancer was again claiming its own.

When Doc Calvin arrived, several patients with appointments had checked in and were thumbing through old magazines. Doc was apparently surprised to learn we were in the waiting room, because Mary was the first patient he summoned. Maybe he figured it would be bad publicity to have her die in the lobby.

I stood and was prepared to go with Mary, but she shook her head. "You wait here and behave yourself." She smiled. "Don't worry. Everything is going to be all right." She had that confident smile like she knew something I didn't.

I remained in the waiting room, but wasn't happy just sitting. First I tried to read an old magazine, but couldn't concentrate. Then I paced back and forth to the drinking fountain several times and twice used the restroom. I was probably making the patients nervous, but I didn't care.

After an hour long eternity the nurse called, and I followed her into Doc Calvin's office. It was a pleasant room, shelves crammed with medical books along one wall, a dozen framed certificates and diplomas on another, and a pleasantly cluttered desk. However I felt uncomfortable in the Naugahyde chair because this was the room where Doc Calvin had told me Mary was dying.

When he entered a few minutes later, he went directly to the desk chair and flopped down. "I wanted to talk with you while Mary's getting dressed," he said. He looked as stunned and confused as I felt.

"Well, Doc, what's the word?" I asked when he didn't continue. "How is Mary?"

"We're going to have to do some tests before we know for sure." Doc rubbed his eyes like he felt tired.

"I understand that," I snapped, not even trying to keep the impatience from my voice. "But what did you find? Why is Mary suddenly feeling better?"

"I won't know without the test results." Doc attempted to sound professionally detached. He didn't even come close. "I can't find anything wrong with Mary. It's like she was never sick."

"But Doc, that's impossible."

"Damnit, don't you think I know it's impossible?" He shook his head, looked at his hands, then out the window, then back at his hands. "I don't understand what happened."

"There's got to be an explanation. A person dying from cancer doesn't suddenly get better for no reason."

"It could be a remission. That happens sometimes. A person gets better for a while and appears perfectly healthy. But Mary's cancer was too far advanced." He shook his head like he didn't believe his explanation. "I won't know until the tests are back, but I don't think Mary is in remission. I think the cancer is gone."

"Gone?" Contradictory emotions overwhelmed me. I had prayed he would tell me Mary was on the road to recovery, that this wasn't another remission. However the rational part of my mind kept telling me it was impossible for the cancer to simply disappear. "How can it be gone?"

"I don't know." He finally straightened up and looked me in the eyes for the first time. "God, Sam, we go to school and get so damned smart we begin to think we know everything. But we don't even begin to scratch the surface. Sometimes patients get better and we never know why. We do all those things that are so goddamn clever and hotshot scientific. But they don't do any good because when you come right down to it, we don't really know how to heal people. We give them medicine and say positive things, but in the back of our minds we know we aren't really curing them. When they get better it's because their bodies did the job and we just helped a little." He rubbed his eyes again. "It's impossible. I've never heard of anything like this, but I think Mary is cured. Why? I don't know. I sure as hell didn't do it. There's no sense fighting what I can't explain. Just put it down to magic, or a miracle. That's as good an explanation as any."

I'm usually a pretty tough guy, but I began crying right there in the Doctor's office. They weren't sad tears. Just tears of joy and confusion. I had expected Doc Calvin to tell me I had been dreaming, but instead he was telling me my prayers had been answered.

"I haven't ever seen anything like this," Doc said, as if talking to himself. His eyes weren't focused on anything in particular. "I've read about cases, spontaneous cures and miraculous healings at Fatima and Lourdes. But I always believed they were hysterical cures of people who suffered from psychosomatic illnesses. Now I don't know. I just don't know." Doc turned to me like he suddenly remembered I was there. "I should get the test results back tomorrow morning. I want you to bring Mary in so I can examine her again. The tests will have to tell us something definite." He mumbled his last words so quietly I barely heard them. "At least I hope so."

Mary came out of the examination rooms smiling like she'd known all along there was nothing to worry about. I wrapped my arms around her, holding her tightly until she gently pushed me away.

"Samuel Johnson, mind your manners."

I reluctantly released my hug, but held firmly to her arm. "Thanks, Doc," I said.

"I'll see you tomorrow morning," he replied, still looking shaken and confused.

"The test results won't show anything," Mary said quietly as I led her from the room, leaving Doc Calvin staring out the window.

I stopped at the desk and made an appointment for Saturday morning, then walked hand in hand with Mary to the parking lot.

I was eager to get home because I felt exhausted, like I'd run a marathon. However, Mary insisted that since we were already in Elliott we should stop at the supermarket. I was too emotionally drained to protest.

She took her time, examining every aisle, enjoying the mundane mechanics of shopping. I pushed the ever-filling cart; glad I'd brought my checkbook. However, when she began stacking cans of dog food in the cart, I decided it was time to intervene.

"That's a lot of food for one dog," I suggested.

"Mica has to have a balanced diet. Leftovers aren't healthy for a big dog like that."

"But that's way too much food. I don't think Eddy will be around long enough for Mica to eat even half of that."

"Oh, I think Eddy will be staying for a while." The mysterious gleam was back in her eyes.

"Come on, Mary, be realistic. Eddy's a drifter. I'll bet he never stays in one place longer than a few days."

"Trust me, Sam, Eddy will be in Cranston a long time."

I really liked Eddy, but whether or not he stayed around wasn't a major concern at the moment. On this day of miracles, I had no intention of arguing with Mary over a few dollars worth of dog food.

During the drive back to Cranston, I still felt confused, but happy about Mary's health. There was a nagging demand for caution in the back of my mind. Her condition could be some freak twist of the cancer. Even though I wanted to, I couldn't believe unconditionally in the miracle of a cure. This all still seemed like a dream, and I was afraid to talk about it because I expected to awaken at any moment.

"Isn't it wonderful," Mary said when we were about halfway home. Apparently she was confident the cancer was gone and had no reluctance to discuss the cure. "I was so worried about you. First we had lost Albert and soon I would be gone. I knew the loneliness would tear you apart. But now we have our whole life ahead of us."

"Don't set your expectations too high, Mary. Doc Calvin said we wouldn't know for sure until the tests came back."

"It's alright, Sam." There was certainty in her voice. "I know the cancer is gone for good."

"God knows I want it to be true, that our prayers have answered, that God has given us a miracle." I was crying again, the tears running unheeded down my cheeks. "I'm frightened. I was reconciled before, but now I'm afraid to hope again."

"Don't be afraid, Sam. It really is a miracle, and God did answer our prayers. I know how the cancer was destroyed."

"What are you talking about? I'm not sure I'm following you."

"It was Eddy." Mary had that mischievous gleam in her eyes, like she was finally sharing her secret.

"Eddy? What about Eddy?"

"He cured me."

"But Eddy's a hitchhiker, an auto mechanic. How the hell could he make the cancer disappear?"

"I don't know how he healed me. I just know he did. Last night when he came into the room and took my hand I felt a warm, happy feeling going through my entire body and suddenly, for the first time in months, the pain vanished. It was like his touch drew the sickness right out of me. I woke up this morning feeling wonderful, knowing I was strong enough to get out of bed. When I went into the kitchen, Eddy was already up. He said, 'Good morning, Mrs. Johnson', as if he expected me to be up and around. I could see it in his eyes."

"It's crazy. I don't understand any of this. He couldn't have done anything." I was beset by contradictory thoughts. There's nothing I wanted more than to believe Mary had been permanently cured. Maybe I was willing to believe in a miracle, but I just wasn't able to believe Eddy was the source of the miracle. I remembered the warm, happy sensation, the instant bonding, I'd felt when Eddy touched me, but it wasn't reasonable to believe he could heal anyone. "Eddy's just a youngster."

"How old does an angel have to be?" Mary asked. "I don't understand either, but I know Eddy touched me, and I was cured. God sent him in answer to our prayers."

Everything was happening too rapidly for me. I didn't understand, and was afraid if I didn't understand, it wouldn't be true. Miracles happened in the Bible, not in Cranston, on Oak Street.

Four

Although it was a beautiful day, I figured Mary must have been exhausted from the unaccustomed activity, so I took the most direct route home from Elliott. We exited the expressway onto old Highway 16 and drove past my service station. I hadn't even thought about business until I saw Eddy bent over the fender of an unfamiliar car, checking the oil. I felt guilty about driving past without stopping, but I was still disoriented and didn't feel like dealing with customers. I soothed my conscience by deciding I could help Mary unload the groceries, make some sandwiches and take Eddy something to eat.

By the time I had carried eight bags of groceries into the house and Mary had stowed everything in its assigned place, Alma Smith popped in. I figured she must have been watching for us to get home, and had rushed over immediately to satisfy her curiosity. Her questions began while she was still on the back porch. I could understand Alma's concern, but didn't appreciate company when I'd rather have been alone with my wife.

Alma never missed a morning of taking care of Mary during the entire illness. I suppose such a loyal friend had the right to ask questions, but my feelings toward Alma were ambiguous. I appreciated her friendship and support, but her constant chatter drove me crazy. When anyone else was talking, I always had the impression she was impatient to voice her own thoughts. There just wasn't a quiet time in her life. I imagine she talked in her sleep. The closest I ever came to seeing Alma speechless was this morning when she saw Mary out of bed. It didn't surprise me that her husband was the quietest man I'd ever met. He had probably given up trying to get a word in edgewise.

I only half listened to the two women until I heard Mary say, "I know I'm completely cured and I know how it happened."

Alma sat up straighter and I could almost see her getting ready to take mental notes, like she was about to hear the secret of the ages.

"Look you two," I interrupted. "I know you've both got a million things to talk about, and Mary says she's feeling fine, but I think she's had enough excitement for one day."

"Sam, I'm not tired," Mary protested. "I feel wonderful."

"No, Mary, Sam is right," Alma reluctantly agreed. "You need your rest, but before I go, you simply have to tell me what happened to cure you."

"God answered our prayers," I said quickly before Mary could comment. "Isn't that right, Mary?"

We had been married long enough Mary could practically read my mind, so I saw the question in her eyes. "Yes, God gave us the miracle we had been praying for," she agreed, giving me a questioning glance.

Alma was a loving woman, but she had obviously been hoping for something more concrete than prayer and miracles. It would have suited her gossip machine better if Mary had claimed a cure from eating peach pits or lima beans or some other exotic remedy.

"Of course, God cured you," Alma said, reaching over and condescendingly patting Mary's hand. She was obviously disappointed in our explanation. "You lie down now and rest. I'll stop by tomorrow and we can talk over a cup of coffee, just like old times."

"I don't have any intention of taking a nap, Samuel Johnson," Mary said as soon as Alma left. "I've slept more than enough the last couple of months. Why didn't you want me to tell Alma about Eddy?"

"Because it's crazy, that's why," I said. "Except for thinking you felt something when he touched you, there's no sensible reason to believe Eddy had anything to do with this. We haven't even talked to him yet, and when we do, he's going to laugh in our faces. Doc Calvin will get the tests back tomorrow and we'll know what really happened. There's got to be a rational, medical explanation, and there's no sense in telling folks about magic and miracles. Alma's a good friend, but you know as well as I do that she'll spread whatever you tell her all over town. I'll bet she's on the phone right now."

"I understand that you're having a hard time believing, but no matter what you think, I know what happened," Mary insisted, sounding peevish.

"Maybe you do and maybe you don't. But I think we should be careful about telling stories. Hell, first thing you know we'll have people making pilgrimages to Cranston just to see where the miracle happened. We don't need to complicate the situation anymore than it already is."

"All right, I'll keep my opinions to myself if you insist," Mary said. I could tell she was upset. "But I know what I know. When Eddy touched me I felt a warm sensation pass through me. I could sense Eddy's spirit entering my body and mind and cleaning it completely of sickness. It was the strangest and most wonderful feeling I've ever had."

I felt like a complete ass. My most fervent prayer had been answered, giving Mary back to me, warm and healthy, and here I was, on the first day of our new life, arguing with her. After all the pain and suffering she had endured, she was entitled to believe whatever she wanted to believe. I took her in my arms.

"Mary, I'm sorry. I didn't mean to sound gruff. It's just that I'm all mixed up inside. I'm so happy you're feeling better but I'm afraid it's just a freak thing and I'm going to lose you again."

"I know," Mary said, forgiving me for being an idiot like she always did. "We're both going to need time to get used to this. Miracles are hard to accept."

It hadn't been more than half an hour since Alma had left and the phone rang. Mary answered and from her end of the conversation I knew an acquaintance was verifying Mary's recovery. As soon as she hung up, the phone rang again. Mary took five or six calls before she was too emotionally drained to continue.

The phone didn't let up, so I began taking the calls. I talked with people I hadn't heard from in months. There were even a few whose names and voices I didn't recognize. The questions were all the same. Was it true Mary felt better? Was the cancer completely cured? How?

I could have taped my end of the conversations. "Thank you for your concern, but we don't know what happened. Mary is feeling much better, but we aren't sure if the cancer is cured. Doc Calvin made some tests and we won't know anything more until the results are back."

After fielding a dozen more calls, I didn't feel like talking to anyone else, so I unplugged the phone jack. I was startled to see it was nearly four-thirty.

"I hate to leave you by yourself," I told Mary. "But Eddy's been alone at the station all day and I think I should get over to help with the afternoon rush."

"That poor boy hasn't had anything to eat. It's certainly a miserable way of showing our gratitude. You take him a sandwich and I'll fix a nice dinner while you're gone."

Eddy had things under control when I got to the station, but cars were beginning to line up at the pumps. I went right to work while Eddy and Mica ate the food I'd brought for them.

Fortunately most of the customers had been working all day and hadn't learned about Mary's recovery. The few who had heard, and asked about it, got the spiel I had developed over the phone.

Between the volume of business and my being slowed by customer's questions, Eddy and I didn't have an opportunity to talk, so I never told him about Mary believing he was responsible for her cure. Even if there had been time, I doubt if I would have said anything. Watching Eddie work, he appeared as ordinary as any youngster, and the idea of him being a miracle worker seemed ridiculous. I couldn't picture a faith healer with a spot of grease on his nose and an oily rag in his back pocket.

It was past six when I totaled the day's receipts and turned off the station lights. Eddy, Mica and I drove home in silence, but I noticed Eddy studying me like he was curious about something.

When we parked the truck, Mica trotted ahead and watered the apple tree. He joined us before we got to the house, and we entered the kitchen together.

Mary was up, working at the counter, and greeted us cheerfully, as if everything were normal. "Well, the two workers are finally home. You both go and wash up. I've got a casserole in the oven. It'll be ready in five minutes."

Eddy went directly to the downstairs bathroom and I heard water running as he washed up. I put an arm around Mary's shoulders, kissed her on the cheek and took a deep breath. "Smells good."

"Of course it does. Now you scoot out of here and wash your hands." She turned to Mica who was sitting patiently beside the outside door. "And I've got a special treat for you."

Mary lifted a thawed steak from the counter top, set it on a plate, and placed it in front of Mica. "A whole steak just for you."

The dog sniffed the steak, then sat back, his tail wagging, tongue lolling from the corner of his mouth, grinning at Mary. "Don't tell me you're a vegetarian," she said, sounding puzzled.

Eddy walked into the kitchen, saw the situation, and snapped his fingers. "It's okay, Mica." The dog woofed and went to work on the steak.

Mary shook her head. "My goodness. I've never seen such a well trained dog." She turned to Eddy. "He won't eat anything unless you tell him it's okay, will he?" Without waiting for an answer, she turned to me. "Sam, now you hurry up and wash. The casserole is ready."

By the time I returned to the table, both she and Eddy were seated. I took my place and started dishing out noodles and hamburger in a savory sauce. After eating my own cooking for so long, it smelled fantastic and tasted even better. Mary had always been a fabulous cook.

Throughout the meal Mary was on an emotional high, carrying most of the conversation, asking Eddy how the day had gone and such. It seemed a bit odd that Eddy never asked about our trip to the Clinic, but I figured it was because Mary didn't give him an opportunity to interrupt.

We had stuffed ourselves and pushed back our chairs before I brought up the subject that had been hanging in the air all evening.

"Eddy, bear with me a minute before you start laughing," I said, trying to make light of the matter. "I know it sounds peculiar, but Mary believes you did something to cure the cancer."

I don't know what response I expected, but it certainly wasn't the reaction I got. Eddy sipped his milk, staring at the flower design on the sugar bowl, not saying anything.

"Well, did you have something to do with it, or didn't you?" I asked, some irritation in my voice.

Eddy sat quietly, like the question was too hard and he couldn't think of an answer.

Mary reached out and touched his hand. "I know you cured me, but Sam doesn't believe. Maybe if you told him he'd understand. We have a right to know."

"Sometimes it's better not to know" Eddy said, so softly I strained to hear.

"Please," Mary urged.

Eddy looked into her eyes for a moment, then nodded. "Yes," he said, making it sound like a sigh.

"Yes, what?" I demanded. "Yes, you cured her?"

This time Eddy merely nodded.

"I knew it," Mary said, sounding completely vindicated. "I told you so, Sam."

I wasn't satisfied. Years of hard living had made me a skeptic and I'd lost my faith in miracle workers. I didn't expect them to be distinguished by halos, but I didn't imagine they looked like twenty something hitchhikers. "Now wait a minute, I don't understand any of this. Would you mind explaining how the hell you cured Mary?"

"I don't know how it happens." Eddy sighed, like he was uncomfortable speaking about the cure. "You've both been good to Mica and me. I'm truly sorry to have brought this on your heads."

"Eddy, how can you talk like that?" Mary asked, shocked at his attitude. "You have a gift, a wonderful blessing."

"It's a curse!" It was the first time I'd ever heard him raise his voice. "Maybe if I left tonight it wouldn't bring trouble."

"What the hell are you talking about?" I felt totally confused. None of this made any sense.

"It's a long story," Eddy said, his voice calm again, but his tone clearly indicated he would rather not discuss the issue.

"Please tell us," Mary pleaded. "We wouldn't be very grateful if we insisted you do something you don't want to, but you've answered our prayers and we'd love to hear your story."

"Okay." Mica, hearing the resignation in Eddy's voice, laid his chin on Eddy's knee. The boy stroked the dog as he talked. "As far as I know I was born with this...this power in my hands. When I was a little kid, I'd find small, injured animals and nurse them back to health. You know, a bird with a broken wing, or a rabbit injured by a hunter. I touched them and held them, and they got better. I was too young to realize I was different."

"Your parents must have known," Mary suggested.

"I'm pretty certain my parents always knew I had the power, but they never mentioned it. I think they wanted to treat me like I was a normal boy. But as I got older, I began to understand I was different. No kid wants to be different, so I never told my friends or anyone I had this…this power."

"If your family were the only people who knew about your gift, I don't see why it's a problem," I said.

"The trouble came later," Eddy continued. "When I was in high school, one of my friends, Billy Wilda, got sick—with Hodgkin's Disease, I think. I visited him in the hospital, and although kids aren't big on that sort of thing, I held his hand. The next day Billy was okay. I mean there was no trace of the disease. It was the first time I had connected my power with curing a person. As far back as I could remember, no one in my family ever had any kind of sickness—not even a cold—but I'd never paid any attention. After all, who ever notices when people don't get sick?

"Anyway, the doctors said Billy's recovery was a miracle, because there was no medical explanation. But I knew, and Billy sensed what had really happened. He told his parents and some of his friends, but fortunately no one took him seriously.

"It probably wouldn't ever have been a problem, but I touched a neighbor's son who had leukemia, and he was cured. Once word spread I couldn't stop. I couldn't tell some people I would heal them, but not others. So there were several more instant cures. At first people thought it was wonderful, telling me how special I was. The newspaper interviewed me and did a big article with my picture on the front page. Doctors wanted to examine me to determine how I caused the cures. Once a priest came to investigate whether there was some sort of religious aspect to the miracles. My parents were proud and I was something of a hero."

"You are a hero," Mary said, gently touching his hand.

"I was only a celebrity for a little while. Pretty soon I noticed that when people looked at me, I wasn't little Eddy anymore but someone different, and for them different was scary. People smiled and said nice things, but there was fear in their eyes. It isn't pleasant for a teenager to realize adults are afraid of him."

"I'm so sorry," Mary said.

"It wasn't long before the kids at school began avoiding me. No one wanted to sit next to me in class, and everyone had excuses not to hang around with me after school. Girls I'd known all my life refused dates. It was bad enough that people avoided me, but it began affecting my family. My younger brother and sister suddenly had trouble keeping friends. My folks didn't get invited to parties their friends attended. My Dad was bypassed for a promotion he'd earned. Then someone slashed the tires on Dad's car, and some kids tossed a brick through our living room window. One morning we found a sign spray painted on the side of the house. 'We don't want Witches!' Suddenly we didn't have any friends. My brother, my sister, my Mom, my Dad. It was like the entire family had the plague."

Eddy paused so long I though he had finished. Before I could comment, he began again. "As a High School graduation present my folks sent me to New York to visit an uncle. A trip to the big city was a thrill for a small town kid, and I was looking forward to going where no one knew me. By this time I didn't have any close friends, so I don't suppose anyone realized I was gone.

"The night after I left home, someone poured gasoline around our house and tossed down a match. As soon as the fire started it was already too late for anyone to escape. My Mom, my Dad, my sister, and my brother all died in the fire meant for me. The police never discovered who was responsible, but I don't think they looked very hard.

"Relatives offered to take me in, but I couldn't stay in the town that had murdered my family. After the funeral I left for good. Now I travel wherever the road leads, never staying long any place. I've seen a lot of the country during the last five years."

"Oh, Eddy," Mary said, taking his hand, tears streaming down her cheeks. "I'm so very sorry about your family."

Eddy smiled at her. "Thank you. It was a long time ago." He looked at his hands like they were foreign objects attached to his arms.

"Why?" Mary finally asked. "You were doing such wonderful things. Why would people treat you so horribly?"

"They were afraid," Eddy said. "I could see it in their eyes. Maybe it wouldn't have been so bad if I only had the power to cure people, but when I touch them, for a moment I can see into their minds, into the deepest, darkest recesses of their souls. People can sense my ability to see into their hidden places, just like you knew I'd cured you."

"Are you saying you can read minds?" I asked, still skeptical.

Eddy shook his head. "No, it isn't really reading minds. It's hard to explain. I don't read thoughts. I just see hidden things in people's souls."

"It all sounds like magic to me. But I don't understand how it would cause a problem. Seeing people's secrets is a small enough price to pay for being cured."

"It isn't only sick people. It's everyone I touch. Nearly everyone has things locked in their hearts that they hide from the world. When they realize I've seen their secrets, it scares them because they're ashamed. They believe I'll reveal their secrets and everyone will know. When people are afraid of something they don't understand, and they don't know how to handle the fear, they strike out at whatever scares them."

"That's ridiculous," I said. "Mary and I aren't afraid."

"No," Eddy said. "No, you're not."

"And no one around here is going to be afraid," Mary said. "Those people in your home town were horrible. Most folks aren't like that."

"It's happened since then," Eddy said. "Everywhere I've been. That's why I keep moving. As soon as people find out about me, they're afraid. Most people are alone in their little worlds, barely touching other people. You and Sam have your love for each other. That's special and keeps the fear away. Most people don't have that. Neither one of you have any dark secrets or hidden shames."

"Are you saying there's been violence everywhere you've been?" I asked, not willing to accept an aggressive reaction to someone who possibly carried life in his hands.

"No, not always violence, but the fear was always there. I didn't have the courage to face the inevitable hostility, so I moved on."

"That's all behind you now, Eddy," Mary said. "You have a home here as long as you want it."

"Thank you, Mary. You don't know how much that means to me." There was a deep sadness in his eyes and a resignation in his voice, like he knew we would eventually become afraid of him.

Mica had remained beside Eddy, his head resting on Eddy's leg, his eyes never leaving Eddy's face.

"So you and Mica have been wandering all around the country since your family died?"

Eddy ruffled the dog's ears and Mica gave a big sigh. "No, Mica and I found each other about a year ago. He was lying by the side of the road, injured, like someone had thrown him from a speeding car."

"Eddy, both Sam and I want you and Mica to stay with us. You can't spend the rest of your life wandering around without a home."

"The folks around here will turn against you," he said. "I can't see sick people suffering and not help them. I don't even have to cure anyone. All I have to do is shake hands or touch someone and they feel the power. Eventually I'll scare people because they'll know I've seen into their soul and they'll strike out. If you're in the way, you'll be hurt, just like my family was."

I wasn't sure I understood Eddy, the power, the cure, any of it, but I new Eddy wasn't a danger to anyone. "I think you're wrong about the folks in Cranston. We've got room in our house and our hearts, and we'd appreciate it if you would stay with us."

Eddy considered for a minute. "I'm tired of running all around the country, and it would be nice to stay with you for at least a while. But you have to promise not to tell anyone about my power. Let them think Mary's cure was a medical miracle."

"Alright Eddy," Mary said, taking his hand. "We promise. But I think you're wrong about the way decent people will react."

"I hope so," Eddy said, his tone suggesting Mary was mistaken.

Five

The Saturday Doctor's appointment was scheduled for ten, so I had plenty of time to drive Eddy to the station, help with the early rush, and make certain the day's business was organized.

"Saturdays are usually slow at the pumps," I explained, showing him the desk calendar where I scribbled notes. "Gives me time for oil changes and tune-ups. John Baker is scheduled for a nine-thirty oil change, and Elizabeth Petty has an appointment at noon. Since you're the only person in the county who hasn't heard Baker's fish story, he'll likely talk your ear off about the Muskie he caught last year. Tell anyone who comes for unscheduled service that I had to go to Elliott. They can either come back next week or call for an appointment."

"Don't worry about it," Eddy said. "If you give me a price list, I can handle whatever comes up."

I rummaged through my desk drawer for a tattered price sheet. "I haven't updated this for a while, but the prices will be close enough for today. I really appreciate you helping like this. It couldn't be what you expected when you asked for work two days ago."

"That's the plus side of hitchhiking. You never know what's down the road. Don't worry about the station. What I can't handle I'll leave for you."

I was hesitant to run off, but eager to get back to Mary. "I just want you to know I appreciate the help."

"No problem. But if this keeps up, you'll have to add some cash to my room and board." Eddy smiled so I would know he was joking.

"Damnit, Eddy, I'm sorry. With everything else on my mind, I never even thought about wages. We'll sit down this afternoon and work something out about paying you for the past couple of days."

"As long as Mica and I have a roof over our heads and food in our bellies, money is secondary. You go on now. Mary is waiting."

I gave Eddy a house key. "You know how it is at a doctor's appointment. I don't have any idea when we'll be back. If I'm not here by one, you go ahead and close up. Then make yourself at home. There should be plenty of food."

"Don't worry about it. Everything's going to be fine here. You go on now or you'll be late for the appointment."

Hank Bishop's car pulled up to the pumps, giving me an excuse to leave. I waved to Hank while Eddy went to service him.

Mary and I didn't talk much during the drive to Elliott. I felt emotionally drained, and nervous about what the test results would show. I could tell by the way Mary quietly watched the passing countryside, smiling to herself, that she had no doubt the cancer was gone forever. I'm a natural skeptic, but she had total confidence in Eddy's story.

The Lord knows I wanted it to be true, but I wasn't comfortable trusting in miracles. I'd spent a good portion of the previous night staring at the ceiling, thinking about Eddy and his gift. If it were true, it was one hell of a story. I didn't see any reason for Eddy to lie to us. And I couldn't doubt what had happened. It was how it happened that confused me. I had Mary back, happy and healthy, but I secretly hoped Doc Calvin had an answer because the alternative contradicted my life's experiences.

We arrived at the clinic a few minutes early. Doc Calvin was evidently waiting for us, because the nurse immediately led us to his office. As soon as we were seated, Doc Calvin opened a manila file and began talking. He never looked directly at either of us, and I wasn't sure whether that was a good sign. Doc Calvin had a pretty fair bedside manner and the complete absence of preparatory chatter indicated he felt out of control. It made me feel more comfortable knowing I wasn't the only bewildered person in the room.

"I sent the samples to the lab under an assumed name so there wouldn't be any confusion if someone remembered your previous tests," he said. "Unless the samples got mixed up—which is highly unlikely— there's no evidence of cancer. Nothing. Nada. Zip. There isn't even any evidence of the damage the cancer had already caused."

"That means Mary is cured?" I asked, needing a straightforward answer.

"Yes. No. I don't know." Doc rubbed both hands over his face, like he felt tired. "I read a dozen medical journals last night looking for similar cases. There were a few instances of spontaneous remission—the key word being remission. The cancer is still there lurking in the background, and prior damage is still grossly evident." He leaned back in his chair, staring at the ceiling, not the ideal portrayal of the confident young physician. "It's physically impossible for tissue and organ damage to vanish overnight. I couldn't find anything—in any of the journals—that even remotely resembled this case. I was tempted to dig out my Bible because that's where you read about miracles."

Mary smiled at me, and I could see the 'I told you so' expression in her eyes.

"Look, this is a whole new experience for me," Doc continued. "Mary, I want to do a complete medical work-up. I need to know everything you've done, or eaten, or felt for the last month or so. I want you to check into the hospital for observation and testing. It would only be for a couple of days— three at most."

"Hospitals are for sick people, and I'm not sick. I've had enough of nurses and bedpans to last me the rest of my life. I won't go to the hospital, but you can make as many tests as you want here in the Clinic." Mary spoke like she was humoring a child. "It'll be a waste of time. The cancer is gone."

I took a seat in the waiting room while Doc Calvin poked, prodded and tested. Although I wasn't convinced it would make any difference, we had promised, and I was concerned Mary would feel sorry for Doctor Calvin and tell him about Eddy.

Other patients were becoming restless because it took an hour and a half for him to complete Mary's examination. Doc came into the waiting room with Mary and I could tell from his expression he hadn't found an explanation.

"If the tests tell us anything new, I'll call you," he said. "If you feel even a little sick, Mary, You call me day or night. Please make an appointment for next week, Tuesday or Wednesday, so we can see if there are any changes."

It was nearly one when we got back to Cranston and Eddy was still at the station. I dropped Mary at the house where she could spend time yakking with Alma Smith, and I went to help Eddy close up. I had been correct that he wouldn't be very busy. There were no cars at the pumps and he was finishing Elizabeth Petty's oil change.

I handled a fill-up while Eddy ran Elizabeth's charge card.

"Well, how did it go?" I asked when we were alone.

"It was an interesting morning" Eddy said. "Guy wearing a ski mask held us up about eleven o'clock. About eleven-thirty Mica bit some fat lady who complained because you weren't here."

Seeing my shocked expression, Eddy laughed. "Just kidding. Everything went okay. Other than the oil changes, there were maybe ten people getting gas."

"Don't joke like that," I said, flopping onto the desk chair, letting my blood pressure return to normal. "You'll give an old guy like me a heart attack."

"I've gotta tease once in a while to keep you on your toes. How did the Doctor's appointment go?"

"It was great," I said. "There's no cancer in Mary. None at all. I know what you told us last night, but I still find it hard to believe."

"I understand," Eddy said. "It really doesn't make any difference whether or not you believe. The important thing is that Mary has recovered."

I couldn't agree more. "Look, it's past one o'clock. What say we close and go home?"

"You're the boss,' Eddy agreed.

I began counting the receipts while Eddy closed the service bays. A car pulled up to the premium pump before I was even half done. I glanced out the window and saw it was Lisa Bennett's silver Lexus.

"I'll get it," Eddy said, trotting toward the pumps.

I stopped counting and watched because I was worried about Eddy's first encounter with Lisa. Lisa Bennett had a classic beauty that made men stare and women jealous. She was about five six, but seemed taller because of her model slender build. Her hair was long and silken, like burnished gold, framing her tanned, oval face. She had a strong, straight nose, firm chin, and wide gray-blue eyes stippled with green.

As attractive as she was on the outside, Lisa was a spoiled brat, rotten to the core. She was beautiful and knew it, expecting men to accommodate her every whim. Her father, Ernest Bennett, owned Bennett's hardware, about half the real estate in Cranston, and a chain of furniture stores through out the state. I didn't like Ernest, not because he was rich, but because he was a bastard. A couple hundred years ago he would have owned slaves and gotten his kicks by horse whipping them. Lisa wasn't mean like that, but she had never wanted for anything, and expected people to do her bidding, as if the world revolved around her. I doubt whether she had any close friends, unless she's found someone at the fancy Eastern college she attended. There certainly wasn't anyone in this county she considered her social equal. If you weren't on Lisa's social level, she treated you like a servant.

I got along with her better than most people because I was an independent cuss, not beholden to her Father for anything. And I felt a little sorry for her. Lisa's Mother had died when she was only a couple years old, and it couldn't have been a great childhood being raised by a bastard like her Father. He spoiled her with every material blessing and an attitude that no one was good enough to associate with a Bennett. I doubt whether she had ever made mud pies or climbed a tree.

When Lisa had first visited my station and tried to intimidate me, I had snapped back. I had told her, in plain English, if she wanted someone to kiss her feet, she could go elsewhere, but if she wanted service from me, she should act like a lady instead of a spoiled brat. She hadn't cared much for my tongue lashing but she kept coming back. Maybe she appreciated being treated like everyone else and maybe this was the only place where she wouldn't have to pump her own gas. We maintained a truce and she obeyed my ground rules. She didn't always act like a lady, but at least she behaved civilly.

However, Eddy was fresh meat, and undoubtedly Lisa would test him. I was concerned how he would react to being bullied. He didn't seem the type to be awed by Lisa's beauty, but I'd never seen him around a beautiful woman and had no idea how he'd react. A lot of men turn into stammering idiots around someone like Lisa. If Eddy kept his cool and Lisa began verbally pushing him around, I wanted to be handy to prevent trouble. I was still feeling great about the doctor's visit and didn't need Lisa spoiling my day.

The office was close enough to the pumps, so I could hear every word spoken. From the slur in her voice, I knew Lisa had been drinking and must have started early to be half in the bag already. She wasn't an alcoholic, but was headed in that direction. Maybe having lots of money and good looks wasn't everything.

Lisa got out of her Lexus and walked around the back of the car so she could watch Eddy. She was wearing high heels that emphasized her legs, and a blue dress that showed all the right curves. She was definitely worth looking at.

"You new around here?" she asked, leaning on the car to steady herself.

Eddy continued pumping gas, not looking at her. "Yes, ma'am."

"Look at me when I'm talking to you," Lisa ordered in her bossy tone, irritated because Eddy wasn't fawning over her like men generally did.

Eddy looked up, giving her his half smile, one eyebrow cocked. "Yes, ma'am." Then he looked back at the pump dial, watching the numbers rotate.

"Damnit, who the hell do you think you are, ignoring me?" She pushed away from the car, and started toward Eddy like she was going to wallop him with her purse. I was coming out of the office to intercede when one of her heels caught on a buckled piece of concrete and she stumbled.

Eddy grabbed Lisa's arm to steady her until she regained her balance. "Are you okay, ma'am?"

Even from the office doorway I could see the surprised look on Lisa's face as soon as Eddy touched her. There was confusion in her eyes, and I knew she was experiencing the warm, happy sensation. She was so startled she almost said thank you, but caught herself in time. There was a flicker of fear in her eyes because of feelings she couldn't understand. She jerked her arm away. "You keep your hands off me, you bastard."

Eddy topped off the tank and hung up the hose as if the stumbling incident hadn't happened. "We're just about ready to close for the day," he said, his voice soft and soothing. "Would you like Sam to drive you home?"

"Why the hell should Sam give me a ride?" I could tell she was still confused by the feelings she had experienced. "I've got a perfectly good car right here. A hell of a lot better than Sam's ugly old truck."

"You look a little unsteady. Maybe it would be safer if you didn't drive any more today." Eddy's voice never changed from a calm, concerned tone.

"What I do isn't any of your goddamn business," Lisa shouted.

"Yes, ma'am." Eddy went to the front of the Lexus and checked the oil and cleaned the windshield while Lisa did a slow burn. When he was finished, Eddy wiped his hands on a rag. "All set," he said in his calm quiet voice. "The oil's fine. That'll be fourteen seventy-five."

"It's okay, Eddy," I called. "Miss Bennett has a charge account"

"Goddamn right I have a charge account." Lisa wobbled to the driver's side, flopped on the seat, and slammed the door. "If you ever touch me again, I'll see you in jail." She stomped on the gas and peeled out of the station. A good thing there wasn't any traffic or she'd have hit someone for sure.

"Sorry about that, Eddy," I apologized. "If I'd known it was Lisa Bennett, I'd have taken care of her."

"That's okay, Sam. I didn't mind."

"She shouldn't have talked to you that way, but Lisa is a bit outspoken. It isn't anything personal. She's just a spoiled brat."

"No, Sam." Eddy shrugged and gave me a half smile. "There's a lot of pain in that girl. She's lonely and frightened, and that's the way she keeps people from knowing."

"If you say so." Eddy might have the power in his hands, but he sure had a lot to learn about people. If Lisa Bennett was lonely and frightened she had fooled a county full of folks.

Six

I woke Sunday morning with Mary cuddled against me, the fresh clean smell of her hair like perfume. I snuggled the covers around us because the room was cold, even though I could hear the furnace rumbling. Holding Mary and feeling her warmth against my chest was the most beautiful sensation I could remember. It brought home the wonder of her being alive and healthy and vibrant.

"Sam, let's have a picnic," Mary mumbled. "We haven't had a picnic in years."

Mary's nightgown had bunched above her waist and I slipped my hand beneath it to gently stroke her back. Perhaps the skin was not as soft as when we married, but it was still smooth and warm.

"Wouldn't it be easier just to order pizza and watch old movies on TV?"

Mary giggled. "Sam you're losing your sense of romance. Pizza and movies are for cold winter evenings. This is spring and picnic season. I want to get out and smell the grass and flowers."

"We're not likely to see flowers around here for a month." I eased into a badly done, exaggerated Irish brogue. "Sure an' I think you're a bit daft but if it's after havin' a picnic, ye are, then me Colleen, it's a picnic we'll be havin'."

I managed to avoid the pillow Mary swung at me as I rolled out of bed.

A cold front had moved in over night, bringing more seasonable temperatures. After dressing I stepped outdoors and shivered in the chill air. A thin layer of frost tinted the grass on the garage's sheltered side.

"Good morning, Sam." Eddy's breath was visible in a puff of fog as he shivered in his jacket, supervising Mica's morning toilet.

"Good morning. There's a bit of frost in the air," I observed.

"But it feels good" he said. "Crisp mornings always smell fresh and new."

"That depends upon how long you've had to tolerate the cold weather," I complained. "This damned winter's been hanging on too long. I'm ready for less crisp and more sun."

Mica finished his morning duty and led us into the warm house where Mary was mixing pancake batter. She was humming some tune I only vaguely recognized. But it sounded wonderful.

"Eddy, guess what?" she queried, her eyes sparkling like a youngster's. "After Church Sam and I are going to have a picnic. We'd like you and Mica to join us."

"Sure. That's a great idea." He didn't sound entirely convinced.

When we finished breakfast, Mary and I drove to Elliott for St. Mary's ten o'clock Mass. Although we had no idea of his religious affiliation, Mary invited Eddy to accompany us, but he declined. Instead he offered to do the breakfast dishes and begin preparations for our outing.

It had been several months since she had attended Mass and Mary was excited by the prospect. I hadn't gone to Church with her for years because it had always been so much easier to sit home reading the Sunday newspaper. My excuse had always been that I was tired and deserved to rest on Sunday, the only day I didn't have to work. On this Sunday I accompanied Mary because I knew she wanted me to, and it was the right thing to do.

After Mass it took nearly half an hour to make our way to my truck. Friends who hadn't seen Mary in months had to hug her and inquire about her health. She was thrilled by the attention and would have happily spent all morning visiting, but I was afraid she would exhaust herself and have some sort of relapse. I suspected it would take longer than three days for me to really believe the cancer was gone. Reluctantly she allowed me to lead her away from the well wishers and help her into the truck.

"Sam, could we please stop at the cemetery?" Mary asked as I attempted to maneuver through the after church traffic.

"Are you sure you feel up to it?"

"I'd really like to go," she said. "We don't have to stay very long, but it's been months since we've visited Albert."

"Alright, but if you start to get chilled, we're heading right home."

Memorial Gardens, a small cemetery on the far side of Cranston, was divided into two distinct sections. The original portion had tall, mostly granite tombstones dating back a hundred years or more. When I had been a kid a lot of us boys had wandered through the old sector reading inscriptions on those time worn stones. We had even found one monument that claimed the two brothers buried there had been killed and scalped by Indians.

Albert's grave, about twenty yards from the road that meandered through the green acres, was in the modern section where ground level headstones allowed the mowing machines to keep the grass evenly trimmed.

As she did every time she visited, Mary crouched beside the stone, kissed the tips of her fingers and touched them to Albert's engraved name. We both knew our son was somewhere else, that only lifeless clay rested in the grave, but nonetheless we always felt closest to him here.

"Let's sit for a minute," Mary suggested.

"If you're feeling tired, maybe we should go home."

"No, I'm feeling all right. I just want to sit here with you and Albert for a few minutes."

I let Mary lean on my arm as we walked the few feet to the granite bench near the foot of Albert's grave. When we sat, I put my arm around Mary's shoulders and let her lean against me for warmth.

"Sam, I have a confession to make," she said. "When I knew I was dying I really had been looking forward to being with Albert again. After all these years, I still miss him terribly.'

"I understand," I agreed. "He was such a big part of our lives that his death left an empty place that won't ever be filled."

She squeezed my hand and smiled up at me. "I only had two regrets. It broke my heart to know when I was gone you wouldn't have anyone. And I've always regretted not being able to give you another son."

"As long as I have you, that's all I've ever needed."

Mary squeezed my hand again. "That's sweet, and I know you mean it, but I've always realized how much you wanted a son to carry on your name. Even after all these years I feel like I've let you down."

I kissed her cheek. "You've never let me down. I love you, Mary Johnson, and having you here beside me is all I've ever wanted. You make my life complete."

Mary snuggled closer and we sat silently for several minutes. The sun slid behind a cloud and there was an immediate chill in the air. I was about to suggest we leave, when Mary spoke.

"You know, Sam, it's hard for me to remember Albert as a grown man. I still see him as a tiny baby, so soft and helpless. The warmth of him as he nursed at my breast is still so vivid sometimes it makes my heart ache. When I close my eyes I can see him taking his first awkward steps and reaching out to me for support. As a baby he needed me in such a special way. He made me feel necessary and important. In some way I've never been able to understand, he made me feel complete. I always hated the thought of him growing up and not needing me anymore. Was that selfish of me, Sam?"

"Yeah, it probably was selfish," I said. "But I'm sure all mothers feel that way. Fathers are just as selfish, but about different things. I couldn't wait for him to be old enough to go fishing. And I was looking forward to him working at the station with me. It made me feel pretty important when he was young enough to believe I had the answers to all the world's problems."

Mary snuggled closer. "Wouldn't it have been wonderful if we'd had grandchildren? Do you realize if things had been different, our grandchildren would be almost as old as Eddy?"

I didn't feel comfortable talking about what might have been. "Maybe we don't have any grandkids, but we have each other and that's enough for me."

"You're right. I don't know why I suddenly felt so morbid." Mary patted my hand and stood up. "This should be a happy day, and if we stay here any longer, I'm going to start crying. Eddy must be wondering where we are, and we've got a picnic to attend to."

The picnic never materialized. A heavy cloud cover had accompanied the front, keeping the day dark and cool. Mary was willing to bundle and picnic anyway, but I had no desire to spend the day shivering. Even though Mary was getting stronger, it had only been three days since she had gotten out of bed and I figured it was too soon for her to risk a chill. I convinced her to settle for a backyard cookout by promising we would picnic at the lake on the first warm Sunday.

I hauled the grill from the garage and got a good bed of charcoal going. Mary made a potato salad while I barbecued some chicken. We bundled in blankets and sat on the back porch, eating off paper plates. The chicken was slightly over cooked, but it tasted good anyway.

I don't know if it was by mutual consent or just the way things happen, but we never talked about Mary's cure or Eddy's gift. It was Sunday, a time for expressing gratitude, but I think we all wanted to pretend Mary had never been sick.

It turned out Eddy had a reservoir of adventures and a talent for making them sound funny. He had spent some time in Montana, and his description of learning how to ride a horse had both Mary and me laughing so hard we nearly fell out of our chairs.

I thought the sound of Mary's laughter was better than a chorus of angels. The world was a beautiful place and I loved everyone and everything. Even as it was happening, I knew this Sunday was going to be one of those days that dwelt in a special niche of memory.

Seven

I was still enjoying a warm glow when Eddy and I opened the station Monday morning. The glow dimmed considerable about ten-thirty when Sheriff Henry Simpson pulled his cruiser into the parking spot next to my truck.

I'd known Henry all his life. He wasn't the smartest guy in town, but he wasn't stupid. He'd been a high school football star and had worked at the lumberyard after graduation. Henry had been a wild youngster, enjoying his share of tavern brawls until he married Molly Barker. She held a tight rein over his wild streak and encouraged him to take the exam for the county police department. Law enforcement suited him, and two years earlier he'd run for Sheriff when John Winkowski had retired. With Winkowski's backing, he had won election by a sizable margin.

Henry was a big man, about six-one and two hundred twenty pounds. Although he kept himself in good shape, a gut was beginning to lap over his pistol belt. His nose had been broken a couple of times, never healing straight. The defect added character to his rather plain countenance. His face was square, outdoors tan, with a gray-blue sheen of heavy beard kept close shaven. His hands were huge, the fingers looking blunt and stubby.

Since County Sheriff was an elective office, anyone hoping to keep the job had to satisfy the political powers. In our county the political power was Ernest Bennett. Henry liked being Sheriff, and was willing to kiss Bennett's ass, but overall he was a good sheriff, fair and honest. There wasn't much crime in our rural county, partly because Henry came down hard on law breakers. People considered twice before stepping over the line.

The sheriff eased his bulk from the cruiser and took his time settling the cowboy style hat perfectly on his head. He was vain about his short curly black hair beginning to thin in the back.

"Morning, Sheriff," I called, pushing up from the chair I'd placed in the sun. "Need an oil change?"

"Not this morning, Sam. I'm here on business." Henry's deep voice rumbled from way down in his chest. He generally spoke softly, but I'd seen him intimidate people when he raised the volume a notch.

"Not much in the line of police business around here," I said.

Henry inclined his head toward the service bay where Eddy was doing an oil change on Bart Timm's old Cierra. "I have a complaint concerning your new employee."

That raised my curiosity level because I knew Eddy hadn't done anything illegal since he'd come to Cranston. "What sort of complaint?"

"I'd rather talk to him about it. Would you please ask him to step out here?"

"Sure, why not? Hey, Eddy!"

Eddy poked his head around the hood. "Yes, sir?"

"Could you come here a minute, please."

"Be right with you." He grabbed a rag and wiped his hands as he walked toward us. There was no hesitation in Eddy's stride, although I noticed a look of resignation cross his face when he saw the Sheriff—like he was accustomed to being hassled by the law. "What do you want Sam?" He spoke to me, but his eyes watched the Sheriff.

"I want to talk to you, son," Henry said. The Sheriff looked relaxed, but his thumbs were hooked on his belt so the right hand was poised in front of his service revolver. I noticed the restraining strap over the hammer was unsnapped. "What's your name?"

"Eddy."

"Eddy what?"

"Just Eddy."

"Look, son, we can do this the easy way or the hard way." Henry's voice had gone up a notch. "The choice is yours. I want to know your name, and for your own sake, I suggest you cooperate."

Eddy didn't seem intimidated, just resigned. "Foster. Edward Foster."

"There, that wasn't so difficult was it? Let me see your driver's license."

"I don't have a driver's license."

Mica had roused from the shade of the service bay and come to sit by Eddy's right leg. Mica was the gentlest dog I'd ever known, but I had the impression if Sheriff Simpson touched Eddy, Mica would go right for his throat.

"Do you have any type of identification?" Henry asked, one eye on Eddy, the other on Mica.

"No, sir."

"Not even a social security card?"

"No, sir. I lost it."

"Sam," Henry said, turning to me. "How do you figure to keep the paperwork on this kid if he doesn't have a social security card?"

I shrugged. "We haven't gotten that far. He's only temporary until we see if it works out."

"How old are you, son?"

"Twenty-three.'

I was surprised. I hadn't bothered to ask, but I figured Eddy to be a couple years older. Maybe the wandering life had aged him.

"Any proof of that?"

"No birth certificate, if that's what you mean."

"Don't get smart with me, son." There was an edge to Henry's voice.

"I don't want to interfere with the due process of the law," I said. "But what sort of complaint do you have against Eddy?"

"Assault," Henry said.

"That's ridiculous." I would have laughed, but Henry was official serious. "Someone's pulling your leg, Sheriff. Eddy hasn't been out of my sight for a single minute since he's been in Cranston. I know he's never attacked anyone. Just for laughs, who's he supposed to have assaulted?"

"Lisa Bennett." Henry was biting off his words like he wanted to obtain information, not give it.

"That's ridiculous," I protested.

"She doesn't think so. Swore out a complaint, and it's my duty to act on it."

"When did this alleged assault take place?" I asked. "Saturday noon, right?"

"That's what the complaint states."

"Well the complaint is wrong," I said. "I was here Saturday when Lisa stopped to get gas for her Lexus. She'd been drinking and was barely able to stand up. She stumbled and Eddy caught her arm to keep her from falling. No matter how you bend it, that isn't assault. Maybe you ought to be talking to Lisa about drunk driving."

"Maybe the assault happened the way you say and maybe it didn't. I have a complaint from a citizen concerning a drifter, and it's my job to investigate." Henry seemed embarrassed. He knew my word was good, and in a normal situation my statement would have been enough to end the matter. But an elected official couldn't ignore a complaint from a Bennett.

"What do you mean by investigate?" I asked. "There were only three people there, so it'll be my word against Lisa's. There's nothing else to investigate. You sure as hell aren't going to check for fingerprints."

"Sam, just keep out of this. I don't know this youngster, and Lisa has lived in the county all her life. I'm going to take Eddy to the station where I can run a check and determine if he's got a record. If he's clean, I reckon the Judge will decide about the assault charge."

I was becoming angry. I understood Henry's position, but after what Eddy had done for Mary, I couldn't let him get hassled on a bogus charge. "If you're taking him I'm coming along to make sure he doesn't fall down the stairs or something."

"That's uncalled for Sam." Henry had been known to rough up drunks from time to time when they resisted arrest, but he took his job seriously, and generally avoided using unnecessary force.

"Maybe it is, but I'm coming along."

"Suit yourself." He turned to Eddy, who had been patiently waiting throughout the exchange. "Are you going to come along peacefully, or do I have to put cuffs on you?"

"I won't cause any trouble," Eddy promised. "Do you mind if I wash my hands before we go?"

Simpson took a moment to consider the request. "Okay, but don't try anything funny."

While Eddy went to the restroom I began closing the service bays and removing the money from the till.

"Sam, you don't have to come along." Eddy said when he returned. "I'll be okay."

"I'm coming. The Sheriff's office is in Elliott, and you'll need a ride home when this bullshit is over."

"Thanks. I'd appreciate that." Eddy turned to Mica, who was watching Sheriff Simpson like he was a peace of steak, waiting for Eddy's signal so he could take a bite. "Mica, you ride with Sam."

Mica looked at Eddy, then at Sheriff Simpson. If he had been human I would have figured he was deciding whether it was a good idea to leave Eddy alone right then. Finally he gave a little woof and trotted over to my truck. I swear that dog could understand Eddy as well as I could.

Sheriff Simpson grabbed Eddy's arm to lead him to the squad car. He immediately jerked his hand back like he'd gotten an electrical shock. From his surprised expression I knew Henry had experienced the warm tingly sensation. I couldn't help wondering whether Eddy had seen into Simpson's soul and whether the Sheriff had any dark secrets that would make him Eddy's enemy. I did notice that Henry avoided touching Eddy again.

Henry waited until I locked the station and hung the 'out to lunch' sign on the door. Then Mica and I followed the Sheriff's cruiser to the County Sheriff's Department in Elliott. Simpson drove around back to the employee parking lot, and I pulled into the small visitor's lot at the side of the building. I left Mica in the pickup and waited in the lobby. A female officer had taken my statement by the time Sheriff Simpson appeared, escorting Eddy. They hadn't been in the back very long, so I didn't think they'd given Eddy the third degree.

"Is there bail or something?" I asked. Mary would never forgive me if I let Eddy spend a night in the county jail.

"No," Sheriff Simpson said. "I've given Eddy a citation requiring appearance in court Wednesday. I'll hold you responsible for getting him there." Henry seemed relieved to have completed this duty, leaving further action in the hands of the Judge—another elected official beholden to the Bennetts.

"Come on, Eddy," I said, making sure everyone could hear the disgust in my voice. "Let's get out of here before I get sick."

Sheriff Simpson just stood beside the desk watching us leave.

When we climbed into my truck, Mica gave a little woof and settled with his head on Eddy's lap. Eddy sort of absent mindedly stroked his ears.

"I'm sorry about this, Sam" he said. "The trouble's starting sooner than I thought it would."

"Hey, don't worry about it. There isn't going to be any trouble. That Lisa Bennett is stirring things up because you didn't kiss her ass. As soon as the Judge hears our side, he'll dismiss the charges."

Eddy stared out the window a long time. "Maybe," he finally said, so softly I wasn't sure I'd heard him. Made me wonder if he knew something I didn't.

Eight

I've never been much of a deep thinker. Like most folks I'd always considered my life controlled by luck, or some mysterious force over which I was powerless. There couldn't be any other explanation for a benevolent God allowing so much suffering. But I would have to be brain dead to miss the wake-up call issued during the last several days. I could no longer simply cheer the good luck, curse the bad, and hide from reality in front of a TV. My life and my outlook had been permanently altered—hopefully for the better.

It didn't make me very proud to realize how selfishly I had behaved concerning Albert's death and Mary's cancer. It had taken a miracle to give me the kick in the backside I needed to wake up from a life long lethargy. For the first time I was beginning to understand what lonely creatures humans really are, insulated inside self-constructed shells, reacting to the world—to the people in our lives—only as they affected us, not particularly concerned with how we affected the world.

So much remained murky and confused, but now I was aware of a deep guilt because I had been consumed by my own sense of impending loss when Mary was dying. It hurt to strip away the pretense of nobility and realize much of my distress evolved from the fear of losing something precious, from my suffering, from my dread of living without Mary, from my anxiety about being alone. There had been too much I and me beneath the suffering. There should have been more concern for the fear and pain Mary was enduring.

This new self-awareness, this looking inside my soul, had begun when I shook hands with Eddy, feeling that warm, happy sensation flooding through me. Just as Mary knew with certainty Eddy had cured her, I was beginning to believe he had healed something inside me; some mental aberration I hadn't realized was there. Without a doubt, I wasn't the same man I had been a week ago.

All life's little nuances that I had taken for granted, assumed a new significance. I'm too much of a realist to believe my egotism will ever completely disappear, but I could sense myself growing, expanding beyond my shell. It was a good feeling—but scary, as if I were exploring uncharted oceans.

No doubt there would always be a sense of guilt because I hadn't been the perfect father to Albert and because I had taken Mary for granted. It was too late to change anything concerning Albert, except to attempt to forgive myself. I knew self-forgiveness would be the most difficult thing I'd ever done. But Eddy had given me the opportunity to show Mary how much I loved and appreciated her. I intended to do exactly that.

My new awareness made me acutely aware of my obligations to Eddy. He was a stranger who had walked into my life and given me a gift beyond value. I had not asked for his help—not even realizing it was available. He had performed a miracle and asked nothing in return. A week ago I would have looked for an angle, figuring no one gave without hope of gain. But Eddy had touched me and I was a better person. He had touched Mary and she was whole again. Without understanding how, I knew I owed Eddy more than I'd ever owed anyone. I promised myself I would give him back at least a small piece of what he had given me.

The court appearance Wednesday would be an opportunity to stand with him as a friend. Going against the powerful Bennetts could have unpleasant consequences. I didn't know if they were true, but I'd heard rumors about folks losing their jobs or having businesses fail when they had crossed Ernest Bennett in some way. However I didn't think there was any way Bennett could harm me, and I knew it was time to reach out to someone else and be less concerned about myself.

Monday evening after supper Eddy went outside to toss a tennis ball for his dog. I grabbed a beer for myself and a diet soda for Eddy and sat on the back steps.

The sky was overcast, the clouds blocking even the faint light from moon and stars. Way off to the north I could hear the rumble of thunder, but it didn't feel and smell as if we were going to get any rain.

"Eddy," I called. "Could we talk for a minute?"

"Sure, Sam." He came over and sat one step lower, taking the soda I offered. "What's on your mind?" Mica dropped the ball at Eddy's feet then lay down, panting heavily.

I sat for a while without saying anything, not knowing how to begin. "You told Sheriff Simpson you were twenty-three," I finally said.

Eddy looked a little embarrassed. "Well, actually I won't be twenty-three until next month, but I figured it was close enough for government work."

"You must have graduated from High School when you were about eighteen," I suggested.

He nodded.

"I'm not great at math, but I calculate you've been traveling around the country for five years. That's a long time to be by yourself. Don't you get lonely?"

"I have Mica." At the sound of his name, the dog sat up, put his head on Eddy's knee and pushed with his nose until Eddy began petting him.

"That's quite a dog," I said. "When I was a kid I had a mongrel a lot like Mica. We were inseparable, but it isn't the same as human companionship. Don't you miss having a home and friends? Maybe finding a girl and starting a family of your own."

He shrugged and didn't answer.

"Come on, Eddy, talk to me. I want to be your friend."

"I'm satisfied with Mica, Sam." Eddy sipped his soda, then studied the lights from the kitchen window reflecting off the aluminum can. "He's my friend, and doesn't care who I am or whether I have a curse or blessing. He just accepts me. Sometimes that's almost enough."

"But surely, in five years, you've met people who welcomed you."

"There have been a few who accepted for a while, but people change, Sam. When their friends start pointing and whispering and avoiding them they're afraid of becoming isolated. It isn't human nature to be grateful for long. It makes people feel edgy."

I understood how it felt to be uncomfortable because of the way I had been since Eddy arrived. But I didn't think my discomfort was the same thing he was describing. "That's a pretty cynical attitude, isn't it?" I asked.

"Maybe, but it's the truth as I've seen it. I read somewhere that if you want someone to be your friend, don't do something for him, ask him to do something for you. If someone does you a favor, it makes him feel good, as if he's in charge. People are more likely to be friendly to someone they feel superior to. If you do a favor for someone else, he feels obligated. Most people are uncomfortable having an obligation. It's hard to be friends with someone you owe something to. Eventually you begin to avoid that person because you don't want to be reminded of your debt. Pretty soon there is actually fear or dislike."

I let that settle in my mind for a moment. "I never really thought about it, but I can appreciate your point. I guess it's hard for me to believe helping people will eventually lead to the problems you've talked about."

"I don't know all the answers," Eddy said. "But I've seen the reaction to my power and I've done a lot of soul searching. When I heal people it makes them nervous because they don't understand it. I can't blame them for that since I don't understand the power myself. But the healing is just an obvious excuse for people to feel uncomfortable. It's my curse of seeing into their souls that causes the problem—that generates the fear."

"I can understand people being nervous about things they don't understand," I agreed. "I just don't see why anyone would be afraid of you."

Eddy shook his head, a sad quality to his voice. "Everyone is afraid of something, Sam. The world is like a huge masquerade ball; everyone hiding behind a mask, terrified someone will get too close and find out who they really are. Those masks hide a lot of things. Insecurity. Dreams and ambitions they believe others will laugh at. Things they're ashamed of. Everyone's frightened of losing their mask because they'll feel naked, exposed."

"I still think you sound pretty cynical for a youngster."

Eddy gave his little smile. "Yeah, I suppose I am. But when I touch people I can sense their fears, their pain. I can see into their souls." He took a drink of soda. "That scared you, didn't it? We shook hands and you're wondering what I saw in your soul. You're frightened that I know your secrets, that I've seen behind your mask."

My instinct was to deny it, but he was right. I don't know if it was fear, but it certainly was uncomfortable knowing he might have seen into my soul. I suppose everyone has demons they aren't proud of. "Well, it does take some getting used to." I gave an embarrassed laugh. "But I don't imagine I'm hiding any terrible secrets."

"No, Sam, you aren't. You have deep pain, but no terrible secrets."

It wasn't necessary to ask Eddy about the pain, because I knew he'd seen the hurt and emptiness I'd felt since Albert's death.

We sat quietly for a few moments. I wanted to talk, to understand Eddy, but didn't know what to say. His life and his power were simply beyond my comprehension.

"I'm curious," I finally said. "You don't have to answer if you don't want to. When you touch someone, does it happen right away? I mean, do you see into their minds in an instant?"

"It depends." I sensed Eddy wasn't comfortable talking about his power. "If I just bump into someone nothing happens. Usually it takes a few seconds to establish contact. Like when I shake hands."

"Did you...uh...make contact with Sheriff Simpson when he grabbed your arm?"

"Yes, but just a flash," Eddy said. "I really don't want to talk about this. When I sense a person's inner secrets it's as if I'm invading their privacy. Maybe it's similar to a priest hearing a confession. Part of my curse is an obligation to keep all those secrets to myself."

"I didn't mean to pry." We sat quietly while I considered what a tremendous burden it must be to carry so many people's secrets.

"Tell me about Mica," I finally said. "How'd you two hook up? I think you told me you found him."

"Mica was lying in a roadside ditch where someone must have thrown him from a speeding vehicle. Apparently he had become inconvenient to his owners, and they discarded him, not caring whether he lived or died. A decent person would have taken him to the pound where he would have had a chance to find a new home.' Eddy's voice took on a hard edge I'd never heard before. "I can excuse a lot of things people do without thinking. Long ago I forgave the thugs who killed my family. But I can't find it in my heart to pardon the bastard who discarded Mica like a bag of garbage. Can you imagine how it must hurt to be thrown from a speeding car onto a gravel road? Mica was more dead than alive, cut and bleeding and starving. He couldn't have been in the ditch very long, or he would have died, so I figure he hadn't eaten for a long time before he was tossed out." Eddy was silent a moment and his voice softened. "I've taken care of Mica since then, trying to give him the love and attention he never had. He responds by returning my love without question, without judgment. Can you understand that, Sam?"

"Sure, I understand," I said, knowing I really did. "But Mica is a dog. People need people. Don't you ever think about stopping somewhere and putting down roots?"

In the darkness I could see Eddy nod. "Sure. Moving from town to town isn't what I wanted out of life. At first I thought maybe I could begin fresh somewhere. A couple of families I stayed with treated me well because they were grateful for the power in my hands." He looked at his hands, then wiped them on his legs like they were dirty. "But it never lasted. I imagine they felt an obligation and it made them uneasy. If something makes you uncomfortable you want it to go away. So when the troubles began it gave them an excuse. They always said something like, 'Eddy, we're sorry, but you understand how it is. We have our families to think about.' And I did understand. So I moved along. Now I don't expect anything more than a place to rest for a while. I don't look for people to be grateful or to be better than they are."

"Have you ever considered working in a hospital?" I asked. "With your gift you could do a lot of good."

"Yeah. I've thought of that. In fact I did get a job as an orderly in a hospital shortly after my family died. It didn't work out."

I waited for Eddy to elaborate, but he remained silent. "Tell me about it. Why didn't it work?"

"With just a High School Diploma I couldn't be a doctor or nurse, but I figured it didn't make any difference what type of work I did as long as there was access to sick people. I discovered my ability had to regenerate ever time I used it, like my battery needed recharging. I couldn't cure everyone in a day. I was forced to make decisions on who would live and who would die. It was hard, Sam, choosing who to save."

I already knew Eddy was sensitive, and I could imagine the agony of deciding. "So you decided not to work in hospitals."

"No, that wasn't the reason. It was difficult, but I could reconcile myself to that. I didn't tell anyone what I was doing, but of course, the patients knew, just like Mary knew. The series of miraculous cures had already caused a sensation, and one of the people I healed told her doctor I was God's instrument. Her words, not mine. At first no one believed her, but when more of the cured patients were questioned, my power was discovered. Doctors are a very jealous group, protective of their niche in society. There was talk about arresting me for practicing medicine without a license. Can you believe that? Here I was curing hopeless cases and they wanted to put me in jail because I wasn't a doctor, a member of the fraternity."

"Not all doctors are that way," I said. I was enough of a cynic to believe a lot of physicians could be jealous of a healer. An orderly miraculously curing terminal patients would certainly erode their professional status. Plenty of doctors wouldn't think twice about crucifying a kid who healed people without charging a penny.

The whole subject was too depressing, so I decided to lighten the discussion. "Mary and I have talked it over and we agree you can stay with us as long as you want," I announced.

"Thanks, Sam, I appreciate that." I could tell from his tone he didn't believe we'd stand by him.

"You think the court appearance is the beginning of trouble, don't you?" I asked.

"It's started this way before."

"But not this time. The Bennetts are upset because you didn't fall all over Lisa and kiss her feet. Mark my words. The Judge will dismiss the charges and it'll be over. Besides, it doesn't have anything to do with your power."

"In a way it does. Lisa Bennett knows I saw into her soul. It confused her and made her angry. Anger is a symptom of fear."

"You don't have to say anything if you don't want to, but I'm really interested in the power," I said, thinking perhaps understanding it would help me to be a better friend. "How does it work?"

"I honestly don't know. I've had it as long as I can remember. When I touch hurt and injured creatures, I feel a sensation of warmth coming from my hands. It's like their illness flows from them into me. I don't know what happens to the disease. Maybe it goes into the twilight zone." I thought I heard him chuckle. "I just know it doesn't make me sick—only very, very tired."

"Does it work for everyone?" I asked.

"No, not everyone. There have been failures. I don't know why some people aren't cured or why I can't sense everyone's pain. Maybe God sent suffering to certain people for a reason, and doesn't let my power work. Maybe in some people the fear is too strong." Eddy finished the soda and stood up. "If you don't mind, Sam, I'd rather not talk about this anymore."

I heard Mary moving around in the kitchen, so I took the empty cans into the house. I didn't know whether I understood Eddy any better, but he had given me some things to ponder. I knew I would lay awake that night thinking about masks and fears.

Nine

A light rain passed through Cranston Wednesday morning, leaving a cloudy, windy day, with a predicted high of fifty degrees. For this time of the year, the temperature was about normal, but the unseasonably warm snap had whetted my appetite for spring. My mood was as cloudy as the weather, and the necessity of driving to Elliott for a needless court appearance didn't help my attitude.

The day began with two arguments concerning who would attend court. Because of her special interest in Eddy, Mary wanted to accompany us. I had been at court appearances before and knew there would be a long, boring afternoon of sitting on hard wooden benches in an overheated courtroom. It took a while to convince her she wasn't strong enough to face the ordeal and she finally agreed to stay home with Mica.

Then Eddy argued the citation was his problem, not mine, and since I had already missed enough business during the last week it wouldn't be necessary for me to waste another half day. With rising impatience I explained there were several reasons he couldn't go by himself. He didn't have a driver's license, and would have to hitchhike or walk the fifteen miles. He didn't know his way around Elliott and might not find the courthouse. And finally, neither Mary nor I were going to let him face Judge O'Hearn alone. If the case went to trial, an assault charge could result in a heavy fine or even jail time. Being a witness to the alleged assault, my testimony would quickly resolve the case. I could tell Eddy felt as if he were imposing, but he couldn't argue against my logic.

Eddy and I serviced the early morning commuters, and at eleven I hung the 'out to lunch' sign. We stopped at the house for a sandwich, with Mary hovering over Eddy like he was a condemned man. She was worried about the impression he would make because he didn't have a suit and tie. None of my clothing would fit him, and I didn't believe it was necessary to impress anyone. We both dressed in clean shirts and jeans. It was a relief when we were finally on the road.

The Henderson County Court House occupied an entire block in the center of Elliott. The main granite building was three stories tall, the entrance flanked by Doric columns. It had been constructed over a hundred years ago, mimicking government building of that era and for a time had been the pride and joy of the entire county. Within the last twenty years, annexes had been built against both sides and the rear to expand the building's capacity. There had been no effort to reflect the earlier architecture, so the sprawling structure looked half-modern, half-ancient, and completely ugly.

The additions housed the county clerk, the tax office, and all of Elliott's municipal government. The courtrooms were in the old portion, probably because the marble lined foyer and wide, double stairway presented a solemn, judicial atmosphere.

Judge O'Hearn's courtroom was on the second floor. Because it was only quarter to one when we arrived, the courtroom doors were locked. A mob a twenty or so people lounged in the hallway, nobody talking, except an occasional lawyer in whispered consultation with a client. It was easy to identify the lawyers because they were the only people wearing suits. Two police officers were evidently also waiting for court, lounging together, isolated from the civilians.

Wednesday afternoons were reserved for misdemeanor offenses and preliminary hearings to decide which cases could be settled on the spot, and which ones would be go to full trial. Everyone was required to be there at one o'clock and wait for his case to be called. I knew from experience the law fraternity would take care of their own, so the defendants with lawyers would be heard first. Since Eddy and I weren't in that group, we would have a boring wait.

At precisely one o'clock the courtroom doors were unlocked and litigants hesitantly entered. The room was small, maybe forty by forty, with no resemblance to the spacious courtrooms in Perry Mason movies. Five rows of polished wooden benches, capable of seating twenty or thirty people if they squeezed together, filled half the room. The benches ended at a three foot high barrier, separating the area reserved for defendants and lawyers, which boasted two tables and six wooden chairs. The Judge's bench was a raised platform to the left side of the room, a black plastic sign with white letters announced, Benjamin J. O'Hearn, Henderson County Court. Upright poles holding an American Flag and a State Flag flanked the Judge's chair.

The benches filled from the back, forward. Eddy and I waited our turn to enter and consequently were squeezed into seats in the front row. Before I sat, I looked over the crowd, but didn't see the Bennetts or anyone who looked like he might be representing them. I was beginning to hope they wouldn't show and the charges would be dismissed.

There was the same hushed murmuring as in Church before services while we waited another fifteen minutes. A middle-aged lady, carrying a stack of manila folders, took her place at the stenographer's desk a moment before Judge O'Hearn entered and climbed the three steps to his lofty throne. No one ordered us to stand, like you see in the movies, but the Judge's appearance silenced the crowd's murmuring.

Judge O'Hearn, sans the traditional black robes, was wearing a navy blue suit, white shirt and red tie. His elevated position above the room made him appear larger than his five six, one hundred seventy pounds. His face, red and slightly puffy from excess weight, was fringed by distinguished silver hair that I suspected had been tinted. He wore half glasses positioned toward the end of his nose so he could easily see over them.

O'Hearn briefly glanced at this audience, then leaned over and talked in a soft voice to the stenographer, who handed him a manila folder. He opened it, shuffled some papers and finally called the first case—a young man charged with drunk driving.

Surprisingly the cases involving the police officers were called first and disposed of quickly. O'Hearn probably wanted the officers back out on the street where they could catch more lawbreakers for his court.

Then, as I had expected, cases represented by counsel were called next. There was no pattern to the order of appearances. Perhaps the more affluent attorneys got preference. Certainly the cases weren't scheduled alphabetically. The first case was Swanson, and the next Adams. Traffic tickets, drunk and disorderly, vandalism, and assorted petty offenses were all handled identically. When Judge O'Hearn called a case, if no one answered his call, or if only one party to the dispute was present, he entered a judgment or dismissed the charge, depending on whether the accuser or accused was present. In a couple of cases he issued a warrant for the accused who had failed to appear.

If both parties were present, they stepped forward, O'Hearn read the charge or complaint, then demanded a plea. Guilty, or no contest, he disposed of with the appropriate fine or judgment. O'Hearn listened to arguments on not guilty pleas, deciding whether the case merited further action. Some he dismissed, some he entered a judgment on and some he scheduled for later trial. He moved the proceedings along as rapidly as possible, but it was still a slow process.

By two-thirty most of the litigants had been heard. The courtroom was nearly empty and the Bennetts were still not present. I was beginning to wonder whether Eddy's case had been over looked. Judge O'Hearn slowed the pace, glancing occasionally at the courtroom door, like he was expecting a visitor.

Besides Eddy and me, there were only two other people remaining when Ernest, Lisa, and their attorney entered the courtroom, taking seats in the first row, across the narrow aisle from Eddy and me. Judge O'Hearn nodded almost imperceptibly at the Bennetts and I figured he had been waiting for them to appear. I didn't think it boded well for Eddy, but I sure as hell wasn't going to let political cronies railroad him.

Lisa was as beautiful as ever, but looked nervous, like she'd rather have been somewhere else. She avoided looking at Eddy, but gave me an embarrassed smile that lit the room like a hundred flash bulbs going off.

Ernest Bennett glanced at his watch a couple of times as O'Hearn finished the case of a speeder, which he resolved by imposing a fine. Ernest was tall, almost gaunt, but looked like a man who worked out regularly. The one time he looked in Eddy's direction there was a smug expression, reminding me of a shark eyeing a snack.

While the young man was paying his fine, Judge O'Hearn consulted briefly with the stenographer, took a manila folder, and looked in our direction. "Edward Foster," he called.

"Here, your honor."   Eddy walked to the defendant's table and I accompanied him.

The Bennett's attorney took his place at the other table. Lisa and Ernest Bennett remained seated in the gallery.

"Who are you representing, Mr. Allen?" O'Hearn asked Bennett's attorney.

"Lisa Bennett, your honor," Allen said. He was a tall man, something over six feet, and tending toward being fat. I judged from the quality of his suit that he was a high priced attorney. The lawyers in our county generally weren't so well dressed.

O'Hearn fixed his judicial stare on me. He had been in my station a few times and knew who I was. "What are you doing here, Mr. Johnson?"

"I'm Mr. Foster's employer and witnessed the alleged assault," I said.

"This area is reserved for litigants and their attorneys. Please have a seat in the gallery. We'll call you if we require your testimony.'

My blood began to boil and I was about to make a caustic comment when Eddy put his hand on my arm. That warm, happy feeling instantly calmed me.

"It's alright, Sam."

I reluctantly retreated behind the barrier.

When I had seated myself, Judge O'Hearn studied the contents of a manila folder, then glanced over his glasses at Eddy. "Mr. Foster, according to the citation, on Saturday, April 26th, at approximately noon, while working at Sam Johnson's service station in Cranston, you serviced an automobile driven by Miss Lisa Bennett. After filling Miss Bennett's gas tank, you forcefully took her by the arm, attempting to coerce her into Sam Johnson's truck. Miss Bennett broke loose from your grip and sped away, fearing for her safety." Judge O'Hearn took off his half glasses and fixed judicial stare at Eddy. "Are you represented by an attorney, Mr. Foster?"

"No, sir."   Eddy's voice was soft and respectful, but I could see he wasn't intimidated by the judicial presence, only resigned to the process.

"Do you understand you may plead guilty, not guilty, or no contest? And do you understand each of these pleas?"

"Yes, sir."

"Then, how do you plead?"

"Not guilty, your honor."

"I will enter a not guilty plea and set a trial date. The charges against you are serious, and I encourage you to engage an attorney. Do you have any questions or comments before I set the trial date?"

"It didn't happen the way the citation says," Eddy patiently explained.

"That's why we have trials, son, to determine what actually happened."

"Your honor," I interrupted. I figured this fiasco had gone far enough, and had no intention of allowing O'Hearn to set a trial date. "I respectfully submit that a trial would be a complete waste of time and taxpayer's money. I witnessed the alleged assault and want to set the record straight."

"Would you please identify yourself," O'Hearn ordered.

"Hell, Ben, you know me." I said.

"For the record, please." Judge O'Hearn gave a tolerant smile, like he was addressing a child. "Despite the informal nature of these proceedings, this is a court of law, and you will address the bench in proper form."

"Sorry, your honor. My name is Sam Johnson. I own Johnson's Premium Service in Cranston, and was present during the entire incident. Not one damn word of that citation is true."

"Objection!" Allen said in a loud voice.

O'Hearn looked over his glasses at the attorney. "And what are you objecting to, Mr. Allen?"

"I object to Mr. Johnson giving testimony in this preliminary hearing without being properly sworn."

"Overruled. I would like to hear what Mr. Johnson has to say." O'Hearn fixed his judicial stare on me. "Mr. Johnson, you are not under oath, but the stenographer will record your comments. If your statement today doesn't coincide with testimony given under oath should this matter be held over for trial, you may be liable to charges of perjury. Do you understand?"

"Yes, your honor. Wouldn't want it any other way."

"Then, if you would please have a seat in the witness chair, we'll hear what you have to say"

I made my way to the front of the courtroom and sat in the chair to the left of Judge O'Hearn.

"Now, please tell the court, in your own words, what you saw and heard."

So I told them exactly what had happened.

"Objection!" Allen said. "Mr. Johnson was not in a position to see and hear what actually occurred"

"Overruled. I will remind you this is a preliminary hearing and somewhat informal. Even though Mr. Johnson is not under oath, you are welcome to cross examine him."

"Thank you, your honor. Mr. Johnson, exactly where were you when the incident took place?"

"I had been in the station's office counting the day's receipts when Miss Bennett drove in. Before Mr. Foster began servicing her car I stepped into the doorway to watch."

"And how far was the office from where Mr. Foster and Miss Bennett were standing?"

"About fifteen or twenty feet. But I could hear everything they were saying."

"I understand your gas pumps are on an island, parallel to the station, with room on each side for cars to fuel. Were Mr. Foster and Miss Bennett on the side of the pumps toward the office, or were then on the far side of the pumps?"

"They were on the far side of the pumps."

Allen turned to Judge O'Hearn. "Your honor I contend that Mr. Johnson was not in a position to observe what actually happened."

"Damnit, I could see perfectly well what was happening," I protested.

"Mr. Johnson, watch your language," O'Hearn said. "I won't warn you again.

"Sorry, your honor," I said, trying to sound humble.

O'Hearn addressed Bennett's lawyer. "Mr. Allen, I remind you this is an informal hearing and I'm interested hearing Mr. Johnson's testimony. Twenty feet wasn't so far that he couldn't observe what was happening. Have you finished your questioning?"

"No, your honor." Allen turned back to face me. "Mr. Johnson, do I understand you observed Mr. Foster catching Miss Bennett's arm when she allegedly stumbled?" Allen said.

"That's right."

"Then Mr. Foster suggested that you give Miss Bennett a ride home?"

"Yes, sir, that's exactly what happened."

"I'm not entirely clear why Mr. Foster suggested you give Miss Bennett a ride. Was there a mechanical problem with her car?"

"No, sir." I didn't think it was a good idea to say Lisa was drunk. "Miss Bennett appeared unsteady, shaken from her near fall and Eddy thought it would be in Miss Bennett's best interests if I drove her home."

"Thank you, I have no further questions." Allen turned to O'Hearn. "Your honor, I contend that this matter should go to trial. Mr. Johnson was not in a position to really understand what was happening. Much of his testimony is based on supposition."

O'Hearn ignored Allen's remarks and looked over at Lisa. "Miss Bennett, do you have any comments regarding Mr. Johnson's statement?"

Lisa stood up, avoiding eye contact with Eddy. "There was some confusion at the time. The incident may have occurred as Mr. Johnson testified." Lisa looked relieved, but there was only anger on Ernest's face.

"Thank you, Miss Bennett. Mr. Johnson, you may return to the gallery."

While I was walking back to my original seat, Judge O'Hearn opened the file again and addressed Eddy. "Mr. Foster, Sheriff Simpson ran a background check on you after issuing the citation. According to the replies he received, you do not have a criminal record—at least no criminal convictions."

"No, sir, I've never been in jail."

"From the numerous responses Sheriff Simpson received, it would appear you've traveled a great deal for someone so young. Do you have a permanent address?"

"No, sir."

"If your honor pleases," I said. "Eddy is staying with me and my wife and is gainfully employed at my service station."

"Thank you, Mr. Johnson," O'Hearn said before turning back to Eddy. "Mr. Foster, I've known Sam Johnson for many years and am taking into account his speaking in your behalf. It would appear there has been a misunderstanding in this matter. Therefore I am going to dismiss the charges. However, I warn you, if you ever come before this court again, I will not be so lenient."

"Your honor," Ernest Bennett said, standing up. "I protest your decision. This homeless drifter assaulted by daughter, and you're letting him off without punishment. When decent women aren't safe in public places, you aren't representing the sort of law we expected when you were elected." There was a strong emphasis on the word 'elected'.

Judge O'Hearn heard the emphasis and the color rose in his cheeks. "Mr. Bennett, I appreciate your parental concern. However I understand you were not present during the incident. Is that correct?"

"No, I wasn't there, but my daughter doesn't lie. When she came home she was extremely upset."

"The court is not questioning your daughter's honesty, simply her interpretation of the incident." Judge O'Hearn addressed Lisa. "Miss Bennett, do you have any further information to enter in evidence? Do you object to the charge being dismissed?"

Lisa shook her head. "No." Her voice was so soft I had to strain to hear.

"Obviously there was a misunderstanding on your daughter's part, Mr. Bennett. Mr. Foster intended no harm, and I am dismissing the charges."

"You may be sorry for that decision," Bennett threatened.

"I will pretend I didn't hear that comment," Judge O'Hearn roared. "However, if there's another word from you I will cite you for contempt of court."

Ernest shut up then, but he grabbed Lisa by the arm and nearly dragged her out of the courtroom.

Lisa and Ernest were in a heated discussion, their voices low, but urgent, when Eddy and I stepped into the hallway. I tried to steer Eddy away, but Ernest had seen us and moved to block our path. He was a vindictive person who didn't like to lose. I'd already guessed it was Ernest, not Lisa, who had pressed charges against Eddy.

"This isn't finished, young man," Ernest threatened. "If you ever so much as talk to my daughter again, I guarantee you'll be sorry."

Eddy completely ignored Ernest, looking directly into Lisa's eyes, reaching out to touch her arm. "Don't be afraid to let people see your true self," he said. "You're a beautiful person."

Ernest pushed between Lisa and Eddy, grabbing Eddy's hand and pulling it away from his daughter. Ernest's expression registered shock and anger, and I realized he hadn't experienced the warm, happy sensation everyone else felt upon touching Eddy. I wondered if it was because the contact had been too brief, or whether Ernest had sensed Eddy glimpsing some of his shameful secrets.

I grabbed Eddy's arm and dragged him away. A confused look lingered in Lisa Bennett's eyes and she opened her mouth like she was going to say something, then changed her mind.

Ernest Bennett was so angry I thought he would have a heart attack. Maybe Lisa wore a mask, hiding a good person, but not Ernest. He was a bastard, with or without a mask. I was afraid Eddy hadn't heard the end of this matter.

Ten

We never did open the service station Wednesday afternoon because I make the mistake of stopping at the house first. Mica was always unhappy when Eddy wasn't around, so we only intended to stop long enough to pick up the dog. I should have known Mary would insist on a word for word account of our day in court. Since her recovery, I just couldn't refuse her anything. Eddy took Mica outside while I sat at the kitchen table and gave her as complete a report as I could remember. By the time she was satisfied it was nearly six.

Mary had never been good at just sitting and having a conversation, so she busied herself preparing supper while I talked. Eddy came in and we both washed up. Mary and I wrapped up the discussion while we ate.

Eddy and I began stacking the dirty dishes in the sink as Mary rummaged through the kitchen cabinets like she had lost something.

"Sam, I've completely run out of salt. I can't imagine where it all went. I could have sworn we had an extra box in the pantry. But I've checked everywhere and there just isn't any. Without seasoning, you're not going to be happy with your eggs tomorrow morning. Would you please run over to Sal's Diner and pick up some salt?"

Although Cranston didn't have a grocery store, Sally Winthrop kept a few essentials on hand at Sal's Diner for the convenience of her customers. A few years ago I had considered adding groceries to my stock at the Service Station, creating a small convenience store like they had in the newer gas stations along the highway. I had decided I didn't want to bother with the extra inventory and longer hours or worrying about the freshness of products.

"Damnit, Mary, I don't feel like running to the store." I was tired and was looking forward to a beer and relaxation. Maybe I was a more considerate person since Eddy had touched me, but I still became irritated by disruptions to my routine. It was going to be a while before I reached perfection—if ever.

"Can't you get along without salt tonight?" I whined. "Make something for breakfast that doesn't need salt and I'll go in the morning after Eddy and I open the station."

"Of course, I have to have salt," Mary insisted. "The only thing I can make that doesn't need seasoning is instant oatmeal, and you don't like oatmeal. I'm not going to have you complain my cooking is bland. So you just put your beer back in the refrigerator and get yourself down to Sal's. It won't take more than fifteen minutes."

"I'd be happy to go, Mary," Eddy said. "Mica and I would enjoy the walk. The fresh air and exercise will be good for us."

"You get plenty of fresh air at the station," I said, hearing myself sound grumpy. "I'll go."

"No, Sam," Eddy insisted. "I'd really like to go. I need to take Mica for a walk."

"Thank you Eddy, I'd appreciate it," Mary said, as if the matter were decided. "If you pick up a box of salt and a gallon of milk at Sal's Diner, it should tide us over until I can get my lazy husband to take me shopping in Elliott."

"No problem," Eddy said, slipping into his jacket. "I should only be a few minutes. Come on, Mica."

The dog jumped up and down in excitement, his tail going a mile a minute, as he preceded Eddy out the door.

"You should be ashamed of yourself, Samuel Johnson, making that poor boy walk over to the Diner in the dark," Mary scolded after Eddy left.

"Eddy wanted to go," I protested. "And you know I would've gone after I griped a little."

"If you say so," Mary said, pouring herself a cup of tea and sitting at the table. "Alma Smith told me there was an argument with Ernest Bennett after court. You never mentioned anything about that."

"How the hell could Alma have already called you about what happened in the courthouse? It was only a couple hours ago."

"She phoned just before you and Eddy got home. You know her sister works in the courthouse."

"There wasn't any trouble, and Alma Smith has a big mouth."

"Samuel Johnson, that's no way to talk about Alma. She's the best friend we have. She just knows a lot of people and she hears thing."

"And repeats everything she hears."

"Now don't try to distract me by bad mouthing Alma. I want to hear about the trouble."

I sighed, knowing Mary would keep after me until I told. Truthfully I hadn't decided in my own mind how significant the confrontation with Ernest Bennett had been. Although I'd never personally had a run in with Ernest, rumor had it that he was the last person you'd want for an enemy. If you could believe half the stories, Ernest was responsible for some pretty serious, unsolved incidents of physical violence and intimidation. I don't know how much of the gossip I believed, but I had no doubt Ernest was capable of almost anything. I just hadn't decided whether the courthouse confrontation would have any consequences. I decided to down play it for Mary because she had a tendency to get exited over trivial events.

"There wasn't any trouble, just an exchange of words," I said. "I've already told you, when Judge O'Hearn heard my side of the story, he dismissed the charges. Well Boss Bennett didn't like that very much. He told Eddy if he so much as talked with Lisa again, there would be trouble."

"The Judge said that?"

"Not Judge O'Hearn. Ernest Bennett. He confronted us in the hallway outside the courtroom."

"That Ernest Bennett has gotten too big for his britches," Mary declared. "Just because he's got a pile of money, he thinks the world revolves around him. I take that back. Even when he was a little tyke, and his family was dirt poor, he acted like he was better than anyone else." Mary sipped her tea. "I can understand Ernest being nasty, but I don't understand why Lisa wanted to get Eddy into trouble. Despite the negative things I've heard, I've always liked her."

"I don't think she did anything," I said. "I got the impression the citation was Ernest's idea. Lisa didn't look like she wanted to be in court and when

O'Hearn asked if she agreed with dismissing the charge, she jumped at the chance."

"That makes sense," Mary agreed. "She was always such a sweet little girl. I believe she acts tough now because she doesn't know how to stop. It must be terrible for her, living with a tyrant like her Father. Things would have been different if Linda were still alive. A girl needs her Mother. I'll bet when Lisa's at school she's an entirely different person."

"Maybe you're right. Lisa never said a word when Ernest confronted us. I thought Ernest was going to have a heart attack when Eddy touched Lisa's arm and spoke to her."

"What did Eddy say?"

"He spoke quietly, like he does, and I was concerned with getting him out of there so I didn't hear it all. It sounded like he told Lisa not to be afraid, that she was a good person. I don't know whether Ernest heard Eddy, but Lisa looked confused by it. Maybe Eddy senses something in that girl no one else does."

"He senses a lot of things none of the rest of us notice."

"If he weren't such a good kid, he'd be scary."

Mary glanced at the kitchen clock. "I wonder what's taking him so long." There was concern in her voice. "Going to the Diner and back should only have taken a few minutes."

"Maybe he stopped to talk with Sally. She could use some cheering, with her husband dead and her son dying."

"Do you think Eddy is touching Johnny? Wouldn't that be wonderful for Sally?"

"Johnny's in Elliott at Memorial Hospital," I said. "More likely business is slow at the Diner and Eddy is visiting with Sally."

"Sam, I've got a feeling something's wrong." Mary reached across the table and squeezed my hand. "I'd feel a lot better if you'd drive to the store and give Eddy a ride home."

"What could possibly happen walking over to the Diner?'

"I don't know, but I have a feeling something's wrong. Stop being obstinate and go."

"All right, but you're getting worked up over nothing." I was reaching for my jacket when Mica scratched at the back door and barked. "Sounds like Eddy's back," I said. "Strange though, I've never heard Mica bark before."

"You'd better check," Mary said anxiously. "Sam, I'm frightened. Maybe a car hit Eddy. I just know something terrible has happened. I can feel it in my bones."

"Now, Mary, don't let your imagination get the best of you. The dog probably ran on ahead."

"You check anyway, Sam. I'm worried. Mica never leaves Eddy, and you know it."

"Okay, I'll see what's up," I said, knowing I sounded peevish. "But Eddy's going to resent us fussing about him taking a short walk."

I slipped into my jacket and stepped onto the back porch, pausing while my eyes adjusted to the dark. Mica whined, tugged at my trouser leg, ran off a ways, stopped, came back, and barked. Obviously the dog wanted me to follow and that frightened me. Maybe something had happened to Eddy.

"Okay, Mica, I'm coming," I said, walking as fast as I could in the dark. "Lead the way."

Clouds had again moved in with sunset. Without the illumination of stars or moon, it was pitch dark away from the house. We didn't have the luxury of streetlights in Cranston, and I hadn't thought to bring a flashlight. I would have missed Eddy if Mica hadn't shown the way.

Eddy was lying in the ditch beside the driveway, attempting to raise himself onto his hands and knees, so he could crawl toward the house. Mica was at Eddy's side, whining and licking his face.

"Damnit, Eddy, are you alright?" I asked, knowing the words were stupid even as I spoke.

"I've been better," Eddy said, his voice thick, edged with pain. He wasn't having any luck lifting himself.

"Here, let me help." I grabbed under his shoulders, lifting him to his feet. He didn't say anything, but a sharp intake of breath indicated the movement hurt. I tried to be gentle as I lifted his left arm over my shoulder and half carried him toward the house. I couldn't see well, but Eddy's jacket felt wet, and I knew it was blood.

"Lay him down on the couch," Mary said, taking charge when we stumbled through the kitchen door. She never panicked in emergencies, and didn't faint at the sight of blood like some anemic females.

"I'll get your sofa dirty," Eddy protested.

"Never mind the sofa. Sam, help Eddy take off his jacket. It's all covered with blood. I'll get some water and bandages."

I eased Eddy onto the couch and helped remove his jacket. The strain of lifting his arms hurt him and his breathing was shallow, like a deep breath would be painful. The shirt underneath was also drenched with blood. I helped take it off, and then held the shirt against a gash above Eddy's right eye that was bleeding badly.

Mary returned with a pan of water and began wiping away blood with her good dishtowels. As she cleaned his face, I saw a small cut over his left eye. His upper lip was swelling and there was a thin trickle of blood from his nose. "You took terrible, Eddy. What the hell happened?"

"Four guys decided they didn't like the way I looked," Eddy said, attempting a smile that turned into a grimace. "They tried to rearrange my face."

"Sam, you get on the phone and call the Sheriff," Mary ordered, her voice angry. "We'll have to take Eddy to the hospital. I think he might have broken ribs and he's certainly going to need stitches."

"I don't need a doctor," Eddy protested. "I'll be alright if I can just lie here a few minutes."

"Don't argue with me, young man." Mary was crying, but the tears didn't interfere with her nursing. "I raised a boy of my own, and I know when it's time to go to the hospital."

"Yes, ma'am." Eddy sounded too tired to argue.

I used the phone in the kitchen and called the Sheriff's office first. After three rings a female answered. I explained that Eddy had been beaten, and an officer should meet us at the hospital. Maybe the police were accustomed to this sort of call because she took the information without a shred of emotion in her voice. I had an urge to yell, to shake her from the lethargy, but knew it wouldn't accomplish anything.

I took a deep breath to calm myself before calling Memorial Hospital to warn them we were coming. The duty officer at the Sheriff's Department had been hysterical compared with the nonchalance of the hospital operator. I got the impression she didn't care whether or not we brought Eddy in for treatment. I made a mental note to punch her in the nose when we got to the emergency room.

I hung up and took several deep breaths trying to get my blood pressure under control.

Mica was hovering beside Mary and Eddy. I could hear a low whining and noticed clotted blood in the fur on his head and neck.

"Come here, Mica," I said. "Let me look at you."

"Mica's all right," Eddy said, his voice cracking like it hurt to talk. "When those guys attacked me, Mica lit into them like an avenging angel. I'm pretty sure he bit at least two of them before one of the bastards hit him with something—maybe a baseball bat. I healed him." He said it nonchalantly, like healing injuries caused by a club were the most normal thing in the world.

I realized if Eddy said Mica was okay, he was okay, but I checked the dog anyway. Other than a clot of dried blood on his head and neck, there was no evidence of any injury.

"Why don't you heal yourself?" I asked.

"It doesn't work on me," Eddy said, grimacing at a sudden pain. "I sure wish it did."

"Samuel Johnson, you're wasting time with all this gabbing. You back the truck up to the porch, while I put on a coat and wrap Eddy in a blanket. Then you come back in and help me carry him out."

"I can walk," Eddy said.

"No you can't. If your rib is broken, we don't want to puncture a lung. Now, Sam, don't just stand there, get a move on."

"You wait here, Mica," Eddy said, ruffling the dog's ears despite the pain. "I'll be all right. You did just fine. I'm proud of you."

The dog flopped down beside the sofa, like he understood every word. His head rested on his front paws and there was the saddest look in his eyes I've ever seen on a dog. It was like he knew he hadn't done everything he could. That he should have died before allowing Eddy to be hurt.

Eleven

I had purposely avoided requesting an ambulance because we would make better time in my truck. If one of the two county ambulances had been available, the drive to Cranston, then back to Elliott, would have taken at least forty or fifty minutes. If both were already on calls, it's anyone's guess how long we'd have had to wait. When Joan Timberlane broke her hip it had been nearly two hours from the 911 call until she finally got to the hospital.

Memorial, the only hospital in the county, was a small facility, three stories of rooms, labs, and housekeeping services, but the staff was first rate. If I thought Eddy wouldn't receive the best care, I would have driven the additional thirty miles to Wentworth.

It was pretty crowded in the truck's cab. I had considered having Eddy lie down in the pickup's bed, but decided he would be too cold and bouncing around back there wouldn't help his injuries. Mary cushioned him in her arms and tried to make him as comfortable as possible. I drove like a maniac, ignoring the speed limit and the light evening traffic. I was mentally kicking myself every mile, and feeling pretty guilty. If I hadn't been so lazy, I'd have gone after the salt and we wouldn't be rushing Eddy to the hospital.

Fifteen minutes after leaving Cranston, I screeched to a halt in front of Memorial's emergency entrance, where the signs read, 'Ambulances Only'. Maybe the hospital operator hadn't been as apathetic as I had thought, because an orderly met us with a gurney as we were helping Eddy from the truck. The sight of all the blood must have caused a sense of urgency. The orderly wheeled Eddy through the automatic doors without wasting time covering him. Or maybe he didn't want to get blood on a hospital blanket.

Mary and I were following the gurney toward the cubicles at the end of the hallway when a buxom nurse intercepted us.

"You aren't allowed in the treatment rooms," she said in a commanding voice.

Her authoritarian tone would have stopped most people, but I was prepared to push past until Mary put a restraining hand on my arm.

"We'll take good care of the patient," the nurse said, assuming a more neutral tone after establishing control. "You can help by providing information." She pointed toward the emergency reception desk.

"Thank you," Mary said, firmly directing me toward the long counter.

A girl, who didn't look old enough to be out of high school, smiled at us. Acting very official in her crisp, white pants suit, she began making entries on a long form. I answered the standard questions—name, address, age— with no problems. When she asked about Eddy's medical history—blood type, previous illnesses, allergies, sensitivity to medications— I didn't have the foggiest idea. The girl, who probably believed Mary and I were Eddy's parents, looked at me like I was simple minded until I explained we were only Eddy's friends.

When she asked how the bill would be handled, I did some quick thinking, knowing the days of altruistic medicine were long past. Now hospitals operated like businesses, requiring credit references. I intended to pay for Eddy's treatment out of my own pocket, but being a friend, not a relative, and because Eddy was of age, the hospital would require more assurance of payment. I explained Eddy was my employee, covered under a group policy. I gave my insurance information, knowing the insurance company would reject the claim. Later, when the hospital's accountants began yelling and screaming, I would make other arrangements.

When the young lady was satisfied she wouldn't get any further useful information, she thanked me, suggesting Mary and I take seats in the waiting area. She assured us Doctor Calvin would speak to us as soon as he finished examining Eddy. I was pleasantly surprised Doc Calvin was the physician on call because I had confidence in him.

Mary sat on one of the plastic chairs while I parked my truck in the small emergency lot. Sheriff Simpson had arrived and was sitting beside Mary in the waiting area when I returned. A large, wall mounted TV was playing, but no one was watching. Except for the Sheriff and Mary, the room was deserted.

"You want to tell me what happened?" Sheriff Simpson asked.

"Working a little late, aren't you?" I had expected one of his deputies to handle an evening call. Maybe he already suspected who was responsible for Eddy's injuries, and anything concerning the Bennetts rated the Sheriff's person attention.

He shrugged. "Some days are longer than others. What happened?"

"Four men attacked Eddy and beat the hell out of him," I said.

"Did you recognize any of them?"

I shook my head. "I wasn't there. We didn't ask Eddy a lot of stupid questions because we were busy trying to keep him from bleeding to death."

"Then how do you know four men attacked him?"

"Because Eddy told us. Just look at him. It doesn't require a genius to see he was worked over. The bastards almost killed him."

"Just tell me what you know about the fight," Simpson said, like he would rather have been home in bed.

"It wasn't a fight. Not with four against one. That's a beating."

Sheriff Simpson was irritated, but trying to remain patient. "We'll make more progress if you stick to the facts and keep opinions to yourself. I want to find out what happened, not what you believe happened."

"After supper tonight, Eddy walked over to Sal's Diner to pick up some salt and milk," Mary interrupted realizing both the Sheriff and I were getting angry. "About an hour later his dog came whining and scratching at the door. Sam went to check and found Eddy lying in the ditch beside our driveway."

"Thank you, Mary." Simpson scribbled in a spiral notebook. "Had Eddy been drinking?"

"What the hell does that have to do with anything?" I demanded.

Mary put her hand on my arm. "The Sheriff is just doing his job. If you can't be civil, at least be silent." She turned to Simpson. "Eddy doesn't drink."

"Okay. Did Eddy tell you anything besides having a fight with four men? Did he tell you how the fight began?"

"We didn't ask him," Mary said. "But Eddy is a gentle boy. Whatever the reason for the fight, he didn't start it."

"Did he tell you anything that might help me?" Simpson asked, sounding frustrated.

Mary thought for a moment. "Eddy told us his dog bit at least one, maybe two of the hoodlums."

"Then, as far as you know, the dog might have attacked someone, and that started the fight."

"No, Sheriff," Mary said firmly. "Mica—that's Eddy's dog—wouldn't attack anyone unless they were threatening Eddy."

"But it could have happened that way," Sheriff Simpson insisted.

"This is a bunch of bullshit." I couldn't sit silently while Sheriff Simpson attempted to blame Eddy for the beating. "We both know Eddy was beaten up by four thugs, and we both know why."

Sheriff Simpson was not in a good mood. "I don't know a damned thing. And I won't until I have some facts to work with."

"You know Judge O'Hearn dismissed the charges against Eddy, don't you?" I asked.

Simpson nodded. "I received a report."

"When Eddy and I were leaving the Court House, Ernest Bennett threatened Eddy. I was there and heard every word. I'd bet my bottom dollar Bennett hired those thugs to teach Eddy a lesson. You know as well as I do Ernest Bennett has things his own way around here. If he doesn't like someone, they had better watch out."

"I'd be careful with that kind of talk if I were you," Simpson warned. "You don't have any idea what really happened. Making accusations without proof could get you into trouble."

"Trouble," I said, scornfully. "Like maybe Bennett will send his thugs to beat me up? He tries that and you'll find out what trouble really is."

"Now, Sam, you cool down," Mary said. "That isn't what the Sheriff meant, and you know it. Losing your temper isn't going to help anyone."

"I suppose if Bennett is behind this, it'll just get swept under the rug like it always does. Boss Bennett runs this county and everyone walks carefully around him."

"Now, Sam, I told you to cool down." Mary sounded like she was getting irritated. "You know Sheriff Simpson will do everything he can to catch those hoodlums." She looked at Simpson. "You will, won't you?"

"I'll do my job," Simpson agreed. "I'll see what Eddy has to say when the Doctors are finished. But right now I don't have anything to work on or a place to begin."

"You could begin by checking all the doctors in the area to see if anyone needed treatment for dog bites," I suggested. "Eddy's dog probably bit at least one of those bastards before he was bashed with some sort of club."

"Don't tell me how to do my job," Simpson said, obviously not interested in my opinions or advice. "I plan to check on the bites as soon as I finish talking with you." He stood up. "And I'm finished now. I suggest you keep groundless accusations to yourself, or you'll end up being sued."

Sheriff Simpson left us and walked over to the reception desk to talk with the nurse. Mary and I sat quietly, making small talk for about half an hour before Doctor Calvin came from the treatment room.

"How are you feeling, Mary?" he asked. "Still no sign of a relapse?"

"I'm fine, Doctor," Mary answered. "I'm not going to have a relapse."

"What about Eddy?" I asked. "How is he?"

"I assume Mr. Foster doesn't have family in the area," Doc said, like he was uncomfortable sharing patient information with people not related.

"He doesn't have family anywhere," I said. "He's been living with Mary and me, so I guess you could consider us family."

Doc Calvin hesitated, like he was making a decision. "Eddy's not in any danger, but he's going to be sore for a while. It took forty stitches to close the facial cuts. His nose isn't broken, but x-rays show a cracked rib, and a mild concussion. He does have some painful bruises on his torso, and the cracked rib will slow him down for a couple of weeks. I'd say he was a lucky young man not to have more serious injuries after such a severe beating." Doc Calvin rubbed his eyes, like he was tired. "And this wasn't the first time. Did you know he's been beaten before?"

"No." Mary and I looked at each other, both thinking about the violence Eddy had encountered in the past.

"The x-rays showed evidence of earlier trauma. There is scaring on his back and chest. I'd say this isn't even the worst beating he's suffered."

Mary was crying softly. "That poor boy. Why do people treat him that way?"

"Doctor Calvin, can I talk with your patient?" Sheriff Simpson asked, walking over from the reception desk.

Doctor Calvin nodded. "Yes, but please keep the questioning as brief as possible. Mr. Foster is in pain, and needs to rest. I couldn't give him a general pain medication because of the head injury."

"Is he still in the treatment room?" Simpson asked.

Doc Calvin nodded.

"Okay, thanks." Simpson turned and walked toward the cubicles at the back of the room.

"I'd like to keep Eddy overnight," Doc Calvin said.

"Then he is seriously hurt," Mary said, concern in her voice.

"No, not really. At least nothing life threatening. We always have to be careful with head injuries. I'd just like to keep him overnight in case there are complications." Doc Calvin saw the alarm in Mary's eyes. "But honestly, I don't expect any problems. It's just a precaution."

"Can we see him?" Mary asked.

"I don't see why not. I'll arrange for him to be moved into a room. As soon as he's settled, you can visit for a few minutes. Like I told the Sheriff, he needs to rest."

"I get the impression you're not telling us everything," I suggested. "Is there something more serious?"

"No, nothing else about Eddy," Doc said, almost as if talking to himself. "But when I was stitching the abrasion on Eddy's forehead I experienced the strangest sensation."

"Like what?" I asked, suspecting he had experienced the Eddy effect.

"Oh, it was nothing. Just a passing sensation. It's been a long day and I'm tired."

"You've been working too hard," Mary suggested. "Was it a dizzy feeling?"

"No, it was like nothing I've ever felt. It was strange, like a sense of well being, complete peace."

"Well, at least it wasn't a cramp." I wanted to change the subject before Doc Calvin associated the sensation with Eddy. I didn't think the beating had anything to do with Eddy's power, but the fewer people who knew about his gift, the better. "Will Eddy be able to go home tomorrow?"

Doc Calvin acted like he was coming out of a trance. "What did you say?"

"Will Eddy be able to go home tomorrow?"

"Unless there are complications, I don't see why not." Doc took a deep breath. "I have to get him scheduled for a room. Please check with me when you visit him tomorrow."

Doc Calvin walked to the reception desk just as Sheriff Simpson came out of the treatment room. The sheriff gave a half wave, but didn't come over to talk before leaving the building.

After another ten minutes Doc Calvin returned and directed us to Room 231. In parting he cautioned us to stay only a few minutes.

Eddy was in a semi-private room, in the bed closest to the door. A privacy screen had been positioned between the beds so we couldn't see the other occupant.

Eddy looked small and helpless with a large white bandage on his forehead, contrasting with the dark color of his bruises. His lips were swollen and the doctor had coated them with a thick salve.

"I'm sorry to cause all this trouble," Eddy mumbled.

"No trouble," I said.

"You rest now so you'll get better." Mary took his hand and held it against her cheek. "I wish I had the power."

"Yeah, me too." Eddy tried to make it sound like a joke, but he was obviously concerned. "Sam, I don't have any money. I can't pay for all this."

"That's the least of our worries," I said, smiling. "The way I see it, you're going to have to hang around Cranston until you work off your hospital bill."

"Might be a few days before I can work," Eddy said, attempting a smile that turned into a grimace.

"The doctor said we could only stay a minute," Mary said. "We'll come back tomorrow. He thinks you'll be able to come home then."

"I hope Mica doesn't make a fuss,' Eddy said. "We've never been separated over night."

"Mica will be fine," I assured him. "I'll even let him sleep in our room"

"I'd appreciate that."

Mary kissed him on the cheek and we headed for the door.

"Sam. Mary. Thanks for everything."

After all Eddy had done for Mary and me, it felt good to know we were able to do a little something for him. It wasn't nearly enough, but it was a start.

Twelve

It had been after midnight before I'd crawled into bed. I couldn't remember the last time I had been up past ten-thirty or so, and I was exhausted. Even so, the adrenaline high of rushing Eddy to the hospital kept me tossing and staring at the ceiling.

I couldn't shake the idea that Ernest Bennett was behind the attack on Eddy, yet the more I thought about it, the more it didn't make any sense. Not that I believed Ernest wasn't capable of hiring thugs to beat up someone. The problem was that no one could have known Eddy would be walking over to Sal's Diner after supper. However, it also wasn't logical that four hoodlums would have been cruising the streets looking for trouble and Eddy had been the victim of opportunity. That sort of thing might have happened in Elliott or some larger city, but not in Cranston. And how likely was it that random attackers would choose a victim walking with a large dog?

That left me with the thought that the punks had been watching the house, waiting for an opportunity to confront Eddy. If that were the case, what would they have done if Eddy hadn't walked to Sal's? Would the thugs have come to the house, or would they have jumped him at the station, maybe as part of a fake robbery?

When the alarm beeped I had an almost overpowering urge to turn it off and roll over for a couple more hours sleep. My practical nature and a little kick from Mary forced me out of bed.

After a week of short hours, I couldn't afford to not open the station for the commuter rush. My regular customers weren't likely to permanently abandon my place in favor of the highway stations, but with Eddy's anticipated medical bills, every dollar counted. Also I was a creature of habit. After thirty years of opening the station every morning, I knew I'd feel guilty lying in bed. I was already eager for a return to my normal, predictable life. If a handful of short days made me nervous, I wondered what would happen when age forced me to retire. Maybe I was one of those guys destined to die with a gas pump in one hand and wrench in the other.

Maintaining a grumpy attitude, I dragged myself to the station, serviced the morning commuters, and did an oil change for Edna Henley. Although Cranston didn't have a newspaper, news traveled fast, and most of the customers had heard about Eddy's beating. I answered questions as curtly as possible, leaving no doubt I didn't want to discuss the matter. Sid Jessup sensed juicy gossip and made a pest of himself until I chased him away and closed the station at ten-thirty.

When I stopped at the house, Mary was already waiting, wearing a spring dress that made her look young and beautiful. I think she enjoyed the idea of going to the hospital as a visitor, not a patient.

Mica sensed we were leaving, and let me know he wasn't happy being left behind. He acted as if I were punishing him for not protecting his master. Normally I'm not sentimental, but that dog was so lonely and incomplete without Eddy, I felt guilty shutting the door in his face. If I could have figured some way to sneak the dog into the hospital, I would have taken him along.

We parked in Memorial's nearly empty front lot and used the main entrance. The hospital lobby was a vast expanse of gleaming vinyl floors that looked as if no one ever walked on them, and groupings of chrome and Naugahyde furniture no one ever sat on. Hospital lobbies reminded me of motels, more show than function. Except the hospital odors of floor polish, flowers, bland food, and medicine, triggered images of sickness and death, reminding me of Mary's lingering illness.

No one challenged us as we bypassed the front desk, going directly to the chrome doored elevators. On the second floor, we stopped at the nurse's station to ask whether Doc Calvin had left orders for Eddy's release.

A cute brunette nurse, probably a year or two out of school, checked the charts, shaking her head. "Doctor Calvin didn't leave release orders," she said, glancing at her practical looking watch. "He should be making rounds in about an hour. If you'd like to talk with him, I'll leave a note."

I thanked her, left a message, and walked arm in arm with Mary to Room 231. From the doorway we could see Eddy had an early visitor. Her back was toward us, but the tight little figure and the golden hair identified her immediately. I was ready to burst in and say something, but Mary tightened her grip on my arm and shook her head.

"I'm glad you're feeling better, Mr. Foster." Lisa Bennett had a package in her hands, and there was a box of sampler chocolates on Eddy's night stand.

"Please call me Eddy," he said, noticing Mary and me standing in the doorway. "Hey, Sam and Mary come on in and join the party."

Lisa spun around, her cheeks coloring, no doubt feeling uncomfortable being discovered in Eddy's room. "I have to go, Eddy," she said. "I have an appointment. Please get well quickly."

"Don't let Sam and Mary chase you away," Eddy said. "You can't leave before Johnny gets back."

Lisa hesitated, obviously embarrassed to be confronting me after our day in court. "Maybe I can stay another minute or two."

"Sam and Mary, isn't it thoughtful of Lisa to visit? She even brought some candy." Eddy indicated the box of chocolates.

"Did you come to see your handiwork?" I asked. After the citation, Eddy's beating, and a sleepless night, I wasn't in the mood to be pleasant or forgiving.

Mary gave me a look that would have curdled cream. "Sam, you mind your manners." She took Lisa's hand and gently patted it. Mary had a knack for putting people at ease. "Don't pay any attention to Sam. He's always grumpy when he hasn't had enough sleep. And now he's forgotten how to be polite. It was very thoughtful of you to visit Eddy."

"Thank you, Mrs. Johnson." Lisa looked more comfortable.

"Please call me Mary. I think friends should use first names, don't you?"

"Thank you, Mary. Actually I came to see my cousin, Eddy's roommate." Lisa held up the second box of candy as evidence. "Johnny's in therapy, so Eddy and I were visiting while I waited." This bright, thoughtful girl wasn't the Lisa Bennett I knew. "I haven't made a very good impression the couple of times we've met, and I wanted Eddy to know I didn't have anything to do with...with this."

Before I could make one of my famous acid comments, an orderly pushed a wheel chair into the room. I recognized Johnny Winthrop although I'd only seen the boy a few times. He was small for a ten year old, and his robe appeared to be a couple sizes too big. His complexion was yellowish and his head completely bald. The orderly helped the boy into his bed, adjusted the pillow, and started to place the privacy screen.

"Its okay, Bob, we don't need the screen," Eddy said.

"Okay with me, Eddy." The orderly shrugged. "Just make sure you two trouble makers don't cause mischief and get me into hot water."

"We'll be good," Eddy promised.

"Hey, Johnny, aren't you going to say hi," Eddy called when the orderly left with the wheel chair.

"You've got company," Johnny answered, his voice a whisper, like he was reminding Eddy of hospital protocol.

"Hey, buddy, when I have company, we both have company. Besides, Lisa is here to visit you." Eddy turned to include us in the exchange. "Sam and Mary, I want you to meet my good friend, Johnny. We've decided when we both escape from this place I'm going to teach my buddy about fixing motors. Right, Johnny?"

"Sure Eddy." The boy didn't sound like he believed.

"We already know Johnny," Mary said. He was Sally Winthrop's son, and lived with his mother above Sal's Diner. "How are you feeling, Johnny?"

"Therapy always makes me tired, but otherwise I'm okay. I've got leukemia, you know." Johnny said it in a matter of fact tone, like he had come to terms with the illness, or maybe didn't understand the seriousness. "That's why my head is bald. Radiation makes my hair fall out."

"Would you believe I had cancer?" Mary said. "This time last week I was so sick I couldn't even get out of bed."

"Are you in remission?" Johnny asked. He had been in treatment a long time, and cancer patients tended to learn a lot about the disease. "I've been in remission since last Christmas, but I still have to come in for treatments."

I felt a tightness in my throat. The youngster had the same aura of resignation I had sensed in Mary when she knew she was dying.

"I almost forgot," Lisa said, bridging an uncomfortable pause. "I brought you some candy." She handed Johnny the box. "I don't know if you can have chocolate."

"I'm not supposed to," Johnny said, ripping off the wrapping. "But what the doctors don't know won't hurt them."

"Johnny had a bad night and we held hands," Eddy said. "There's no better way to become friends than for a couple of guys to stay up late, sharing secrets. I told my good buddy he was going to get better, but he doesn't believe me. He doesn't have faith. Why don't you perk him up, Mary?"

"You don't mind?" Mary asked, referring to the promise we had both made concerning Eddy's power.

"I think this is a special case, Mary." Eddy attempted a smile. His lips weren't as swollen as last night, but it was obviously still painful to grin. "Johnny and I don't have any secrets, do we pal?"

The boy's face lit up like it made him feel good to be included in adult camaraderie.

Lisa had been looking back and forth between Eddy, Johnny, and Mary, a troubled expression on her face. "I don't think you should give Johnny false hope," she said. Although she wasn't her usual bitchy self, she obviously didn't appreciate the direction the conversation was taking.

Mary patted Lisa on the shoulder. "Don't worry, Lisa. I promise you it will be all right." She walked to the far side of Johnny's bed and took his hand in both of hers. "Let me tell you a story." Her voice dropped to a whisper to keep the conversation private.

There was an awkward moment when Eddy, Lisa and I didn't know what to say. Eddy gave me a look that had a hint of disapproval. Suddenly I felt ashamed for the way I had behaved. I'm usually a stubborn old man, but I knew it was the right thing to do, so I apologized to Lisa.

"That's all right, Sam. I understand how you feel, after going to court and every thing. It must look like all this is my fault, but I truly didn't have anything to do with the beating."

"We never thought you did," Eddy said. He gave me a look that demanded I make a positive comment.

"No, I never figured this sort of thing was your style." I didn't think Lisa was guilty, but I would have bet my service station against a dollar bill that her father had hired the thugs.

Lisa turned to Eddy. "Well, I have to go now. I really do have an appointment."

"Thank you for coming, Lisa." Eddy held out his hand and Lisa took it in both of hers. "And please don't be afraid to be yourself. You're a truly beautiful person inside. Just accept it."

Lisa had that strange confused look on her face, and I knew she was experiencing the warm, happy feeling. She didn't want to let go of Eddy's hand.

"Hey, Eddy," Johnny called. His face was positively glowing and it was evident he was excited. "Is it really true?"

Eddy gently pulled his hand away from Lisa. "Yeah, pardner. You don't think we'd pull the wool over your eyes, do you?"

"Is what true?" Lisa asked. She was still having the warm happy feeling, but I could see she wasn't comfortable with Johnny's sudden happiness. I figured she must think we were telling the boy something to give him false hope.

"It's a secret," Johnny said.

"Eddy, I'm going to see if I can corner Doc Calvin and get you released from this joint," I said, not wanting Lisa to begin asking Johnny about the secret. "I'll walk you to the elevators, Lisa."

I could see her debating with herself before she decided not to pursue the secret the rest of us seemed to be sharing. "I'd like that, Sam," Lisa said, planting a quick kiss on top of Johnny's head, then hurrying out before she began crying.

"Johnny's such a brave boy, and I hate what's happening to him. It doesn't seem fair for him to..." She gave a big sigh. "Hell, Sam, you know what I mean."

"Yeah, I know," I said, thinking of the helplessness that had overwhelmed me when Mary was dying. "But I've got a feeling Johnny's going to be okay."

"Don't patronize me Sam." Lisa said sharply, sounding more like the Lisa I knew. "I know Johnny is going to die. He isn't in remission and the treatments aren't helping anymore. The Doctors think he might have a month. Maybe less."

"I'm a grumpy old man, like Mary said, but I'm not patronizing you," I insisted. "The Doctors are wrong. You wouldn't believe me if I told you how I know, but trust me in this. Johnny is going to live long enough to be as old as I am."

There was nothing else I could say so we walked to the elevators in silence.

Before she pushed the down button, Lisa turned and looked directly in my eyes. "You don't like me very much, do you, Sam?"

I considered lying, but decided Lisa wanted an honest answer. "Frankly, I've always thought you were a spoiled brat. If you were my daughter, I'd have turned you across my knee and given you a good spanking."

Lisa surprised me by laughing. "Thanks for your honesty. I have been a spoiled brat and didn't like myself very much. I don't know why, but during the last several days I've taken a hard look, and what I saw didn't make me feel very good. I want to change, to be a better person, but I'm not sure I can do it alone. Would you and Mary please be my friends? I'm going to need people who will be honest when I need it."

"I haven't ever been your enemy," I said.

Lisa nodded. "I know. You never liked me very much, but you always treated me like a person, and I appreciated it—even if I didn't show it."

"If you want honesty, we'll sure as hell give you that."

Lisa pushed the down button. "Thanks, Sam." She came up on her tiptoes and kissed me on the cheek. Then she stepped into the elevator and before the doors closed I saw tears on her cheeks.

I stood there a long time, knowing how confused Lisa must feel, wondering about the changes that were swirling through my world. Damnit if I wasn't beginning to believe in miracles.

Thirteen

Doctor Calvin had decided to keep Eddy in the hospital one more day, so I wasn't able to pick him up until Saturday morning. Mary and I were both impatient to have him home, but not if it would endanger his recovery.

I have to admit my heart went out to Mica. I was afraid the dog might die before Eddy got home. He wasn't eating at all, no matter how much Mary coaxed him. Mostly he either lay on Eddy's bed or beside the kitchen door. I put him on a leash when I let him outside to do his duty because I was afraid he would run away. Mica had never been to the hospital in Elliott, but my guess was that somehow he'd find his way there so he could be with Eddy.

Business had been booming at the station on Friday. In fact it had been one of the best Friday's I'd had in a long time. Maybe it was because everyone had heard about the beating and that type of violence was so rare in Cranston, they were curious about what had actually happened. I didn't make many of them happy with my laconic replies.

I had considered calling Billy Thornton and asking him to watch the station Saturday morning. Four years ago, before the expressway, Bill had worked for me during the afternoons while he was in High School, and was familiar with the routine. Since graduation he had been working at the Cranston Co-op and I knew they were closed on Saturday. It was tempting to ask Billy, but I decided there wouldn't be enough Saturday morning business to justify his wages. Nearly everyone in Cranston who needed gas had been to the station Friday, so it wasn't likely I'd miss many customers.

Mary wanted to go with me to pick up Eddy, but I didn't think it was a good idea. It had only been a week since she'd been out of bed and I still believed she needed to gain back her strength. Of course, deep in my heart I hadn't adjusted to the idea that she was whole again Besides, it would be awfully cramped in the front seat of my pickup with Mary, Eddy, and me. Fortunately Mary didn't argue too vehemently, only putting up a brief struggle before she agree to stay home with Mica and make a nice meal for Eddy's homecoming.

She did insist I take Eddy an entire set of clean clothes. I hadn't even considered that the clothing he had at the hospital was dirty, bloody, and torn. If it'd been left to my planning he would have come home in a hospital gown.

I stopped at the station on my way out of Cranston and hung the 'Gone Fishing' sign on the door. People had seen the sign before and most of them would know I had to pick up Eddy.   One of the advantages—and disadvantages—of a small town was that everyone knew everyone else's business.

There isn't much traffic on Saturday mornings, so I made good time on the drive to Elliott. It was a few minutes before nine when I parked my pickup in the main lot.

Eddy was sitting on the bed, dressed in his shabby old clothing when I arrived. Johnny Winthrop's bed was empty, but unmade.

"Where's Johnny?" I asked.

Eddy glanced at me with that knowing expression of his. "They've taken him for some tests."

I didn't have to ask why they were giving Johnny tests, and I could tell Eddy didn't want to talk about it. "Mary insisted I bring you some clean clothes," I said. "Why don't you change and we'll burn those old rags."

While Eddy was getting dressed I noticed his chest and ribs were wrapped in bandages. He winced whenever he raised his arms, but otherwise seemed to be in good shape. There was still some swelling on his face where the stitches were visible, but the ugly bruising had nearly disappeared.

We were just about set to leave when a cute young nurse entered the room pushing a wheelchair. "Are you ready to go, Eddy?"

"Sure am. I loved your hospitality, Betty, but I'm looking forward to getting out into the fresh air again."

"We're going to miss you," she said. From the dreamy look in her eyes I suspected she had a little crush on her patient. "You be sure and visit us once in a while."

"I promised, didn't I?" Eddy frowned at the wheelchair. "I don't need that, Betty. I'm perfectly capable of walking."

"Hospital rules," Betty said. "We can't have you falling down and hurting yourself on hospital property."

"I guess orders are orders. Wouldn't want to break any rules." Eddy dutifully sat in the chair. "I just hope you know how to drive this thing."

Betty laughed and began pushing him toward the elevators. She turned to me. "Mr. Johnson, did you hear about Eddy's roommate, Little Johnny Winthrop?" She was obviously excited regarding what must have been big news in the hospital.

I acted like I didn't have a clue what she was talking about. "What about Johnny?" I asked. "Has he taken a turn for the worse?"

"It's just the opposite," Betty said. She sort of tossed her head, like she didn't quite believe her own story. "It was the strangest thing. When the technician came yesterday afternoon to take him to therapy, Johnny wouldn't go. He insisted he felt fine and didn't need therapy anymore. Fortunately Doctor Calvin was making rounds and he heard the commotion. After what happened to your wife, he decided to give Johnny a complete exam. He couldn't find a trace of the leukemia. Johnny's been downstairs having x-rays and blood tests again this morning. The word is that he's completely cured, just like your wife. It's absolutely amazing. Two miracles in a week. It sort of gives me a funny feeling in my stomach."

I didn't know how to respond, and before I opened my mouth and said something stupid, Eddy spoke up.

"Isn't it wonderful, Sam? Johnny told me last night he was feeling better."

"Yeah, that's great news. I sure hope he's as lucky as Mary was." I would be the last person in the world to begrudge Johnny's recovery, but I had to wonder about the timing, coming so soon after Mary's miracle. Pretty soon we'd have people lined up at our front door begging to be cured.

That would be an aggravation, but somehow I didn't think it was the trouble Eddy had predicted.

We arrived at the entrance and Eddy jumped out of the chair. He shook Betty's hand and I could tell she was having that warm, happy feeling. If he didn't want people to know about his power, he would have to stop healing folks or shaking hands. She was still standing in front of the hospital, looking confused when we drove out of the parking lot.

"Who's watching the station?" Eddy asked.

"Closed her up for the day," I said. "Didn't have anything scheduled and it's always slow on Saturdays anyway."

Eddy sounded sad. "Business isn't so good you can afford to be closed."

Of course he was right. Insurance had paid a big portion of Mary's expenses, but it'd still take a few years to zero the account. Combined with Eddy's bill, I needed every dollar I could get. But I'm too ornery to admit it. "Business isn't so bad that I'll go bankrupt if I close for one day."

I could tell Eddy didn't believe me but he didn't say anything. We drove to Cranston without further talk about money or medical bills. Mica heard my truck pull into the driveway and was jumping at the passenger side door before I stopped at the house. His tail was going so fast I though it'd tear off his hind legs. Eddy climbed out, squatted by the dog, and gave him a big hug while Mica licked him all over the face.

Mary was waiting at the kitchen door and also gave Eddy a hug. I saw him wince from the pressure on his ribs, but he hugged her right back. It made me feel good. Like my own son was returning home.

* * *

Although his ribs caused pain when he moved, Eddy insisted on going with me to the station on Monday. After being laid up since Wednesday, he must have been getting restless. For the last five years Eddy had worked a multitude of jobs, scratching for a day-to-day existence, and had never learned to deal with idleness. Maybe he felt being active would aid his recuperation.

The warm weather had returned, and after we ate the lunch Mary had packed, Eddy convinced me I should take an hour or so and make sure Mary was all right. I'm pretty certain he sensed in his special way that Mary and I needed time together as we developed a deeper, stronger relationship. It didn't seem right to leave him alone while he was still hurting, but I knew if there were any problems he could phone and I would be back at the station in minutes. More than likely he understood I still worried about Mary. Some things are just hard to get into my head.

It was such a beautiful day that Mary and I decided to sit in the backyard and hold hands like a couple of teenagers.

Along about three o'clock, Sally Winthrop stopped at the house.

I didn't know Sally very well, although I admired her hard work and accomplishments. She was a single mother, her husband having been killed in a car accident when Johnny was about four years old. I'd heard she was distantly related to the Bennetts by marriage. I think her husband had been the son of Ernest's brother-in-law's sister. It they were related, it didn't move Ernest to help when she was widowed. But Sally had the strength to meet the challenge, using insurance money to open Sal's Diner. She and Johnny lived in an apartment above the restaurant. She wouldn't ever get rich, but the Diner was moderately successful with a loyal clientele of farmers and local residents. She was a great cook. Not as good as Mary, but better than average.

Sally was pretty in a hard worked sort of way, and I expect she could have remarried, but the idea apparently didn't appeal to her. Between supporting her son and operating the restaurant, she kept herself occupied.

"I hope I'm not interrupting," She said nervously. She was wearing her waitress uniform and little apron, obviously taking a break from work.

We had three lawn chairs in the yard so Mary, Eddy, and I could sit out during the evenings. "Of course you aren't interrupting," Mary assured her. She indicated the vacant seat. "Please sit down. Can I get you something to drink?"

Sally sat on the edge of the chair. "No thank you. I can't stay very long. I have to get back to the diner." She self-consciously folded and unfolded her hands in her lap, like she didn't know what to do with them. "I wanted to talk about Johnny." Sally seemed about ready to start crying. "I don't know how to say this."

Now I'm not much for handling women on the verge of tears, so I kept my mouth shut and let Mary do the talking.

"You don't need to say anything," Mary said. "I know why you came."

Mary's statement didn't seem to surprise Sally. "Johnny doesn't have leukemia anymore," she said. "The doctors have examined him every possible way, and they can't find a trace. Johnny told me about Eddy and how you had cancer and Eddy cured you and that it was Eddy who cured him." The words come in a flood. Then Sally cried without make a sound, her head down, her shoulders shaking. When she finally looked up, tears glistened on her cheeks and her eyes were red.

"I'm sorry," she said. "I didn't mean to cry. I told myself all the way over here that I wouldn't let myself go."

"That's alright," Mary said. "A wise man once said crying is good for the soul."

Sally took a handkerchief from her apron pocket, wiped her eyes, blew her nose, and smiled. "I'm all right now." Another sniffle and a straightening of her shoulders. "Since George was killed, Johnny has been my entire life. It was tearing me apart that he was going to die, and I can't begin to tell you how grateful I am that he isn't sick."

Mary reached across and patted Sally's hand. "But you're confused and you find it impossible to believe. I understand exactly how you feel."

"I had to talk with you because I can't believe what Johnny told me. I know he's not sick, but he's had temporary improvements before. The doctors say this isn't remission."

No," Mary said. "It isn't remission. I'm sure the cancer is gone."

"I realize I should be talking with Eddy, thanking him for curing my son, but Johnny told me he'd made a promise not to tell anyone how he was cured. I didn't want Eddy to think he had broken a promise."

"I'm sure he wouldn't mind Johnny telling you," Mary said.

"I don't know whether I can believe what Johnny told me," Sally said. "I don't think he would lie, but it just seems impossible. If it's true, I don't understand why Eddy wants it to be a secret. It's the most wonderful gift I've ever heard of."

"I know," Mary agreed. "Eddy made us promise to keep it secret also. He's afraid when people find out about his gift there will be trouble. He said that's the way it always begins."

Sally shook her head. "It just doesn't make any sense. I still can't believe it really happened, but Johnny is well again, and I feel like I owe

Eddy for giving back my son. If he wants it to remain a secret, that's the least I can do."

I stood up. "Why don't I leave you gals alone with your girl talk?"

"Please don't go, Mr. Johnson. I wanted to talk with you also. To ask a favor."

"Please call me Sam," I said, reluctantly resuming my seat. Before I'd met Eddy I wasn't much of one to grant favors. Even now I wasn't sure there was anything I could do for Sally.

"You know Johnny hasn't had a male role model since his Father died, and I think a boy should have a man to look up to. He thinks Eddy is the greatest guy he's ever met." Sally took a deep breath and sort of rushed into continuing. "While they were in the hospital Eddy had told Johnny he would teach him how to fix cars. When Johnny's out of the hospital and he's feeling strong enough, I was wondering if it would be alright for him to stop at the station once in a while so he could visit with Eddy?"

"I don't know, Sally. A service station isn't a very safe place for a kid. If he got injured my insurance probably wouldn't cover it."

Sally looked like I had just punctured her balloon. "I understand."

Mary sat bolt upright in her chair. "Samuel Johnson you should be ashamed of yourself." She put her hand on Sally's arm. "Of course Johnny can stop at the station and visit with Eddy. Isn't that right, Samuel Johnson?"

Mary only called me by my full name when she was upset about something. I'd rather pet a rattlesnake than have Mary angry with me. I wasn't happy with the idea of having a youngster running around the grease racks, but it was better than facing Mary's criticism. "Sure Sally, Johnny can come over to the station any time. I'll just make certain he doesn't hurt himself."

Sally's face lit up with a huge smile and it appeared as if a couple of years had lifted off her shoulder. It sure is easy to make people happy when you just try a little.

"Oh, thank you, Mr...uh...Sam. Johnny was really looking forward to working with Eddy, but I told him I'd have to ask you first." She stood up and straightened her skirt. "Thank you so much. I have to get back to the diner now. Thank you again."

"If you need someone to talk with, you come back any time," Mary said.

"You tell Eddy that Johnny and I want all of you to come to the diner for my best meal, on the house, to celebrate Johnny's recovery."

"We'd love that," Mary said.

I was feeling pretty pleased with myself when I headed back to the station to finish the afternoon. What a difference the last few days had made in my attitude.

With all the curious customers flocking to my station, it looked as if my tired old business was going to be even more profitable than it had been before the expressway opened. Maybe paying doctor's bills wasn't going to be so difficult after all.

Fourteen

About four o'clock Wednesday afternoon the school bus stopped in front of the station and Johnny Winthrop jumped down.

"Hi, Mr. Johnson," he called. He still looked frail, and his bald head was hidden under a baseball cap, but his color was good and he appeared to have an abundance of energy. "Mom said you gave permission for me to work with Eddy."

"Sure did," I replied. "But does your Mom know you're stopping here today? I'll bet this is your first time back at school."

"I went to school yesterday afternoon, and Mom said it was okay for me to visit Eddy today. She'll pick me up at closing time."

Sally kept the diner open until eight or nine most nights, and I figured it would be inconvenient for her to come for Johnny. After all, six o'clock was prime time at a diner. "I'll call your Mom and tell her you got here okay and I'll give you a ride home after we close." I sure was getting soft in my old age.

Eddy came out of the service bay wiping his hands on a rag. Johnny's face lit up like a flash bulb and he ran over to give and get a hug. Then Mica patiently let Johnny hug and pet him as Eddy introduced the boy to his dog.

Although I wasn't convinced it was a good idea having a youngster hanging around the service bays, I really didn't mind as long as no one got hurt. In order to minimize the chances of an accident, I called Johnny and Eddy into the office and explained the rules. The boy could watch and learn, but he couldn't do any actual work. He was a good kid, but I figured a youngster like Johnny would quickly lose interest and stop coming to the station. However, after observing him and Eddy for a few minutes I wasn't so certain Johnny would be bored.

The boy obviously worshipped Eddy, and watched him with the same intensity Mica did. If being a mechanic was good enough for his idol, then Johnny was determined to learn all there was to know about repairing cars. He hung on every word, like he was listening to the wisdom of the ages, and handed Eddy tools as he asked for them. When Eddy went to pump gas both Johnny and Mica were right at his side. It gave me a good feeling to see them so devoted to Eddy, but I have to admit I felt a touch of jealousy. It was reminiscent of how Albert had followed me around and helped at the station when he was Johnny's age.

By closing time, when Eddy, Johnny, Mica and I squeezed into my pickup so I could drive the boy home, I had decided maybe it wouldn't be so bad having a youngster hanging around after all.

"Thanks, Mr. Johnson," Johnny said as he hopped out of the truck. "See you tomorrow, Eddy." He was still standing in front of the Diner, waving when I drove away.

* * *

I don't know how Lisa Bennett learned Eddy was alone at the station during mid-afternoons. She began arriving every day just before I left to be with Mary, and generally remained until the school bus dropped off Johnny.

After getting an oil change, a tune-up, and having the exhaust system checked, she abandoned pretenses and just came to talk with Eddy. There was a boy-girl aspect, but I sensed Lisa was seeking something more, like she was drawing strength and sustenance just being with Eddy.

I had mixed emotions about her visits. I wasn't so old I couldn't recognize the value of female companionship for a young man. Now that Lisa's attitude had undergone a change she proved to be bright, cheerful, and intelligent. There was always the possibility the relationship might blossom into romance. It would be an incentive for Eddy to put down roots and make Cranston more than a brief stop in his wanderings. That would have pleased both Mary and me.

It was the thought of her Father that made me uneasy. I knew Ernest Bennett had taken a strong dislike to Eddy and I was still convinced he was responsible for Eddy's beating. The attack might have been triggered because Ernest didn't like to lose, and we had defeated him in court on the assault charge. Or Eddy might have seen something in Ernest's soul that frightened the bastard. Or it might have been because Ernest didn't believe Eddy was the proper sort to associate with his daughter. I figured he might go ballistic when he learned Lisa was hanging around the station every day socializing with a grease monkey. No doubt Ernest was capable of causing a lot more trouble.

I had given up hope the law would curtail future problems from Boss Bennett. I called Sheriff Simpson several times to keep track of his investigation into Eddy's beating. As far as I could determine, there was no investigation. Simpson hadn't made any progress locating the hoodlums and I suspected the case was going to remain unsolved. According to Simpson, no area doctor had treated anyone for animal bites, and the deputies hadn't been able to locate witnesses to the attack. I had a feeling the Sheriff wasn't trying very hard. If the cops didn't find evidence of his connection, Ernest Bennett was going to avoid prosecution. The thing that worried me was if Ernest got away with hiring thugs, he might try something worse. I could only hope the beating was enough to satisfy the bastard.

Tuesday afternoon Lisa came later than usual. I had already returned from my afternoon visit with Mary when her Lexus drove into the station parking area. She must have picked up Johnny at school because he hopped out of the car as soon as it stopped moving. In just a few days the boy was looking more like a normal kid. He had gained weight and was no longer the sad looking, pale youngster I had seen in the hospital. The hair lost during radiation treatments was already beginning to grow, although Johnny still kept the fuzz hidden under a blue and white baseball cap.

"Hi, Mr. Johnson," Johnny called, running toward the service bay. "Is it okay if I help Eddy?"

"If it doesn't bother him, it doesn't bother me," I called. Asking permission was an unnecessary ritual that pleased me. Most kids would have become too casual, trying to call me by my first name and barging around like they owned the place, but Johnny never forgot his manners.

Lisa waved as she followed her cousin into the service bay. She looked like a high school student, her hair pulled back in a ponytail, secured by an aqua ribbon. She was wearing jeans and a sweater, filling them out in all the right places. A man would have to be brain dead not to enjoy the view.

Eddy gave Johnny a hug, being careful not to put greasy hands on the boy's clean shirt. He smiled a greeting at Lisa, and I could tell from the look in her eyes she would have liked a hug.

Mica nosed Johnny, insisting on some attention. Satisfied, he wandered over to Lisa and gave a canine grin when she crouched, hugged him and ruffled his ears.

Eddy was doing a tune-up on Clem McDonald's car, and talked while he worked, explaining each step for Johnny's benefit. The boy's eyes shinned with pleasure as he handed Eddy tools when asked. I could tell Johnny would have loved to pitch in and help with the repairs, but he faithfully followed my rule about not doing any actual work.

Lisa stood off to one side, just watching. I figured she really wanted to be near Eddy, because she wasn't the least bit interested in things mechanical, nor what made a car engine work. After watching Eddy and Johnny for a few minutes, she wandered over to talk with me.

I had always been a poor bookkeeper and housekeeper, leaving invoices and notes all over the desk, never wiping off the accumulation of grit. Since Lisa had begun stopping regularly, I had cleaned up the office area so it was fit for a visitor. The clutter was gone from the desk, and I had even scrubbed the dirt and grease from the metal surface. Lisa had taken to sitting on the desk, her ankles crossed, while I leaned back in the desk chair. We talked nearly every time she stopped, unless Eddy didn't have a car to work on. Then I would take a folding chair and sun myself beside the pumps while she and Eddy talked in the office.

"Sam, if I ask you something, will you give me an honest answer?" Lisa selected a soda from the vending machine and hopped up to sit on the desk.

"Depends on the question," I said.

"Is there something wrong with me that I've missed?" The way she asked, I knew this was a boy-girl problem concerning Eddy.

"Nothing as far as I can see." Except for Mary, Lisa was the prettiest girl I'd ever met. Since that first visit, when Eddy had touched her, she had changed into a new person, and I decided I enjoyed having her around. For one thing she no longer acted like a first class bitch, and I hadn't even smelled a hint of liquor on her breath.

Lisa nervously nibbled her lower lip while she organized her thoughts. "I didn't think it was me. I don't want to sound egotistical, but I know I'm pretty and have an above average figure. Now that I'm trying to be a better person, I think I've got a lot to offer a man."

I nodded, but didn't say anything. I figured Lisa was being modest. If I weren't a very happily married man, my ego would have suffered from being treated like a Dutch uncle.

"I've never had a problem with men wanting to date me," she continued. "Honestly, none of them interested me very much. Either they were attracted by my Father's money, or they wanted to get into my pants. Or both."

I nodded again, feeling a blush rising in my cheeks, embarrassed by the boy-girl talk kids handled so easily. But I had to agree with her. Unless boys had changed since my younger days, there must have been a list of fellows as long as the telephone book begging her to give them a chance.

I figured Lisa must be pretty desperate to ask me for advice on dating. Maybe she didn't have anyone else to turn to. I couldn't imagine her having a father-daughter talk with her Dad. But Mary was the only girl I'd ever dated, so I didn't have a great deal of experience.

"Eddy is the first man I've really felt attracted to, and he won't give me a tumble. I even asked him for a date. I've never asked a guy for a date before, and it wasn't easy to swallow my pride. He turned me down. I've thought about this a lot, Sam. After deciding I'm not a turn-off, I have to wonder if Eddy has a problem. You know him better than anyone around here." Lisa took a deep breath. "So, I was hoping you could tell me why Eddy won't date me."

Eddy's refusal had obviously hurt Lisa's pride and self-esteem. She felt confused and needed someone to bolster her ego. Since I was never much of a lady's man, and didn't know whether I had any answers, I didn't say anything.

"I don't think it's the citation," she continued. "I explained it was my Father who called the Sheriff, and I think Eddy believes me. Damnit, Sam, I'm trying to be a better person."

"I'd say you've been pretty successful," I acknowledged.

"Did I tell you I dropped out of school for this semester and I've taken a summer job working as a volunteer at the hospital?" Lisa asked. "A month ago I wouldn't have believed I'd ever do anything like that. But I really like it. There are gross parts, like emptying bedpans, but it's fun meeting people who don't know who I am or who my Father is. They accept me as just another volunteer. There are times when it's sad working with really sick people. You know there's nothing you can do for them, so you try to smile and be friendly and as helpful as possible."

"Yeah, I imagine it feels good doing something useful on your own. I always figured helping folks was better than bossing them around."

"I was pretty bossy, wasn't I," she said.

I nodded. "Bossy enough."

"I'm really trying to change."

"I know, and you're doing a good job of it."

Lisa finished her coke, dropped the empty in the trash bin, and took a deep breath. "So, what is it about Eddy? Is he gay? Is he married? Does he have a girl friend back home? What?"

"As far as I know Eddy's a normal, healthy man, and doesn't have a wife or girlfriend hidden somewhere," I said, wondering how I could explain Eddy when I didn't understand him myself. "I know Eddy believes you're a special lady."

"He sure doesn't act like it."

"He told me he thinks you're beautiful—inside where it counts."

"Then why won't he date me?"

I thought about it a moment, then shook my head. "I don't know for certain. If I were thirty years younger, I'd sure as hell ask you out. The way I see it there are at least two possibilities." I couldn't tell Lisa about Eddy's power, although she probably suspected something. Eddy had touched her, and I knew from personal experience his touch could be unsettling. "First, you're from totally different worlds, and it scares him. You have roots, your family has money and you're getting a college education. Eddy is a wanderer, with no money, no roots, and no family except Mica. He barely has a high school education, although he's about as smart as anyone I know. He probably thinks he doesn't have anything to offer a girl with your looks and position."

"But none of that's important. I can't help having money. I'm not asking Eddy to marry me, only to go out socially."

"Maybe it's not important to you, but it is to Eddy. You've been wealthy all your life. He understands what it's like not to have a home or career and to wonder where his next meal is coming from. You don't."

"Eddy could have a home here. He could study and be anything he wants to be."

"I know a little about his background," I said, speaking cautiously to avoid the subject of his gift. "He's been so deeply scarred by his past he's afraid to develop any attachments. He's even concerned about his relationship with Mary and me. Did he tell you about his family?"

"Only that his entire family died in a fire." Lisa was on the verge of tears, but took another deep breath and controlled herself.

"They died in a fire when Eddy was away from home. Now he blames himself for the tragedy because he wasn't there to save them, or because he didn't die with them."

Lisa thought a long moment. "I can understand his grief, but that was years ago. It wasn't easy but I got over my Mother's death."

I nodded. "I suspect Eddy had other tragic involvements I don't know anything about. Mary and I have offered him a home for as long as he wants to stay. Maybe that'll help." I saw the same qualities in Lisa I had discovered in Mary, and knew she would be good for Eddy. "Be patient, Lisa. Give him a chance to put down roots, to heal those hurts he carries in his heart."

"I'm not very good at being patient," Lisa said.

"Young people never are. But if you're there when he needs you, it'll be worth the wait. I know he likes you. His refusal hasn't got anything to do with you personally. He's afraid of any attachments."

"I just wish I could convince him to try one date," Lisa sighed. "I don't know what to do. I can't drag him off to dinner."

"Well, I'll see if maybe I can put in a good word," I said, feeling sorry for both Lisa and Eddy. An idea was beginning to form. Perhaps if Eddy did go out with Lisa, he would discover advantages to staying in Cranston. If Ernest got upset because his daughter was dating below her social class, we would just have to deal with it at that time. "I'll talk with Eddy. I can't make any guarantees, but maybe I'll be able to convince him he should do something with his time other than working or sitting around the house."

"Oh, Sam if you could, I'd be eternally grateful." Lisa hopped down from the desk and kissed my cheek.

Even at my age I wished I'd taken the time to shave this morning. "Now you stop that before Mary finds out I'm flirting with a pretty girl. I'll talk with Eddy tonight. But I'm not making any promises."

"All I'm asking for is a chance."

Fifteen

Lisa hopped back up on the corner of my desk when Eddy stepped into the office with Johnny and Mica following right behind. I though if he kept collecting disciples, pretty soon he'd be leading a parade.

"I'm finished with the oil change," he said. "Is there anything else scheduled?"

"Not today," I replied. "Why don't you take a break?"

A cherry red pickup truck with chrome pipes and oversized tires pulled up to the pumps and honked. "Hold your horses," I shouted. Impatient customers always irritated me.

"I'll get it," Eddy volunteered, heading out the door before I could move.

I recognized Joe Black's custom job and didn't feel comfortable with Eddy servicing him. There are some people I just don't take to, and Joe Black was one of them. He was a bully with a mean streak, and we'd had words more than once.

Joe had worked at the Winston Lumber Yard since high school, and I suspect he spent all his money on that damned truck and cheap beer. Physically he was handsome enough, standing about six feet tall with a muscular build from working out. But his shoulder length black hair always looked like it needed to be washed, and his close-set eyes were usually bloodshot from booze or drugs. Even in this cool weather he was wearing a sleeveless T-shirt so he could show off the tiger tattoo on his shoulder.

He climbed out of the pickup when Eddy began pumping gas. "You be damned sure you don't scratch my truck, pretty boy," he warned. There was a distinctive lisp to his words, like he had a minor speech impediment.

When Eddy ignored him he sauntered toward Lisa, who had stepped into the office doorway. "My, my Lisa, you surely do look gooood today," he said drawing out the sound of good as his eyes swept over her body. "Beautiful day like this, why don't you and I go over to the lake and watch the sunset?"

"No thank you." The way Lisa said it, I could tell she didn't like Joe any better than I did.

"I've got a bottle in the glove box. It'll keep us warm until we think of some better way to spend our time—if you get my drift."

I figured Lisa had handled belligerent men before, but I was feeling protective. "The lady said no." I idly fingered the baseball bat I kept next to my desk.

"Butt out, old man. I'm talking to Lisa."

Joe took a backward step when Mica moved between him and Lisa. The fur on Mica's neck stood straight up, his lips were pulled up exposing fangs, and there was a low, rumbling growl in his throat. I had never seen Mica acting aggressively, and I wondered whether he recognized Joe as one of the thugs who had beaten Eddy. Joe was certainly the type to hire out for something like that.

"That'll be fourteen fifty," Eddy said, coming up behind Joe. "The oil's good."

I don't know whether it was the baseball bat or Mica's growl that intimidated him but Joe shrugged, pulled out his wallet, and tossed fifteen dollars at Eddy. "Keep the change, pretty boy."

He swaggered to his truck, revved his engine, threw us a one-finger salute, and peeled out of the station, leaving a strip of rubber all the way to the corner.

Before any of us could comment on Joe's visit, the evening rush began. Both Eddy and I were busy pumping gas and checking oil. I let Johnny clean windshields while Lisa waited patiently in the office and helped ring up sales. When Eddy and I began closing the station, she offered to give Johnny a ride home. I believe she wanted me and Eddy to have some time alone so I could talk to him, man to man.

Johnny wasn't very happy about going with Lisa, but he didn't complain. He would have preferred riding in my truck, although the cab of my pickup was pretty crowded with Eddy, Johnny, Mica, and me crammed on the single seat. I think the boy felt like he was one of the guys when we all squeezed together and joked and laughed during the short drive to Sal's Diner.

If Lisa had planned on giving me an opportunity to talk with Eddy, she hadn't considered that I'm a coward at heart, and wanted to forget the whole thing. I'd never had a man-to-man conversation with my son, Albert, and didn't know how to broach the subject. So in my usual straightforward manner, I procrastinated until we were home and settled at the kitchen table. I was hoping Mary would understand and pick up the conversation. Women are always better at boy-girl stuff, and Mary was an expert.

"Seems like Lisa Bennett is more than a little interested in you," I said as casually as possible, helping myself to a portion of Mary's fantastic Yankee Pot Roast. After subsisting on frozen food and sandwiches while Mary had been sick, it was a joy eating her cooking.

"She's just being friendly," Eddy said, passing off my comment as idle table talk.

"I may be getting old, but I'm not deaf and blind. There's friendly, and there's interest. I'd say Lisa is interested."

"I haven't seen Lisa Bennett since that day in the hospital," Mary said, an eyebrow raised in my direction, like she was wondering why I was bringing up this topic. Sometimes I think Mary can read my mind, so she followed my lead as if we had planned it. "I've always thought she was a lovely young woman. She will certainly make some man a wonderful wife. Alma told me she met Lisa at Wal-Mart the other day and couldn't believe the changes that have taken place. She said Lisa was like a new person, thoughtful and caring."

Eddy continued eating without comment, probably thinking if he ignored us we would change the subject.

I didn't have the patience to be subtle, and Eddy wasn't responding, so I jumped right in. "Lisa and I talked today while you and Johnny were working on Fisher's car. She can't understand your lack of interest. Most guys are chasing after her, but when she flat out asked you for a date, you turned her down."

Eddy waited until he had chewed a mouthful of tender beef. "I didn't actually turn her down," he mumbled. "I said I'd think about it."

"Sounds like a turn down to me."

Eddy shrugged. "I suppose you're right, but I don't see any point in dating Lisa."

"You don't see any point? Are you deaf, blind, and stupid? If I were your age and single, I'd have asked her for a date long before she had a chance to ask me."

"Lisa's a very special person," Eddy agreed, ignoring my remarks. "She's going to make some man very happy, but I'm not that man."

"So now you're a psychic," I said. "You can see into the future."

Mary had begun to understand my purpose, but she instinctively knew I was handling it wrong. "A pretty girl like Lisa probably has plenty of men chasing after her. A lot of women are attracted to men who aren't paying so much attention to them. Edna and Bill Cooper are a perfect example. She thinks the sun rises and sets on him and he always acts cool toward her. But they seem to be perfectly happy."

"That's beside the point," I argued. "It doesn't make any difference how the Coopers get along. Eddy, I think you should at least try a date with Lisa and see how it goes."

"It would be pointless," Eddy said without conviction.

"Eddy, Sam isn't often right about this sort of thing but this time he is. Since you've been in Cranston, you've never gone out and met any young people. You really need to be around boys and girls your own age. If Lisa's interested in seeing you socially, I think you should date her. It isn't healthy for a young man to spend all his time with old folks like Sam and me."

"Are you trying to get me out of the house so you and Sam can be alone?" Eddy asked, a twinkle in his eye.

Mary blushed and dropped her gaze. "You know that isn't what I meant."

"Eddy, can you give me one good reason why you don't date Lisa?" I asked.

He pushed a piece of carrot around in the gravy. "You know my reasons."

"No, I don't. You're gonna give me some crap about not going out because you're afraid of commitments. You think you're going to be leaving Cranston one of these days and don't want to have ties. So what? Just because you don't stay anywhere very long doesn't mean you have to be a hermit and let the world pass you by. Neither Mary nor I are suggesting you get married. We're just saying you'll never have a life of your own if you don't get out and meet people. An evening with Lisa would be good for both of you."

"Sam, when the time comes, it's going to be hard enough leaving Cranston. You and Mary have been like a family to me, and Johnny acts as if I'm his big brother or something. Some places I abandon without a backward glance. Some places I leave a part of myself behind, and it hurts. I don't need to complicate my life with any more emotional attachments."

"Damnit, Eddy, you can't avoid emotional attachments. They just happen. Who knows, maybe if you see Lisa socially you'll decide you can't stand each other. Or maybe you'll fall in love. But you'll never know for certain if you don't try"

Eddy was obviously unhappy with the conversation. "There's no future in it. It just means more people will get hurt."

"The way I see it, not going out with Lisa will hurt her just as much. Since you've been in Cranston she's changed a lot. You remember that first day at the station, her being half drunk and acting like the Queen of Sheba. That's the way she was all the time, drinking too much, treating people like dirt, acting like a snobbish little bitch. I doubt whether Lisa even liked herself very much. She was probably lonely and unhappy, but didn't know any other way to act. I don't understand how your power works, but when you touched her, you caused those changes. Now she's attempting to be decent, even volunteering at the hospital. For the first time in her life a man she's interested in acts like she's a fence post. You know as well as I do you healed something inside her. You can't make people change and then turn your back."

"Oh no, don't put that burden on my back," Eddy protested. It was the first time I had seen his temper flare and it startled me. He hadn't even been angry when those four men beat him up. "I didn't make Lisa change. My power isn't some sort of remedy for all the world's ills. I can't get rid of greed and hate and every negative attitude just by touching them. People make their own choices. Don't you think if I could change people for the better I would have done that when I was a kid and my family would still be alive? No don't try to put the burden of curing evil on me."

"Now, Eddy, don't get upset," Mary soothed, reaching over to touch his hand. "I know Sam has a bad habit of mixing into things that are none of his business. Sometimes he's worse than a preacher."

"I'm sorry for blowing off steam," Eddy said, calm again as the flash of temper passed.

"I didn't mean to upset you," I said. "But you have to admit people do change when you touch them."

"Not everyone. I don't know why some people change when I touch them, but it isn't because of my power. Maybe they become more aware of themselves and that makes them want to be better. But I don't heal anything inside them. They change because they want to."

"Okay, I grant that your power doesn't make people change," I said, "but that still doesn't answer the original question. Why won't you open up your life a little and take Lisa to dinner?"

"It hurts too damn much to get close to someone and then have to leave," Eddy explained.

"I think you owe it to Lisa, and yourself, to at least have dinner with her," I said.

"Damnit, Sam, do you think I enjoy my life? Do you think I don't want to go out with pretty girls and laugh and have fun?"

"You said people change because they want to, that they are more aware of themselves and decide to be better. Well, it's time you became aware of yourself and changed. Stop running and start living."

"I don't know what to do," Eddy said. "I like Lisa and don't want to hurt her, but this is a no win situation. There's no way I can date her, or not date her, without causing pain to her or myself."

"I know you don't need any more sadness in your life," Mary said. "Maybe you're never going to find happiness for yourself. Some people are destined to bear that cross and it's a heavy burden. But Sam is right. You'll never know if there can be contentment for you unless you take a chance. Maybe Lisa can be your happiness. Maybe destiny brought you to Cranston."

"Excuse me," Eddy said, pushing back from the table. "I need to think. If it's all right with you, I'm going to play with Mica."

"What was that all about?" Mary asked when Eddy took the dog outside. "You haven't ever been a match-maker that I know of, but you were pushing that boy to date Lisa Bennett. And you upset him."

I helped Mary clear away the dirty dishes and leaned against the kitchen counter while she began washing them. "It's because of Eddy that I have you back alive and well and I'm trying to do something for him" I put my arm around Mary's shoulders and kissed her on the cheek.

"Stop that Samuel Johnson. You're going to get soap suds all over the kitchen."

I gave her another peck on the cheek and then picked up a dishtowel to begin drying dishes. "Lisa asked me to talk with Eddy, sort of like father to son, and I agreed because I think it's a good idea. I owe Eddy more than I can ever repay. We both want to give him a home here in Cranston because it's the only way we can even begin to settle our debt. He needs a permanent place so he can begin to live his own life. You and I have talked ourselves blue in the face trying to convince him it will be safe to stay, and it hasn't done any good. Maybe if he develops feelings for Lisa he'll decide to hang around—to make this his permanent home. I know for a fact that once a beautiful woman gets her hooks into a guy, he's never gonna want to stray from hearth and home. It happened to me, didn't it?" I leaned over and kissed Mary on the cheek again.

"Now stop that, Sam Johnson," Mary protested, giggling like the young girl I had married. "You certainly are in an amorous mood tonight."

"Wouldn't you like Eddy to have what we've got?" I asked.

"Of course I would, but you can't just push people into liking each other. I think you should apologize to Eddy."

I knew Mary was right. I'd handled the situation poorly and upset Eddy needlessly. I'd spoken my piece, as I'd promised Lisa, and now it was time to butt out of their lives.

When we finished the dishes, I left Mary to complete her chores and stepped out onto the back porch. There was a full moon casting enough light for Mica to see the tennis ball Eddy was throwing. Eddy took the saliva-coated ball and tossed it again before he looked up.

"I didn't mean to pitch into you so hard" I said. "But I still think it's a good idea for you to go out with Lisa. At least it's worth a try."

"That's okay." Eddy threw the ball again. "I'm not upset. The more I think about it, the more I believe you're right. It isn't going to go anywhere, even if I wish it could, but I probably do owe Lisa an explanation. At least I can tell her about my curse. Then when I have to leave she'll understand it has nothing to do with her."

"Maybe I was a bit harsh saying you owed her, but it would be a kindness if you explained to Lisa. If you do leave some day, it'll help her over the rough spots."

"That's enough Mica," Eddy said, taking the ball from the dog and setting it on the porch. He stood up and wiped his hands on his jeans. "It isn't going to change anything but the next time Lisa comes to the station, I'll ask her for a date."

"Eddy, you've got problems I don't even begin to understand, but you won't regret deciding to go out with Lisa."

"Yeah, you're right."

Mica had found the ball on the porch and was nosing it toward Eddy like he wanted to continue playing. Eddy reached down and ruffled his ears. "No more tonight," he said. "You've had enough chasing"

"Did you recognize Joe Black today?' I asked, changing the subject. "Was he one of the guys who attacked you?"

Eddy shook his head. "I don't know. He could have been, but it was too dark to see and the whole thing happened pretty fast. Why do you ask?"

"I just had a feeling about him. He's the type who might do something like that, and Mica was just about ready to rip out his throat."

"If Mica recognized him, I didn't. He could have been one of the men, but I really don't know. Mica was probably just being protective of Lisa."

We stood for a moment, neither saying anything. Now that the sun was down, there was a chill in the air, and we weren't wearing jackets. I shivered and rubbed my bare arms.

"How about going inside and we'll see if I can finally beat you in a game of chess?" I asked.

Sixteen

Lisa didn't visit the station on Thursday. That was unusual, but I figured there could be several good reasons. She was volunteering at the hospital and might have had to work the afternoon shift. Or perhaps she wanted to give me plenty of time to talk with Eddy.

By Friday's mid-morning lull Eddy had obviously decided not to wait any longer for Lisa to stop at the station, because he asked if he could use the telephone. Being a nosy old man, I stepped into the service bay to give him a sense of privacy, but remained close enough to hear his end of the conversation.

Apparently Lisa wasn't home, and it sounded as if Eddy reached the maid. The Bennetts were the only folks I knew who had a maid and a cook. He left a message for Lisa to call the station before six, and my house after six, giving both numbers although Lisa probably already had them. Leaving a message made me nervous because I felt certain Ernest Bennett would learn about the call. The less he knew about Lisa and Eddy, the better.

No doubt Ernest was aware Lisa had been spending a lot of time at the station recently, and he was smart enough to realize she wasn't visiting me. He must have been livid about her showing an interest in a foot loose young man like Eddy. I figured Bennett would want Eddy to pull up stakes and leave Cranston before Lisa got serious about him. Since the beating hadn't scared Eddy out of town, I was afraid Ernest might do something even worse.

Lisa returned the call in the early afternoon when Eddy was taking a break in the office and I was busy pumping gas for Mrs. Wiley. It couldn't have come at a better time to prevent me from eaves dropping.

"Well, I set up the date," he said when I came into the office to make change. "We'll go out for a coke and burger tomorrow evening."

"It's about time," I said. Although I was worried about Ernest's reaction, I was pretty certain Lisa would be good for Eddy. I figured we could deal with Ernest when the time came. "Do you need to borrow a suit or tie?" The waistline on my suit's trousers would wrap around Eddy twice, and there'd be enough room in the suit coat to conceal a sofa cushion. At any rate, there weren't any eating places within a reasonable drive where folks would even consider getting dressed up for dinner. But I felt like a father with his only son going on a first date and wanted Eddy to make a good impression.

"No, thanks. I told Lisa we'd have to go some place casual because I didn't have clothes for a fancy restaurant. She suggested the Burger House in Elliott. We don't need to dress up for a burger."

Word had gotten around that Eddy could work magic on a car engine, so we had several tune-ups scheduled. When Johnny came after school, Eddy was working on Bill Smith's new Chevy. After greeting both Mica and me Johnny stuck his head under the hood and watched Eddy work. It was still slow at the pumps, so I began taking inventory and straightening the shelves.

Because I had an armful of oil filters, Eddy went to service the customer who had pulled up to the pumps. A brief glance out the front window convinced me it wasn't a customer. Ernest Bennett was the only person in the county who drove a late model BMW. Since he never bought gas at my station, I figured his arrival meant some sort of trouble. Maybe he'd already heard about Lisa's date. I dropped the filters and hurried toward the pumps.

Ernest had gotten out of his BMW and was obviously angry, standing almost nose-to-nose with Eddy. However, I noticed he stayed back far enough to avoid physical contact. "I'm only going to warn you once," he said. "I want you out of this county. We don't need your kind around here."

"Do you want a fill?" Eddy asked in his usual quiet voice, like he hadn't heard Bennett's tirade.

"You aren't listening to me," Bennett hissed, Eddy's calm infuriating him. "I want you gone and I want you gone today."

Mica had assumed a protective stance beside Eddy. The dog wasn't growling, but he obviously knew his master was being threatened. I was pretty certain if Ernest touched Eddy, Mica would rip him to pieces.

"What's this all about?" I asked, trying to squeeze between the two men.

"You stay out of this," Ernest warned. "It's none of your damned business."

"When you threaten my employee, it becomes my business," I said, suddenly on the verge of losing my temper. I was getting tired of people telling me to butt out in my own station.

"Unless you want more trouble than you can handle, I'd suggest you mind your own business," Ernest growled. His tirade seemed excessive, but Ernest was the kind of man who had to be in control. Most likely he would cause trouble for anyone he didn't consider suitable for his daughter.

"Don't you think Lisa is old enough to make her own decisions about boy friends?" I asked, trying to keep a grip on my temper.

For a moment Ernest looked startled, as if Lisa and Eddy were the furthest thing from his mind. Like a flash bulb going off in my head, I realized Ernest wasn't here because Eddy had a date with Lisa. Whatever had triggered Ernest's tantrum, it had nothing to do with his daughter.

Eddy laid his hand on my arm and I immediately felt calmer. "It's okay, Sam, I can handle this."

"There nothing to handle," Bennett hissed. "You have one day to get as far from Cranston as you can or there's going to be serious trouble."

Ernest shook his finger in my face. "I own this county and no one tells me what to do."

"You don't own this station. I'm not going to tell you again to get the hell out of here." If Eddy hadn't been touching my arm, I'd probably have punched Ernest in the nose.

Mica had begun growling and Bennett glanced nervously at the dog. He pointed his finger at Eddy and when Mica began edging toward him, Ernest hastily climbed in the BMW and slammed the door.

"You just remember what I said. If you aren't out of this county by tomorrow you'll be sorry." He put his transmission in drive and peeled out of the station, nearly running me down

"I'm sorry for the trouble," Eddy said softly, squatting to pet Mica and calm him.

"It isn't your fault," I said. "Ernest Bennett is an ass. His bark is a hell of a lot worse than his bite."

"Not always," Eddy said, like he knew things I didn't.

Johnny, who had been watching the altercation from the service bay, looked like he was about to cry. Eddy walked over and gave him a one armed hug. "Come on, good buddy, let's finish that tune-up."

I went back to my inventory and began picking up the filters I'd dropped. I had been looking for trouble in the wrong place. Now I was pretty certain something more serious than a boy friend was bothering Ernest. I knew enough about Ernest Bennett to realize he didn't make idle threats.

While I put away the filters, I was close enough to the service bay to overhear the conversation between Johnny and Eddy. Eddy hadn't seemed intimidated by Bennett, but it sounded like he must have taken the threats seriously. My ears perked up and I listened more closely.

"Johnny, you know I'm a drifter and never stay very long in one place," Eddy began. "I might leave Cranston some day to see what's down the road."

"Don't you like it here?" Johnny asked. It didn't sound as if he were taking Eddy seriously.

"Sure, I like it here, but my feet get itchy and I just have to move along."

"You aren't going to leave because of what Mr. Bennett said, are you?" Johnny sounded unsure; like he was afraid his hero might be frightened.

"No, of course not," Eddy said.

"Then why don't you stay here forever?" Johnny suggested. "We could open a garage together and make a million dollars."

"There isn't much call for another garage in this area. There isn't even enough work here to keep two people busy. Sam only has me helping out because he's my friend."

"When you leave I could go with you." Johnny sounded like he didn't really believe Eddy would actually disappear one day.

"I don't think your Mom would approve. And you do have to go to school, don't you?" Eddy held out his hand. "Would you please give me the ratchet and quarter inch socket?"

Johnny passed over the tool and watched quietly for a moment. When he spoke again, he sounded more sure of himself. "What if I get sick again? You wouldn't be here to cure me."

"You're not going to get sick again," Eddy said.

Before I could hear the rest of the conversation I had to service Bill Thompson, who had pulled up to the pumps. Pretty soon Johnny came out of the service area crying, and went to the side of the station with Mica and began throwing the tennis ball.

I thought about trying to comfort him but what the hell can you say to a young boy who just found out he might lose his hero.

We got our big rush shortly after that and Eddy had to help pump gas. When Johnny tired of throwing the ball, he sat on the desk chair and waited for closing. There was no opportunity for him to talk with Eddy, and he never said a word when either of us went into the office to make change or run a charge. Maybe he was pouting.

We all piled into the pickup at six and I drove Johnny home. He kept silent until he climbed out of the truck at Sal's Diner.

"Can I come back tomorrow?" he asked, making a valiant effort to keep from bursting into tears.

"Sure," Eddy said. "There's still a thing or two you can learn about fixing engines. And it might be a long time before I get the urge to move along."

Johnny turned and ran up the outside stairs to the apartment above the restaurant.

"Why did you tell Johnny you might be leaving?" I asked as we drove back toward my house. "Bennett isn't going to run you off, is he?"

"Mr. Bennett is frightened, and scared people do things without thinking. I won't be leaving Cranston today, but there's going be trouble soon, and I want to be gone before it starts."

"I don't think Bennett is worried about you dating Lisa," I said. "It's something else. His temper tantrum doesn't make any sense unless you saw some dark secret when he touched you at the courthouse. I think he's actually afraid of you or something you know."

When Eddy didn't respond, I continued. "Well, did you see something when Ernest touched you?"

I drove past my house and Eddy must have realized I wasn't going to let this go without some sort of answer.

"Sam, you're a Catholic, so you know about confessions," he said. "People go to a priest voluntarily, but even so a priest is forbidden to reveal what he learned during confession, no matter how terrible it is. People don't volunteer their sins to me, but I feel like I have the same constraint. I can't tell you or anyone else what I see in a person's soul."

"It isn't the same thing," I argued. "A priest takes a vow. I don't see where you've taken any kind of vow of silence."

"It doesn't make any difference," Eddy said. "I didn't ask for the power, and I don't want to see into anyone's soul. But I know part of my curse is that I don't have the right to reveal secrets I learn because of the power."

"If I knew what we were facing, maybe I could help," I argued.

"Believe me when I tell you there's nothing you could do about it." Eddy took a deep breath. "For the sake of argument, let's look at a hypothetical example. Say I looked into someone's soul and saw they had committed a murder. There wouldn't be anything I could do. If I went to the cops and said, 'John Doe murdered Jane Doe', they'd laugh at me. I would know the crime had happened, but I wouldn't have any proof."

"Are you saying Bennett murdered someone?" I realized Ernest was a first class bastard, but I'd never believed he'd go that far.

"It was just an example, Sam." Eddy sounded irritated because I'd jumped to the wrong conclusion. "Mr. Bennett didn't kill anyone."

"Okay, maybe he hasn't got any bodies buried in his backyard, but if you saw some other dark secret, he's a powerful man around here, and is capable of causing serious trouble. Maybe together we could find proof of whatever it is and stop the trouble before it begins. Eddy, you can't keep running away. You have to take a stand and fight back. This is the time and place."

Eddy didn't respond.

"Well," I said.

"Sam, I appreciate what you're saying and that you want to help, but I just can't say anything. You may think that's stupid, but it wouldn't be right to babble about things my power had revealed."

"Just think about it," I suggested.

"It won't change anything, but I'll think about it."

I wanted to continue pushing until Eddy allowed me to help, but I realized I had gone as far as I could for the moment. "Okay, if Bennett didn't scare you off then why did you tell Johnny you might be leaving" I asked, changing the subject

"He's starting to get too attached to me," Eddy said with a deep sigh. "It won't be long before I leave and I didn't want it to be a complete surprise."

"He didn't appear to take the news very well," I said when Eddy didn't volunteer any information.

"He was pretty upset," Eddy agreed. "I don't know if telling him was better than just going. Either way he'll get over it. Kids are good that way. But it'll make the next couple of days pretty uncomfortable."

"He might get over it and he might not. He won't ever understand if he thinks you ran away because you were afraid."

"I told him there wasn't enough business at your station and one day you wouldn't be able to afford me." Eddy joked.

"Hey, thanks for making me the heavy."

"No problem. I figured, with your broad shoulders, you could carry the load." Mica licked Eddy's face and he ruffled the dog's ears. "He wouldn't understand my leaving because of the trouble."

"I don't see how he could understand that when even I don't believe it?" Eddy didn't respond. "So, how did it all end?"

"Johnny suggested I wouldn't have to leave because his Mother would give me a job as a cook, and I could live with them."

"That kid sure does have a great imagination. How did you get out of that one?"

"Told him I didn't know how to cook. Of course, he argued that his Mother would teach me. I explained it just wouldn't work—that I was a wanderer and wasn't comfortable staying too long in one place. That's when he went and played with Mica."

After having circled the block twice, I pulled into the driveway and shut off the truck. "Well, I'd be prepared for Johnny to come up with some other plan to find you a job. He really wants you to stay. Just like Mary and I want you to stay."

I decided it was time to stop worrying about Eddy leaving and start doing something to prevent it. There was no doubt in my mind that if trouble came Ernest Bennett would be the cause. Maybe his anger wasn't related to Lisa, but I still believed she could be the key to avoiding further problems from her father. I wasn't sure Ernest had feelings for anyone except himself, but if there was someone who could make Ernest back off, it was his daughter. I make a mental note to have a heart to heart talk with her as soon as possible so I could explain my concerns and enlist her help.

I didn't mention Ernest's visit to Mary. Maybe that wasn't fair. Maybe she had a right to know, but until I had talked with Lisa there wasn't any good reason to upset her.

After supper, Mary and I went to the shopping center in Elliott for a weekly spree. Eddy tagged along and purchased new clothing; jeans, underwear, socks and a couple of shirts he needed for his upcoming date. He sure didn't act like he was planning to leave anytime soon.

Seventeen

Even though Ernest Bennett's threats didn't appear to worry Eddy, by the time we closed the station Saturday afternoon I was a nervous wreck. All morning I had the feeling someone was sneaking up behind me, and I half expected a carload of thugs to roar into the station, rob us at gunpoint, and beat up both Eddy and me. When nothing unusual happened it only increased my anxiety

It would have helped ease the tension if I could have talked with Lisa to enlist her aid in restraining her father. When she didn't stop at the station, I briefly wondered if she had been warned away, but I knew my concerns were making me paranoid. More likely she didn't want to give Eddy a chance to change his mind, or maybe she was occupied at the beauty salon, like women were when getting ready for a special occasion.

Because of the date, Eddy didn't join Mary and me for super. He borrowed my old Spice, and while he showered and shaved, Mary ironed out the store wrinkles in his new jeans and shirts. Since I hadn't told Mary about Ernest's threats, she was her normal cheery self, excited about Eddy's date and fussing over him like a mother hen with chicks.

After Eddy finished sprucing up, he joined us at the table for a glass of milk.

"My, don't you look nice," Mary said. "And you smell good too. I've always liked that after shave on Sam. Albert used to borrow it when he went on a date, but he never really had enough of a beard to need a shave."

Remembering Albert brought tears to her eyes. She covered her emotions by asking Eddy if he wanted more milk.

"No thanks." He nervously pushed a drop of moisture around on the table. From the way he fidgeted I knew he was anxious to be on his way. It reminded me of how Albert had behaved when getting ready for a date; nervous about how the evening would go, and impatient for it to get started. I don't consider myself sentimental, but remembering brought a lump to my throat. Maybe Mary's reaction was contagious.

"At least it doesn't look like rain," Eddy said in an attempt at small talk.

"Rain would be nice," I suggested. "There's nothing as romantic as snuggling with a girl and listening to the rain on the car roof. Mary and I used to love to park at the lake when it was raining."

"Sam, you know perfectly well we never parked at the lake." I could see from the look in her eyes that she was remembering some of those evenings.

"I don't think we'll be anywhere near the lake," Eddy said. "We're only going to get something to eat and talk."

Mary reached over and patted his hand. "Don't you mind Sam. He's just teasing."

About seven, when we heard a car pull into our driveway, a wave of relief washed over Eddy's face. He gulped his milk and was out the door like a shot. "See you later." Mica jumped up to follow. "Stay here," Eddy ordered as the door closed behind him.

"Have fun," Mary called, but I doubt if Eddy heard her.

Mica nosed at the door and gave a low-pitched whine. He wasn't ever going to accept being separated from his master.

After Eddy left, we cleaned up the supper dishes and tried to decide how to spend the evening. Since Mary had recovered, and Eddy had been living with us, we hadn't really had any time alone. We discussed going to a movie in Elliott, but nothing playing at the Cinema 6 appealed to both of us. There was a Steven Spielberg movie I might have enjoyed, but it was an action adventure film, and Mary didn't care much for the violence. Actually neither of us had any desire for an evening out. We'd have been thinking the whole time about Eddy and Lisa. So we popped some popcorn and settled down to watch a National Geographic special about whales. Damned if it didn't remind me of all those nights we'd waited up for Albert to come home from a date.

I didn't pay much attention to the National Geographic special or the mystery movie that followed, as I kept checking my watch. It wasn't likely Ernest would cause trouble while Lisa and Eddy were together, but I still worried. There was no way of knowing what Ernest would do.

About ten-thirty Mica headed for the kitchen, woofing and scratching at the back door. Shortly after that we heard Lisa's car pull into the driveway. It was earlier than Albert had usually come home, but then, I hadn't imagined Eddy and Lisa would actually park at the lake and smooch.

I went up and let Mica out. Then I hustled back into the living room so it wouldn't appear as if I had been waiting for the youngsters to return.

"Is it alright if Lisa comes in for a minute?" Eddy called from the kitchen.

"Well certainly," Mary said, turning off the TV. Neither of us had really been watching the ten o'clock news. There is noting as depressing and boring as TV news.

"You're welcome to sit in the living room if you'd like," Mary suggested as she always had for Albert and his dates. "Sam and I were just going to bed."

Lisa was wearing a lime green, one piece dress that set off the green sparkles in her eyes. Her hair was swept up into a pile on top of her head and she looked as pretty as I'd ever seen her. However her eyes were red and puffy and some of the makeup had smeared on her cheeks.

"Don't go to bed on my account. I can only stay for a minute." Lisa said. "May I use the bathroom?"

"Of course." Mary took Lisa by the hand, leading her to the downstairs bathroom. I suppose she wanted to show her where we kept the clean towels, or maybe she wanted to have some girl talk.

"Well, how'd it go?" I asked when Eddy and I were momentarily alone.

Eddy plopped down on a kitchen chair. He appeared exhausted, like he had after healing Mary.

"It was hard," he said, "but I suppose it went pretty much like I'd expected. At least I told her about my power and that I couldn't get serious because I'd have to be leaving soon."

"How did she take it? It looked like she had been crying."

He shrugged and patted Mica on the head. The dog could sense Eddy's unhappiness and was doing his best to make his master feel better. "Yeah, she was upset at first, arguing I was crazy to think there was going to be trouble."

I figured there had to be more to Lisa's reaction. It isn't every day you find out the man you're interested in can heal people of incurable illnesses and see into their souls. I wanted to ask whether she had been skeptical or accepting or frightened, but Eddy obviously didn't want to elaborate. I'm not usually very patient, but I didn't press for details, figuring I would be able to learn all about the date during slow periods at work.

Mary joined us at the kitchen table a couple of minutes before Lisa returned. Eddy stood up when the ladies entered the room, but I didn't have the energy. Lisa's eyes were still red, but she had obviously splashed water on her face and fixed her makeup, because she looked fresh and clean.

"Well, I have to be going," Lisa announced. "I've got to be at the hospital early in the morning. They have a hard time getting volunteers to work on Sundays."

Eddy opened his arms and Lisa accepted a brotherly hug. I could see the warm, happy feeling going through her and was pretty certain she would have liked a kiss.

"Thanks for showing me around Elliott," he said. "I really enjoyed being with you. I'm sorry it wasn't more fun."

"Eddy, I wish you would at least consider what we discussed." Lisa's eyes were filling again. "Don't run off just because you think some idiot will cause trouble."

"I'll think about it," Eddy said without conviction. Some times you just wanted to reach out and shake him. He was so damned certain things would go bad.

Lisa gave me a half hearted smile. "Sam, would you walk me to my car, please?"

I was dying to know what they had discussed, but wasn't so crude I didn't understand when something isn't any of my business. I didn't say anything as we stepped out into the yard, the porch light throwing a glow across the walk. Lisa waited until we reached the car before speaking.

"Sam, I don't know what to do." I could see the sparkle of tears running down her cheeks. Obviously her fresh makeup was going to get smeared. "I really like Eddy. He's so different from anyone I've ever known. When he told me about his power, at first I thought he was joking. Then he held my hand and I had the warm, happy feeling I always do when he touches me. Maybe I was more receptive tonight, but it was like we were bonding, like we knew each other intimately. There aren't any words to explain that feeling, but I knew for certain he was telling the truth. In a way it frightened me, but in another way it made me happier than I've even been."

"It does take some getting used to" I agreed.

"I sensed Eddy had feelings for me, but…I don't know what I felt. Sam, I want him to like me, but it's as if he had a barrier to keep people away. I have to fight off most of the guys I date, but Eddy didn't even attempt to kiss me."

"It isn't you Lisa. Eddy just doesn't want to get involved with anyone. I think he's afraid it'll hurt too much when he has to leave. He's convinced there's no hope of staying here very long."

"I know. He told me the whole story, about his family and all." Lisa put her hand on my arm and suppressed a sob. "He's so sad and lonely. I really like him, Sam. I know if he stayed in Cranston we could be something more than friends." Lisa took a handkerchief from her purse and dabbed at her eyes. "I wish there were something I could do for him."

I decided there wouldn't ever be a better opportunity to voice my suspicions. "Tonight might not be the time to bring this up but there is something you can do if you really want to help Eddy. Did you know your dad is trying to force him out of Cranston?"

"Why?" she sounded confused. "The only time my Father even met Eddy was at the court appearance." She shook her head. "No, I don't believe he's attempting to force Eddy out of town"

She had already had a poor evening and I wasn't proud about adding to her misery, but I was convinced my suspicions needed to be brought out. "Don't take this wrong, Lisa, but I believe your Dad hired the thugs who beat up Eddy."

She tilted her head to one side and looked at me like I'd just told her the Pope was having an affair. "I know Dad pushed for the citation, but that's over and done with." There was a sharp edge to her voice. "I never expected you to make unfounded accusations."

"I know I don't have any proof, but please just hear me out," I said. "Did you know your father stopped at the station yesterday and warned Eddy there would be serious consequences if he didn't leave town?"

"l don't believe you. Eddy never mentioned anything about my father threatening him. I don't think I want to hear any more of this." She opened the car door and in the flash of interior lights I could see the anger in her expression.

"Eddy must have told you he would be leaving because he expected trouble. If you really want to help, and keep him in Cranston, then you have to hear me out." I took a deep breath and continued before she could interrupt. "I'm convinced your father is going to be the source of the trouble. At first I thought he hired the thugs because the Judge dismissed the charges and he was concerned about your relationship with Eddy. But now I believe your father is frightened by something Eddy saw when they touched at the courthouse." Since Eddy had explained about his power, I was hoping she would understand.

"Are you saying that my father has some terrible secret that Eddy discovered?" I couldn't tell whether she was shocked or angry.

"I don't know what Eddy saw when they touched, but your father is afraid of something. If you explain to him that Eddy won't ever disclose the secret, maybe it would prevent him from driving Eddy away."

"I think you're way out of line," she said, sliding onto the driver's seat and slamming the door. "I thought we were friends, Sam, but you don't sound like a friend. My father would never hire people to hurt Eddy or anyone else, and I don't appreciate you suggesting that he has some dark secret he's ashamed of."

The car window was open and I continued talking while Lisa started the engine. "I'm sorry if I upset you but I'm worried about Eddy. We both want him to stay in Cranston, and the only way we can do that is by convincing him there isn't going to be any more trouble. If I'm right your dad might do something serous. Talk to him. If I'm wrong, I'll apologize."

"Damnit, Sam, you're a bastard to even suggest my father would do anything to hurt Eddy." Lisa put the Lexus in reverse and spun the wheels backing out of the drive. I watched her speed into the road, screeching the brakes before turning toward Elliott, cursing myself for making a mess out of my explanation.

I stood next to the garage, replaying my conversation, but I still didn't know how I could have honey-coated my suspicions so Lisa would have listened to me. Even knowing I had handled it poorly, I wasn't sorry I had spoken my piece. I just hoped it would do some good.

With a sense of helpless frustration, I headed for the house. I sincerely hoped after the first rush of anger had dulled, Lisa would realize my suspicions had some justification and at least confront her father. Lisa was the only person in the world who could talk sense to him and prevent something worse from happening

My last hope was to talk with Eddy and convince him to enlist Lisa's help. But when I entered the kitchen, Eddy had already gone to bed.

"You were out there a long time," Mary said.

I wrapped my arms around her and held her close. "Yeah, it took a while to get my foot back out of my mouth."

Eighteen

I have to admit I felt as if I were on a runaway train headed for disaster. From a relatively sedentary, predictable life I was enmeshed in a series of intrigues and escalating events. It felt as if I no longer had control over my life.

However, the rush of events seemed to have at least temporarily slowed down. If Ernest intended to do something about his threats, he was taking his time about it. There had not been any violent incidents and the deadline was long past. Maybe he wasn't going to do anything after all. Maybe Lisa had talked with him and convinced him to back off. By Monday afternoon I had begun to believe my paranoia wasn't justified. It turned out I had simply been looking in the wrong direction.

I didn't feel comfortable leaving Eddy alone at the station, just in case Ernest or his hoodlums attempted something. As usual, Eddy convinced me I needed quality time with my wife. Consequently, early Monday afternoon I was home enjoying a few hours with Mary. We were sitting at the kitchen table, sipping tea, talking of nothing special, when there was a strong, rapid knocking on the front door. In Cranston everyone uses back doors because they are convenient to driveways, and kitchens are the household's center of activity. Only a stranger would pound on the front door.

"Who could that be?" Mary asked, startled by the sudden noise. "They certainly sound persistent."

"Who knows?" I squeezed Mary's hand. "It certainly isn't any of our friends. The way things have been going it could be someone coming to tell us we've won the lottery. Whoever it is I'd better check before he knocks down the door."

I hurried through the house as the rapping became more insistent. "Hold your horses, I'm coming." Since it was too early in the spring to have put up screens and it was impossible to talk through the thick glass, I pushed open the storm door and stepped outside.

There were two men on the porch. The closest one clutched a small notebook and the other held a large camera in his right hand. Behind them I could see a car parked on the gravel shoulder in front of the house. A magnetic sign on the driver's door proclaimed the vehicle belonged to the Elliott Herald.

"Mr. Johnson?" the man with the notebook asked, and then continued without waiting for an answer. "I'm Jess Thurgood with the Elliott Herald. I'd like to speak with your wife."

Thurgood was about six feet tall and looked like he needed a good meal. He shirt collar was a size too large and his suit had a slept n appearance. He didn't introduce the cameraman who stood silently on the porch step, looking bored, like he would rather have been somewhere else.

I wasn't exactly surprised to find a reporter on my doorstep. Enough hospital personnel knew about Mary and Johnny that eventually the newspapers were bound to become interested. However, publicity would mean more unwelcome attention, and I really wanted everyone to leave us alone.

"My wife isn't available." I was pretty sure a visit from a newspaper reporter wasn't a good omen. I realized at the time that his visit was important, but even now I don't know how anything could have been done differently to prevent the catastrophe. Maybe Thurgood's visit wasn't the main catalyst, but I still feel a sense of frustration knowing it was the moment events escalated beyond my control. "What do you want?"

"I'd like to interview your wife concerning her cure" Thurgood said, his voice squeaky, the words rapid, like he needed to get them out before someone interrupted him.

"There's no point talking to my wife. We don't know why Mary's cancer is gone. There's nothing we can tell you. Pester the damn doctor and leave us alone."

"Mr. Johnson, your wife may be the key to the biggest story to ever hit Henderson County. One miracle cure might be a fluke, and two miraculous cures could be a coincidence, but three recoveries within a handful of days, can't be ignored. I have an obligation to report the news for my readers. Your wife is an important part of the story and I have to interview her."

"Well, my wife doesn't have an obligation to talk to you." I was curious about the third cure but Thurgood's attitude irritated me. "If there's a story, talk with the doctors and leave my wife alone."

I stepped into the house and was about to close the door in their faces when Mary came up behind me. "Sam, let the gentlemen come in. I think we should talk with Mr. Thurgood."

"Thank you, Mrs. Johnson." Thurgood squeezed past, giving me a triumphant look.

I stepped aside for the photographer and reluctantly followed them into the front room. Thurgood and his companion took seats on the couch while Mary sat in her rocking chair. I remained standing.

"Now, Mr. Thurgood, how may I help you?" Mary asked.

Thurgood flipped open his notebook and held a ball point pen poised over the page. "I'd like to hear your explanation. I understand the cancer isn't in remission that it's completely disappeared."

"I don't have an explanation," Mary said, smiling sweetly.

"Let me phrase that differently. Would you please tell me what happened? How did you learn you were cured?"

"There isn't much to tell. Two weeks ago—Thursday night, I slept better than I had in months. When I woke up Friday morning, I didn't feel sick. Doctor Calvin examined me and determined the cancer was gone."

"Certainly you must have an opinion. How do you think you were cured?"

"It was a miracle," Mary stated firmly. "How can anyone explain a miracle? I believe God heard our prayers."

I thought Mary's reply was perfect. It has been a miracle, and our prayers had been answered. She just left out the part about Eddy being God's instrument.

"I don't believe God simply reaches out and cures people at random." Thurgood said. "There has to be something more concrete to this miracle."

"If you don't have faith, Mr. Thurgood, then I don't know what else to say. I woke up and was cured. If God didn't heal me how would you explain it?"

"I can't. That's why I'm here, trying to find a rational answer." Thurgood glanced at his notebook. "Do you know the other people who were miraculously cured?"

Mary nodded. "I've heard that a young boy, Sally Winthrop's son, had suddenly gone into remission from leukemia. I'm not certain he's been cured permanently."

"What difference would it make if we're acquainted with the Winthrops?" I asked. "This is a small town and we know everyone here."

"I don't' know." Thurgood sounded frustrated. "Maybe there's some common denominator—a place you've visited, or something you all ate. Two weeks ago you were mysteriously cured from a terminal cancer, Mrs. Johnson. A week later, Johnny Winthrop's leukemia vanished. Wouldn't you agree that's a bit more than a coincidence?"

"We don't know anything about Johnny Winthrop's supposed cure" I said. "Mrs. Winthrop owns Sal's Diner, but we seldom eat there. We don't socialize with her, so it isn't likely we'd have any common experiences. Have you spoken with her?"

Thurgood nodded. "Yes I did"

"What did Sally have to say?" Mary asked.

"Pretty much the same thing you've told me. She doesn't understand why Johnny feels better. He woke up one morning and the leukemia was gone. She thinks Jesus answered her prayers." Thurgood absent mindedly tugged at his ear lobe. "I'm a good reporter and can sense when people aren't telling me everything they know. Mrs. Winthrop was holding something back. I believe she knows how Johnny was cured, and I think you know how you were cured Mrs. Johnson."

"Despite what you may think, I don't know anything, and I'm sure Sally told you everything she knows. If the doctors don't understand what happened, how would you expect us to?" Mary smiled sweetly. "God or Jesus cured us. Why Johnny and I were selected, I don't know."

Thurgood glanced at his notebook again. "Okay, I'll let that go for now. Do you know Ruth Goldstein?"

Mary and I looked at each other and shook our heads. "I'm pretty certain there aren't any Goldstein's in Cranston," I said.

"Ruth isn't from Cranston," Thurgood said. "She's four years old and lives in Elliott with her parents, Aaron and Helen Goldstein. Until last Saturday she had an inoperable brain tumor. Sunday morning the tumor had mysteriously vanished. I doubt whether Jesus cured her. Ruth is Jewish."

"It's all the same God," Mary said. "Johnny and Ruth are very young and I believe God has a special love for children. If there's any mystery here, it's why He chose to heal me—an old woman."

"That's why I think you're the key to this whole story." Thurgood said. "You don't fit the pattern, and the exception proves the rule. Why don't you tell me the entire story? This is human interest stuff. The truth can't hurt anyone."

"We've told you everything we know," I said. I had never heard of the Goldsteins, but had no doubt Eddy was involved in the cure. I made a mental note to ask him. "Why don't you talk with the doctors? Cures are their business."

"I have talked with the doctors." Thurgood sounded dissatisfied. "They claim not to know anything either, but I sensed Doctor Calvin was also holding something back. Everyone involved in this series of events is acting like there's some deep, dark secret. Mysteries make me curious and I don't let go until the secrets are revealed."

"You're going to have to satisfy your curiosity somewhere else," I said. "Neither my wife nor I have anything further to say. We resent your insinuation that we're lying. Just get the hell out of here and leave us alone."

"I apologize if I've offended you," Thurgood said, sounding genuinely contrite. It raised my opinion of him. "I don't believe you're lying—just that you aren't telling the entire truth."

"We've told you everything we intend to," I said.

"Could Jerry at least take a picture?" Thurgood asked, indicating the cameraman.

"No pictures. I suggest you get off my property before I sic the dog on you." Mica was at the station with Eddy, but Thurgood didn't know that.

"There's no reason to get hostile," Thurgood said. "We'll leave, but I'll be back. There's a story here, and I intend to find it whether or not you cooperate."

I followed them onto the porch and watched Thurgood and the cameraman walk back to their car so I could be certain they actually left. When I went back into the house, Mary was standing at the kitchen sink, crying softly.

"It's going to be okay, Mary," I said, wrapping my arms around her. "Sally didn't tell the reporter anything. We stick this out another day or so, and it'll all blow over. No one is going to find out about Eddy."

"I hope so," Mary said. But she didn't sound convinced.

I was certain I was right. I didn't understand why it was so important not to tell anyone about Eddy. Of course, we had promised, but I didn't believe telling would make any difference. Maybe if people knew about his power, we would have a mob of sick people bothering us. It would be a nuisance, but I didn't think folks learning about Eddy's healing powers was going to cause serious trouble. I still believed Ernest was the source of concern.

When I got back to the station I told Eddy about Thurgood's visit. You didn't have to be a mind reader to see Eddy didn't take the news well.

"I don't see what difference it makes," I said. "Just because the newspaper might run a story about the miracle cures, doesn't mean anyone will find out about you. You have to admit all of this is big news in our little back water county."

"I know you don't believe there'll be trouble," Eddy said. "But I've been there before and seen it develop. It's sort of like the flap over flying saucers. A few people see lights in the sky. Pretty soon they see alien space ships. Before you know it some people have actually seen aliens."

"I don't see what aliens and space ships have to do with a newspaper article about miracle cures in Cranston and Elliott."

"It was probably a poor example, but people jump to conclusions. It was way before my time, but what about that Orson Welles' radio show 'War of the Worlds'? It caused panic all over the country because listeners heard what they wanted to hear. People were actually convinced thousands were going to die from alien poison gas or some such."

"I still don't see the connection. We're talking about two different things here."

Eddy shook his head like he was disgusted because he couldn't explain better or because I was too stupid to see the point. "But it is the same thing. We're talking about fear. Fear is like some sort of weed. The seed is planted and it grows and spreads and pretty soon it pushes out rational thought."

Obviously this argument wasn't going anywhere, but being an obstinate old man I probably would have continued all night. Fortunately, Johnny arrived and I didn't think it was the sort of conversation a kid should have to listen to. He was upset enough with the thought that his hero might be leaving any day. Then the evening rush began and both Eddy and I were busy taking care of customers.

There wasn't a chance to talk again until we dropped Johnny off at Sal's Diner.

"The reporter brought up another point," I said. "There's been a third cure. A little girl named Ruth Goldstein."

Eddy didn't say anything.

"Well, was that some of your doing?"

Eddy nodded. "Yes."

I had gotten pretty protective of Eddy, and although it really wasn't any of my business, I wanted to know what had happened.

"I thought you were going to avoid curing people so you wouldn't arouse suspicions. How did you even happen to touch Ruth Goldstein?"

"Sometimes I just can't avoid getting involved. When I told Lisa about my power she was skeptical—like everyone is. But she knew about Mary and Johnny, and although she didn't understand, she realized my story might be true.

"You know Lisa is working at the hospital. Well, she asked me if I would see this child in intensive care. I tried to avoid doing anything, but this little girl's suffering had really touched Lisa. I finally agreed to go to the hospital with her."

I pulled into the driveway and switched off the engine. "So you touched the little girl," I suggested.

Eddy nodded. "Lisa and I sort of snuck up to little Ruth's room. She was lying in her bed, tubes coming out of her nose and mouth. She was bald and pale and sickly looking—such a sweet helpless little girl. I think Lisa said she was four-years-old—dying before she had a chance to live. I could tell Lisa felt strongly about Ruth. I just couldn't walk away and leave her there to die?"

"Of course not," I agreed.

"Ruth was sleeping when we arrived. I figured I could cure her and be gone without anyone knowing." Eddy shrugged. "She did wake up when I held her hand, but she didn't realize what was happening. No one, not even the nurses on the floor saw Lisa or me in Ruth's room. No matter what happens, no one will ever connect me to Ruth."

"Well, Thurgood is looking into all the cures. He may find a link."

"He can link me to Mary since I'm living with you folks, and he can connect me to Johnny because he was my roommate. But there's absolutely nothing that can associate me with Ruth."

"I certainly hope you're right."

I believe fear and the sense of impeding tragedy must have been contagious. Miracles and healings were completely new to me, but I was learning quickly. Maybe when Eddy touched me and saw into my soul, for a fleeting instant I could sense his inner being. Whatever the reason, between the reporter and Eddy's beating and Bennett's threats, I was developing a feeling of imminent doom. It was a premonition that scared the hell out of me.

Nineteen

The Elliott Herald was an evening newspaper, so Thurgood's article appeared Tuesday afternoon. I grabbed the top paper from the stack as soon as the delivery truck dropped off my daily allotment.

It must have been a slow news day—no wars or disasters—because the article was on the front page under a headline screaming,

MIRACLE CANCER CURES

I thought it was a shallow story, even as newspaper features go. Apparently Thurgood hadn't found the secret he had been searching for because there was no mention of a faith healer. Mary, Johnny, and Ruth were identified, and there were summaries of interviews with Sally Winthrop, Ruth's parents, and us.

According to the story, little Ruth Goldstein believed two angels had come to her in the hospital, had touched her and taken the tumor to heaven. She described the angels as a handsome young man and a beautiful woman. Although I had been worried there might be a good enough description to identify Eddy, I needn't have been concerned. Thurgood must have decided Ruth's descriptions were the imagination of a little girl because he didn't pursue the angel angle any further.

The article did contain interviews with doctors from Memorial Hospital—identities withheld—but supposedly Doctor Calvin and whoever had treated Ruth. Even those interviews were couched in careful tones. The

Doctors confirmed three instances where terminal cancers, for no known medical reason, had apparently disappeared. It seemed to me the clinical histories of Mary, Johnny, and Ruth were discussed in more detail than the average person cared to read. Although hospital administrators cautioned it was too early to determine whether the incidents were massive remissions, the newspaper obviously leaned toward a miracle. They highlighted Ruth's angel, along with Mary and Sally's prayers. The story hinted the truth wasn't yet known, which, of course, was accurate. For Eddy's sake I hoped it never would be uncovered.

After all his concerns that folks would learn about the power, I was totally surprised by Eddy's reaction. Actually I didn't notice any reaction. It was as if he'd been reading the sport's page. Maybe he realized Thurgood's article wasn't going to expose him, or perhaps he already knew where the trouble was coming from and the newspaper story wouldn't make any difference.

Before I could question him, the afternoon rush began and we were busy serving customers. While Eddy and I pumped gas Johnny read the story. He really got excited about seeing his name in the paper. When Eddy went into the office to run a charge, I could hear Johnny voicing his excitement.

"Wow, isn't it great," Johnny said. "I've never seen my name in the paper before. I'll bet all the kids at school will read it and I'll be famous."

"You're a real celebrity now," Eddy replied. "You won't tell anyone our secret, will you?"

"Of course not." Johnny sounded like he was offended. "I promised and I never break a promise."

"I know I can trust you."

Eddy had more confidence than I did. It would be a lot of pressure on a young kid to keep quiet.

As usual, several customers purchased papers on their way home. Since two of the cured people lived in Cranston, I figured the news would spread quickly throughout town. Eddy must have had the same thought.

"I think you should go home," he said during a lull. "Mary is going to need you."

"Why? What's wrong with Mary?"

"Sam." He explained patiently, like I was the youngster. "The newspaper story left a lot of things unsaid. People are going to have questions. Friends will be calling and there might even be contacts from the radio and TV stations. You don't want Mary to face that by herself, do you?"

"But I can't leave you alone. This is the busy part of the day. And what if reporters come here to interview you?"

"Nobody's going to bother me," Eddy promised. "At least not today. My name isn't even in the story. I won't have any problems handling the station. You did it alone for years."

I could see the logic in his argument, but I was torn between being with Mary and the feeling I was deserting Eddy. "I don't know what to do."

"I do. Go home. If anyone asks for you, I'll say you took the day off. Johnny and I know the routine. We'll close up at six and walk home. It isn't far. Don't worry about us. Right now your focus should be on Mary."

I knew Eddy was right, so I grabbed my copy of the Elliott Herald, got in my truck and drove home.

When I entered the kitchen, Mary was on the phone. "I have to go now, Susan," she said. "Thank you for calling." She hung up, looking distressed. "I'm glad you came home, Sam. The phone's been ringing like crazy."

I wrapped her in my arms and kissed her forehead. "I'm sure you've guessed by now that there's a headline article in the Herald." I said. "That's why I came home. Eddy figured we'd get a lot of calls, and maybe even have TV and radio people pestering us."

The phone rang again. I lifted it off the hook, hung up without speaking, and disconnected the jack. "We don't need that damn thing driving us crazy"

"But what if we get an important call?" A person gets dependent on the phone and feels sort of lost without it.

"We never get important calls, and I don't see any reason why today would be an exception."

"What if Eddy phones from the station?"

"Don't worry about Eddy. He can handle anything that comes up."

"I suppose it'll be all right if you say so," Mary agreed, still uncomfortable losing our communication link to the world. "Did you bring the paper home?"

I indicated the Elliott Herald I'd tossed on the table. Mary pushed me away, sat, and opened the newspaper. As soon as she saw the headline, tears filled her eyes.

"What did Eddy think about the story?" she asked, certain Eddy had been frightened by the exposure.

"It didn't seem to bother him at all. If he isn't worried, we sure don't need to be. Now, don't cry, Mary," I said, taking both her hands in mine. Women's tears always made me feel inadequate. "It's going to be all right. One day's headlines and then everyone is going to forget the whole thing"

"But they're going to find out about Eddy." Mary said.

"Maybe not. There certainly isn't enough information in the article to identify him. I can't imagine anyone even beginning to think about a miracle worker. If we weren't directly involved, you have to admit we'd think the idea of a healer as pretty fantastic. No one is going to think of it on their own."

"There are going to be a lot of questions. Maybe something will slip out."

"Nothing is going to leak out," I insisted. "And what if it does? Eddy hasn't committed a crime, you know. Maybe it would clear the air if people knew."

I tried to sound confident for Mary, but a nagging worry began to develop in the back of my mind.

* * *

On Wednesday afternoon, when I arrived home on my afternoon break, there was an unfamiliar car in the driveway. I walked into the house with a sense of dread. Recently we never had strange visitors without precipitating another crisis.

This time our visitor wasn't a stranger. Doc Calvin was sitting at the kitchen table, talking with Mary.

"What are you doing here, Doc?" I demanded, afraid he had discovered evidence Mary's cancer had returned. "Mary, are you alright?"

"I'm fine," Mary said, smiling reassuringly. "Doctor Calvin came over to talk. He's made the connection about Eddy."

"The connection about Eddy?" I asked, trying to sound mystified.

"It's alright, Sam," Mary said. "He knows who healed me and Johnny and Ruth Goldstein. He wants to test Eddy, to determine how he is able to cure people."

"Then why aren't you talking with Eddy?" I asked Doc Calvin. I wasn't convinced he really knew about the power. He had to be guessing because it just didn't seem logical to connect Eddy to any of this. "He's of age. He makes his own decisions."

Doc looked uncomfortable. "I sensed Eddy wouldn't talk to me."

"If he wouldn't talk to you, what makes you think we have the right to discuss him?"

"I don't know. Maybe I had to share my conclusions with someone. Maybe I thought we could talk to Eddy—persuade him to undergo testing."

"You want us to ask Eddy to become a laboratory experiment? To convince him he should let you medical people poke and probe? If he did have the ability to heal people, do you really believe a power like that could be measured with a few tests?"

"No, nothing like that. I don't know what I wanted here." Doc looked at Mary like he expected her to solve the dilemma for him. "You now I treated Eddy after his beating. When I examined him, he appeared perfectly normal except for the injuries. But when I touched him I felt a force, a...I don't know what I felt. There was a feeling of warmth and peace like nothing I'd ever experienced."

"It was late in the evening, and you'd already put in a long day," Mary suggested. "Maybe you were just tired."

"Damnit, it was more than that." Doc sounded agitated and I could see that the sensation had frightened him. "I know it doesn't make any sense, but I felt as if Eddy could see into the darkest corners of my mind and exorcise the demons hiding there" Doc was rubbing his hands together in a nervous gesture. "I know it isn't possible, that it refutes everything I've ever leaned, but it's preyed on my mind ever since. I can't explain it, and I haven't had a decent night's sleep since."

Mary reached over and laid her hand on Doc's arm. "There are some things that just don't have an explanation unless you have faith."

"Maybe that's the problem. I'm a man of science and I've always believed there is a rational interpretation to explain everything."

"Okay, so you had a strange sensation when you worked on Eddy," I said. "I don't see how that connects him with healing anyone."

Doc held up his hand to stop my comments. "No, please let me explain." He took a deep breath and continued. "I knew Eddy lived with you and Mary had experienced an inexplicable cure. Then Johnny Winthrop's leukemia suddenly vanished. At the time I didn't make any connection between events—or maybe I didn't want to. When I read the article in the Herald everything suddenly clicked into place.

"I don't know how or when Eddy visited Ruth Goldstein, but he must have. It's the only thing that makes any sense—if any of this makes sense. I didn't want to believe in a faith healer, but I'm not stupid. Combined with the cures and the power I felt, some instinct told me Eddy was responsible. I had to ask Mary if it was true." Doc shook his head and took a deep breath. "Frankly all this scares the hell out of me." Doc avoided making eye contact, like he was uncomfortable letting us see his fear.

"Why?" I asked. I could almost hear Eddy's voice in my heard saying his power frightened people. Now I was seeing proof of it. "Why would Eddy's ability to heal—provided it's true, scare you?"

"Maybe scared isn't the right word. Maybe I'm confused. If Eddy has this power it's not natural. People aren't really able to cure by the laying on of hands. It's superstitious nonsense. I know there have been evangelists and faith healers, but I always figured their healings were the result of mass hysteria and psychosomatic illness." He shook his head again. "I've actually seen three miracles, and it couldn't be a coincidence."

"Why isn't the ability to heal people a natural phenomenon?" I asked. "Just because we don't understand doesn't mean it isn't real. If we went back a hundred years and showed people penicillin or antibiotics, they'd think those medicines were witchcraft. Maybe Eddy's just ahead of his time."

"But that's different," Doc insisted. "Medicines aren't witchcraft. They're science. What Eddy does is magic."

"See, you're thinking like people a hundred years ago. If Eddy does have the power—and I'm not saying he does— then it's more powerful than magic."

Mary reached out and touched my hand. "It's all right, Sam. I've already told Doctor Calvin that Eddy cured me."

"Okay," I reluctantly agreed. "Say it is true. It still isn't magic. His gift, or power, or whatever, comes from the goodness inside him.   Maybe someday, when we purge the hate and greed and ambition from our own hearts, everyone will be able to do what Eddy does. Maybe there are others in the world, right now, today, who can heal by touching people."

"Then, why don't we know about them?" Doc asked, a pleading in his voice. "Where are those other miracle workers?"

"I don't know. Maybe we don't know about them for the same reason no one knows about Eddy.   Sophisticated, modern man can't handle the unknown, the unexplained. They're scared, just like you and they strike out at what scares them."

"I'm not striking out at Eddy," Doc insisted.   "I'm just trying to understand."

"Maybe everyone doesn't strike out, but it has happened to Eddy. People with the gift have to hide it. When Eddy explained how people reacted to his power, I didn't believe him. He predicted folks would become afraid of him, and I've already seen the fear in action with the bastards who beat him, and now with you."

"I'm not a threat to Eddy," Doc insisted. "A power like that just isn't natural."

"Do you believe in God?" Mary asked. Although I was becoming agitated, Mary was calm, almost serene.

"Of course I believe in God," Doc said. "I don't think you can be a doctor and not believe. How else can we explain the miracle of life and the mystery of death? Are you saying this power is religious in some way?"

"I can't answer that," Mary spoke with the assurance of a true believer. "If you believe in God, maybe you'll find an answer in the Bible. It says, 'I am the Light and the Light shines in the darkness and the darkness knows it not'."

For a moment no one spoke, but I could sense Doc wasn't convinced.

"Anyway, thanks for listening to me," he finally said, standing to leave. "Will you speak to Eddy? Will you ask him if he'll allow testing?"

"No, I won't ask him to be poked and prodded by you medical folks," I said.   "I already know he won't be a guinea pig.   He's undergone examinations before and it was a waste of time. If he has this gift, like you suspect, there aren't any medical tests to measure it."

* * *

Although we weren't especially busy when I returned to the station, I avoided telling Eddy about Doc Calvin until we had closed and were driving home.

He didn't respond immediately. "Maybe it's time for me to leave," he finally said, sounding tired and resigned.

"What are you talking about? I thought we'd decided you were going to stay with Mary and me indefinitely."

"I know, and I'm grateful for the offer—more than you'll ever know. But people are learning about the power. It always begins this way. There'll be trouble soon and I want to be gone before it starts. I don't want you and Mary to be hurt."

"Damnit, Eddy, you can't run away for the rest of your life," I insisted. "I know you've had a tough time in other places, but that isn't going to happen here. Cranston isn't like other towns. The people here are good, hard working, God fearing folks."

Eddy gave a huge sigh, like he realized I wouldn't ever understand. "You said yourself that Doctor Calvin was frightened by the power. He's a medical man. Unexplained phenomenon shouldn't scare a man of science. If he's scared, how do you think the average person will react?"

I parked in the driveway, shut off the engine, and we sat in the truck. By unspoken agreement we wanted to finish this discussion before we went in.

"I'm a pretty average person and I'm not frightened," I said.

"Not everyone reacts in the same way. It only takes a few frightened folks and every town has some small, scared people," Eddy said in a quiet voice, like he didn't want to believe it.

"I'm not the smartest guy in the world," I said. "But I refuse to believe that curing people is going to cause any trouble. If there's going to be a problem here in Cranston, it'll be because of something you saw in Ernest Bennett. Some secret he's afraid of anyone discovering. Don't you think it's time you told me about it so we can face this together?"

"Damnit, Sam, we've already talked about this. If I saw something in Ernest, it has to remain between him and me. There's nothing you could do anyway."

"We can't know that if you won't talk to me." I felt like reaching over and shaking Eddy.

"I have to do what my conscience tells me is right."

"Okay, don't let me help, but at some point you have to stop running away," I insisted. "You've got to settle down. You have a home with Mary and me. Lisa Bennett likes you a lot. Maybe you could even get married and have that family we talked about."

"Lisa's a very special person," Eddy agreed. "She's got a beautiful soul and will touch other people in a good way. But it wouldn't work out with us."

"I don't understand you, Eddy. If I were your age and a beauty like Lisa Bennett was interested in me, I'd be floating on a cloud." I chuckled, trying to lighten the mood. "In fact it did happen to me. When I was your age Mary was the prettiest girl in town. I couldn't believe she saw anything interesting in me. But she did. Now look at what I've got. Maybe Lisa isn't the girl for you but if you put down roots, the right girl will come along."

"I wish I could have a life like yours, Sam. You're a lucky man. Mary was your destiny. My fate has already been decided and it doesn't include a home and family."

"That's bullshit," I said. "I don't believe in predestination. We control our own lives. At least think about it. You're in no condition to go gallivanting around the country. When your ribs are completely healed we can talk again. By then you'll see I'm right."

Eddy opened the car door. "We'd better go in. Mary's going to wonder what we're doing out here." He looked back at me. "I'll stay a few more days. I just hope I don't wait too long."

Twenty

Life is never static. It may seem as if each day is like the one before, but nothing is ever the same. We age, we grow, and the seasons change. Each day the world moves ahead and there is no going back. Sometimes the changes are so gradual, so minute, they are barely noticeable. Sometimes life changes in an instant, like a bursting bomb. Eddy had been an exploding rocket dropping into our lives. From the first day he had ripped out the roots of complacency and nothing would be normal again.

I suppose living in a small town had accustomed me to a slow paced life. But life wasn't leisurely any longer. There had been more excitement in the last few weeks than in the previous ten years. I knew it wasn't going to calm down any time soon. It seemed as if one episode quickly led to another.

Thurgood's article in the Elliott Herald managed to generate a great deal of commotion. Mary reported that on Wednesday and Thursday our home phone rang constantly as curious friends and neighbors wished her well, pestering her for details and tidbits of inside gossip. She complained about not being able to complete her housework because of the constant interruptions, but I could tell she was enjoying herself. After the lengthy illness, when her only companions had been Alma Smith and Connie Childress, speaking with so many people fulfilled a deep need.

It was a good thing Mary enjoyed handling all of her contacts with the outside world because I wasn't able to get away from the station for our usual afternoons together. On both Wednesday and Thursday, Eddy and I were run ragged from opening to closing. Thurgood's article had mentioned my service station, and consequently dozens of strangers pulled in to fill up and ask questions, as if my station was the first stop on a religious pilgrimage. I knew people were inherently curious, but I'd never expected so many to be drawn off the beaten path by a single newspaper story.

Most of the strangers were simply inquisitive, wanting to see the town where two of the miracles had roots. I was grateful for the business and pumped a record number of gallons. The extra traffic was going to help with all the medical bills, but I never expected any of the curiosity seekers to become regular customers, so I didn't make a special effort to win friends. I assumed a grumpy, don't know anything attitude to discourage them, and kept Eddy busy in the service bays as much as possible. I figured the fewer questions he had to answer, the better.

However, some of the strangers were eagerly searching for miracles of their own and I'm not so hard hearted I could be gruff with them. There was an obvious desperation in the eyes of those seeking cures for critically ill loved ones. My heart ached because I remembered how hopeless I had felt when Mary was dying and I understood why they had come to Cranston. Only a couple of weeks earlier I would have grasped at any possibility to save Mary and would probably have attempted to track down miracle cures myself.

Some of them asked to fill water bottles, as if they hoped there was some sort of curative powers in the local waters. I wanted to tell them the miracle wasn't in the water, but in Eddy's hands. However I realized there was so much pain and misery in the world Eddy couldn't even begin to heal it all. So I filled their bottles, and kept my tears inside. There wasn't anything else I could do, although I felt a heavy guilt knowing Mary had been cured and I didn't have the right to help any of these people by revealing the secret.

I figured it had to be even more difficult for Eddy, so I tried to keep him away from the desperate folks. I'm certain if there had actually been dying people in the cars he would have cured them on the spot. For the first time I was able to appreciate what a tremendous burden it must be for Eddy to have the power and not be able to help everyone. No wonder he didn't want his secret revealed.

It became so difficult to face the hopeful seekers that I considered closing the station. However, I knew the public has notoriously short memories, so I figured the flurry of interest would quickly fade and the entire thing would be forgotten. I hoped so because I didn't have the strength to handle much more.

My silent prayer must have been answered because by Friday business had returned to normal. We only had one stranger stop for gas and conversation, and by early afternoon it was quiet enough at the station that I felt comfortable letting Eddy handle it while I stopped at the house to spend some time with Mary.

I had just stepped into the kitchen when Lisa called. I grabbed the phone before Mary could get up from the table where she was working on a shopping list. I hadn't seen Lisa since her date with Eddy, and still didn't know whether she had talked with her father, or if she had forgiven me for interfering. She hadn't stopped at the station to visit Eddy, but that might have been because she was busy at the hospital.

There was a short pause when she heard my voice, like she hadn't been expecting me to be there. "There's been a lot of excitement at the hospital about the newspaper story," she said, "and I was calling to find out how the publicity was affecting Mary and Eddy."

"They're both doing fine," I said. "There's been a lot of activity, but nothing we couldn't handle."

"I was worried about Eddy," she said. "All of this must be difficult for him."

"He's doing all right, but we've been busy with all the curious folks," I said. "We've all been wondering about you. You haven't been around since Saturday."

"I've been busy at the hospital. I think the newspaper article convinced a lot of sick people that if they were in Memorial Hospital they would have a chance for a miracle. At any rate, there've been a record number of admissions and I've had to put in extra hours."

"I though maybe you were staying away because you were angry about our conversation Saturday night."

"No, I'm not angry. I still think you were off base about my father, but I've given it a lot of thought and realize you were just concerned for Eddy's sake. I haven't been around because I've been busy and had a lot of things on my mind."

"Have you talked to your dad about Eddy?" I asked.

"No, and I don't intend to." Her tone was abrupt and defensive.

"After Doc Calvin read the newspaper story he made the connection about the cures and Eddy." I said. "It almost caused Eddy to leave Cranston. If you have feelings for him you really need to talk with your dad. If something else happens, I won't be able to keep him from taking to the road. I need your help."

"Sam, you're wrong about my father and I don't have time to discuss this any further." I could hear anger in her voice. "I'm on my way to the hospital and called to offer Mary my support not to get into an argument."

The phone clicked in my ear and I was left listening to a dial tone.

"What was that all about?" Mary asked.

I knew she was curious after hearing my end of the conversation and decided it was time to tell her about my suspicions. I sat across from her at the table, took both her hands in mine, and told her about Ernest's visit at the station, his threats, and my belief he was the source of our troubles because Eddy had seen a dark secret

"Saturday night I asked Lisa to talk with her father," I explained. "I figured if anyone could help prevent Ernest from doing something desperate, it was his daughter. It doesn't look like she's going to talk with him."

At first Mary looked confused, but as I expressed my concerns I could see fear in her eyes. "Oh, Sam are you certain about Ernest?" she asked.

"I can't be absolutely certain, but I know in my heart it's true. I could scream because everyone thinks there will be problems because of Eddy's ability to cure, and I know the trouble will come from Bennett."

Mary began to cry, so I stepped around the table and held her in my arms.

"Sam, I'm frightened," she sobbed. "What can we do?"

"Damnit, Mary, I don't know what to do," I said, letting the frustration come through. "I'm scared too."

* * *

When there wasn't anything further in the Elliott Herald over the next several days, I pretty much decided publicity about the cures had run its course. I hadn't considered Jess Thurgood's tenacity.

He turned out to be a bulldog, getting his teeth into the bones of a story and refusing to let go. He had attempted to interview Mary a couple more times, but gave up when she politely refused to talk. I know he pestered Sally Winthrop and probably harassed the Goldsteins. When no one could, or would, tell him anything, he became more determined. Somewhere he picked up a thread, because he appeared at the service station Friday afternoon.

I walked over to where he parked his car beside my truck. "Don't you ever give up?" I asked. "I've already told you Mary and I aren't giving any more interviews."

"No, I never quit on a story. But it's obvious I'm not going to learn anything from you or your wife. I'm here to interview your mechanic, Edward Foster." Thurgood looked tired, like he had been working a lot of overtime. It made me wonder if reporters were paid by the hour.

I knew Mary had never mentioned Eddy, so my first thought was Sally Winthrop had told Thurgood something. I immediately dismissed the idea, knowing if Sally had slipped, she'd have told us.

"Eddy is busy," I said. "He doesn't have time to waste answering a lot of stupid questions."

"I'm getting damned tired of people not talking to me," Thurgood complained. "I just get more curious when folks try to hide information."

"We're not hiding anything."

"Then, why can't I talk with Eddy?"

"Because he's on an hourly wage, and I don't plan on paying him to answer questions about something he doesn't know a damned thing about."

"I can always wait until he's off work," Thurgood suggested.

"Not on my property you can't. I don't allow loitering and I'll chase you off with my shotgun if I have to." I didn't have a shotgun at the station, but figured a little white lie wouldn't be held against me.

"Then I can park down the road and wait until he leaves work. One way or another, I intend to speak with Foster. You and I both know he's the key to this whole story."

"I don't know any such thing. If you don't get the hell out of here and leave us alone, I'll talk to a lawyer about a harassment suit."

Our voices had risen above normal conversational tones, and Eddy stepped out of the service bay to see what was happening. Mica took a stance at Eddy's side, his body tensed, like he was preparing to protect his master from a threat.

"It's alright, Sam." Eddy said, walking toward us, wiping his hands on a cleaning cloth. "It had to happen eventually. I might as well get it over with. I'm Edward Foster. Everyone calls me Eddy."

"I'm Jess Thurgood, with the Elliott Herald." Thurgood gave me a triumphant look.

He stepped forward to meet Eddy, and held out his hand. Eddy hesitated, then with a gesture of resignation, reached out with his own. Thurgood was startled, almost jerking back his arm, before relaxing. I knew he was experiencing the warm, happy feeling.

"What did you mean, that it had to happen eventually?" Thurgood asked, wiping his hand on his trouser leg like he had touched something unpleasant. There was a hint of uneasiness around his eyes and I wondered what Eddy had seen in Thurgood's soul.

"Nothing special," Eddy said. "You've talked with everyone else in this county. You had to get to me eventually."

"Okay, I'll accept that," Thurgood said as if making a concession. "No one involved in this series of cures wants to tell me anything. I smelled a conspiracy of silence, so I kept digging until I discovered some solid information concerning you."

Eddy cocked his head to one side, listening intently, but made no comment.

"In this business, after a while you develop a sort of sixth sense." Thurgood sounded like he was proud of his investigative skills and welcomed the opportunity to brag. "The Goldsteins were honestly mystified by Ruth's recovery, but I had a notion both Mary Johnson and Sally Winthrop were keeping something from me. Since the adults wouldn't say anything, I figured Johnny Winthrop as the weak link. And I was right. Kids have a hard time keeping secrets, particularly when they're the center of attention."

I chuckled. "You're getting just a bit desperate for a story, aren't you?" I was glad Johnny hadn't arrived yet because if he learned he had somehow let the secret slip it would devastate him.

Thurgood ignored me and my comment. "Mrs. Winthrop refused to let me interview her son, so I went to Johnny's school. I didn't believe any of the kids would talk with me because I'm a stranger and an adult. However, I figured if Johnny had something to say, he would have told some of his friends and eventually the teachers would hear about it. Again I was right. There's a rumor going around Johnny's school that you had something to do with his leukemia disappearing." He stared hard at Eddy as if he were expecting a confession.

When there wasn't any response he continued. "I didn't know what to make of a rumor like that. It was the first time I'd heard your name, and as far as I knew, you'd never met Johnny. Employing a little basic detective work, I learned you were his hospital roommate. One rumor, one cure, one connection." Thurgood had a smug expression like we should applaud his reasoning.

"But there were three cures," he continued. "I asked Sheriff Simpson if he knew a young man named Edward Foster and he told me you worked for Sam Johnson, lived in his house, and arrived in Cranston shortly before Mary Johnson was miraculously cured. Two cures, two connections. I couldn't find a link with Ruth Goldstein, except that you and Ruth were in the hospital at the same time. Her amazing recovery occurred shortly after your release. Two out of three connections, and one probable. Wouldn't you say that was more than a coincidence, Eddy?"

Eddy shrugged. "I don't see what you're driving at, Mr. Thurgood. It's never been a secret that I know Johnny and Mrs. Johnson."

"The secret is what you had to do with these three miraculous cures."

Eddy laughed, although I could tell Thurgood's argument bothered him. "You've got to be kidding, Mr. Thurgood. I'm a drifter, an auto mechanic. I don't know anything about medicine."

"I'm not talking about medicine. I'm talking about black magic, voodoo—hell, I don't know—something other than medical science."

"Don't you think you're reaching a little bit?" I said. I could tell from Thurgood's attitude he wasn't totally confident about his conclusions. "I can name dozens of people who know both Mary and Johnny, myself included. I don't know the Goldsteins, but some of those people probably do."

"Okay, so I'm reaching. But the rumor concerns Eddy, and a rumor like that doesn't spring up without some basis in fact. There's a story here, and one way or another, I'm going to get to the bottom of it. It'll be easier on everyone if you tell me what you know."

"Get serious," I said, "Johnny and Eddy became friends in the hospital. He thinks Eddy is the greatest thing since chunky peanut butter. He's just a little boy. Any connection to his cure and Eddy is simply some sort of fairy tale he's made up."

"Maybe and maybe not." Thurgood looked hard at Eddy. "You didn't answer my question."

"I'm sorry," Eddy said politely. "I didn't know you'd asked a question."

"Are you a warlock? Do you practice black magic or white magic or voodoo or any of that sort of thing?"

"Do I look like a witch?" Eddy squatted and began ruffling the fur behind Mica's ears because the dog had begun a low, throaty growl. "I thought witches were supposed to have black cats, pointed hats, and warts on their noses."

"Hell, I don't know what warlocks are supposed to look like." Thurgood didn't sound sure of himself. "You still haven't answered my question."

"No, I'm not a warlock." Eddy had a smile that didn't quite reach his eyes. "I don't know anything about magic or voodoo. Does that answer your question?"

"Yeah, I suppose it does." Thurgood sounded disappointed. "If you were some kind of witch or magician, you wouldn't tell me, would you?"

Eddy continued petting Mica. "Probably not."

"Look, Thurgood, I've been patient, letting you ask your dumb questions. I have no idea what you wanted to accomplish, but Eddy's got a job to do. I'm not paying him to stand around talking with you. Now get the hell out of here. I don't want you bothering us at work again."

"Alright, I'll go," Thurgood said. "I don't know what it is, but I still think there's something to this angle. I promise you I'm going to dig until I know everything about Edward Foster since the day he was born. Somewhere, someone has the answers."

We watched Thurgood climb into his car and pull out of the station. The bastard had wasted our time, and didn't even have the decency to buy gas.

"He's going to find out," Eddy said, sounding resigned. "Several newspapers have had stories discussing mysterious cures, complete with the names of people who know about me. In the articles relating to the fire that killed my family there was a lot of speculation concerning the power. If he checks newspaper files around the country, he's going to discover the truth."

"He's not going to learn anything. Hell, Thurgood doesn't even know the name of your hometown. It isn't likely he'll know which newspaper files to check."

"This is the computer age, Sam. Newspapers probably have databases so they can check references. If he finds the right database, everything will be there."

"So what if he finds out?" I asked. "What if he publishes a front page story about you having the power to cure sick people? Maybe we'll end up with a bunch of fanatics camped on my front lawn, but I've never understood why exposure worries you so much."

"You heard Mr. Thurgood. As soon as he thought there might be something besides medicine behind the cures, he talked about witches and voodoo."

"So what? This is the twentieth century. No one believes in magic any more."

"I understand you being skeptical, Sam. Until you've seen it happen, it doesn't seem possible. But people still have all the superstitions. They still want to kill witches."

"Not in Cranston they don't"

"You've heard about the witch trials in Salem, haven't you? You think folks have grown smarter or more tolerant than those poor ignorant farmers in the sixteen hundreds. Today people understand about planes and rockets and TV and a thousand magical things those Puritans never imagined, but we still have superstitions and nightmares about the dark unknown. Folks are still afraid. Believe me; people strike out at what they fear."

"You're wrong, Eddy."

"I wish that were true." Eddy took a deep breath and let it out slowly. "Sam, I'll finish out the week, and then I'm leaving. It'll take Thurgood at least that long to research his story."

"Damnit, Eddy, you're upset. We'll talk about this when we get home tonight. It'll give you time to think sensibly."

"If it'll make you feel better, Sam, we'll talk, but it won't change my mind. Something is going to happen and I don't want you and Mary caught in the middle."

"Eddy, what you have is so wonderful, I don't see why you won't share it with the world"

"Because the world is full of the sick and the hurt and the scared. Over the last couple of days you've seen some of them yourself." Eddy headed for the service bay to finish an oil change as a car drove up to the gas pumps. "I can't help everyone in the world." He stopped and looked back at me, a deep sadness in his yes. "Sam, I'm one of the frightened people."

Twenty-One

Although Mary had cooked a beautiful roast, no one paid attention to the food when our Friday evening meal became a one–sided debate. Mary and I were at a disadvantage, speculating on a shadowy future, but we carried the majority of the discussion. Mostly Eddy refused to argue, simply stating he felt it was time to move along. When he did choose to say something in his own defense, he could cite examples from five years of experience.

We were already acquainted with a portion of his history, but when Eddy filled some of the gaps, I began to sense deep loneliness, fear, and concern for others. Eddy had seldom stayed more than a couple of months in any location, although he had remained nearly a year in a small Montana town. Wherever he went, there was always someone who needed healing. Because it was so easy to relieve the suffering with a simple touch, he couldn't turn his back. One cure inevitably leads to another, and stories about the power spread. People were always grateful for his ability to heal, but slowly realized when he touched them he saw into their souls, into their hidden selves. That scared them. Soon folks began avoiding him, backing away from his touch, looking at him with a mixture of fear and awe. The avoidance, the gradual isolation, were the signals for Eddy to pack his knapsack and seek a location where he was unknown.

"Maybe I missed something," I argued. "Your excuse is that you always moved to avoid violence, but I didn't hear anything about violence or intimidation. What you're really telling us is that as soon as you became uncomfortable, you ran away." I felt inadequate. If I were smarter in dealing with people and their problems, I could convince Eddy it hurt those who cared about him when he just disappeared, that it was time to stop running. I just didn't know how.

"There has been violence," Eddy said. "I've been beaten up a couple of times. Now I've learned to recognize the glances, the attitude, and I've been able to leave before trouble began. No one else is going to suffer because of me." In Eddy's expression were the scars, the burden of not being able to forgive himself for his family's tragedy.

"No one in Cranston is giving you strange looks," Mary said. "I haven't seen anyone avoiding you. Certainly Sally Winthrop and Johnny aren't acting like your power is a curse. You've got friends here. Sam and I aren't afraid of touching you."

"No, but you're different," Eddy agreed. "Neither of you have dark secrets you're hiding from the world, so you aren't afraid of me finding out. But most folks are hiding ugly things. The looks, the attitude will come. People are the same everywhere."

Mary reached across the table and touched his hand. "Eddy, I know you've been hurt and you want to avoid more pain, but please give us a chance. Maybe the story won't ever come out and you're worried about nothing. Even if people learn about your power, you have to allow us to prove we aren't going to turn against you."

"You know it isn't the medical cures that cause trouble," Eddy said. "It's seeing into their souls that scares people."

"Then just don't touch people," I argued.

Eddy shook his head. "Do you realize how difficult it is to avoid touching people? I didn't intend to touch Lisa, but she stumbled and I grabbed her arm to keep her from falling. I didn't intend to touch Doctor Calvin, but he had to treat me for my injuries. I certainly never wanted to touch Ernest Bennett."

"Finally we're at the heart of this whole mess," I said. "We all know Bennett is the problem. I don't know how, but we're going to handle him. Once we've taken care of that, it'll be smooth sailing. Then you'll just have to avoid touching anyone else."

"That's ridiculous." Mary sounded like she couldn't believe I'd say anything so stupid. "Eddy can't do that. Where would I be, or Johnny, or little Ruth Goldstein, if he hadn't touched us? And I don't see how Eddy can avoid physical contact. Who knows how many people he's helped without even suspecting? People who had some disease they didn't even know about yet. Eddy has to use the power God gave him."

"Maybe God didn't give me the power," Eddy said. "Maybe it was Satan."

"I won't hear anymore of that kind of talk," Mary said. I could see she was getting angry. "All good things come from God, and no matter how people react, your power hasn't done anything except good. If bad things happen it's because Satan can't tolerate goodness. I won't stand for you leaving Cranston just because of something that might happen. It's time you stopped running."

"But Mary," Eddy insisted. "When the trouble starts it'll happen quickly and it can be dangerous."

"I don't care. I just won't hear anymore talk about you leaving. You've been in Cranston for less than a month and I simply won't let you go. If it comes to that, I'll have Sam tie you up and lock you in your room."

It isn't likely Mary was serious about making Eddy a prisoner, but she was certainly serious abut him staying. I can't remember ever seeing her so worked up.

"I agree with Mary," I said. "It's time you stopped running."

Eddy didn't look happy. "I don't want either of you hurt. But I'll stay a while longer. We'll take it day by day."

I will always wonder what would have happened if Eddy had left Cranston that weekend.

* * *

Even after our discussion with Eddy, I knew Mary was concerned he would just be gone some morning. And I was afraid she might be right. When we talked about it later, she agreed Lisa was the key to Eddy putting down roots. Mary decided she would play cupid. Maybe Lisa wasn't going to confront her father, but if Eddy fell in love he would have the strongest possible motive for staying.

I don't know much about how the female mind works, but I'm pretty certain all women have an innate desire to see every eligible male married and settled down. I would have preferred to let nature take its course once

Eddy had been pointed in the right direction. But women seem to think nature is too slow if left to its own devices, and needs a shove or two along the way. In this case I couldn't argue. If there was even the smallest chance it would work, it was worth a try.

Although it was short notice, Mary called the Bennett house and invited Lisa to Sunday dinner. I figured having Lisa share a meal was a great idea. Not only would it give her another chance to win over Eddy, but it would also be good for Mary. We hadn't had company for dinner in longer than I could remember, and Mary loved to cook.

Sunday was another one of those days of unseasonably warm weather and sunshine. When Mary and I returned from Mass, she shooed Eddy and me out of the kitchen and began preparing dinner. Mary had never liked men folk cluttering up her kitchen when she was working her own brand of magic on a meal.

There isn't much to do in Cranston on a Sunday. I wanted to take Eddy out to Lipton Lake and see if the fish were biting yet. We would have been able to wet a line and still get back in plenty of time for dinner, but Mary nearly had a fit. She was not going to have the men folk smelling like fish and ruining the dinner. So she put Eddy and me to work setting up the dining room.

Since Mary had been sleeping upstairs again I hadn't gotten around to moving her things out of the makeshift bedroom. Returning the dining room to its original purpose required a fair amount of lifting and carrying, so Eddy and I worked up a pretty good sweat. I wasn't sure we smelled much better than if we had gone fishing. We disassembled the bed and moved the mattress and frame out into the garage. Then we carried in the old dining room table we had inherited from Mary's folks. Of course the table and chairs were dusty from setting so long in the garage, so we washed and polished them. I had to admit it was a good feeling to remove the last vestiges of Mary's illness and to have a dining room again.

Lisa arrived about three, and after a brief exchange of greetings, she joined Mary in the kitchen. The two women chased us out of the house. Eddy and I settled in the back yard with me sipping a beer and Eddy having a soda. Eddy tossed the ball for Mica while I enjoyed the fantastic smells coming out of the kitchen. I would have loved to go in, just to savor the aroma of cooking food but Mary would have none of it

It was at least an hour and another beer before she finally allowed us in the house to wash up

As usual, Mary had outdone herself. The dining room table had been set with the good China, which was only hauled out on special occasions. She had baked a ham, made scalloped potatoes, a French bean casserole, and homemade dinner rolls. When I passed through the kitchen I saw a couple of apple pies cooling on the counter.

We made polite conversation during the meal, but never really did any serious talking until Eddy and I had both finished off a big piece of apple pie and were relaxing over coffee.

"I've decided to move out of the big house and get an apartment," Lisa said.

"Oh, that's wonderful," Mary agreed. "I think it helps to get ready for life if you move out on your own. There comes a time when everyone needs to cut the apron strings."

I was a bit more skeptical but had to agree with Mary. "I think getting away from that mausoleum you live in is a good idea."

Lisa reached over and laid her hand on Eddy's. "I got upset when Sam talked to me about the possibility of my father being responsible for your beating, but I did a lot of thinking about it. I finally got the courage to talk to Dad, and he denied any involvement. We had an argument and I told him if he ever interfered with my life again I would never speak to him. Then I decided the best thing to do was to get a place of my own.

Eddy squeezed Lisa's hand and smiled, but didn't comment.

There wasn't any doubt in my mind that the problems with her father had nothing to do with Lisa, but maybe her talk with Ernest was the reason he hadn't followed through with his threats.

"I might have been wrong about your dad being responsible." I didn't believe for one minute that Ernest was innocent but I did feel a tinge of guilt for having caused a father-daughter rift.

"I know most people believe Dad is a mean person, and maybe that's the side he shows to the world, but he does have a lot of feeling for family. I think telling him I would never speak to him again touched a soft spot. If he had been involved in hiring those thugs, I doubt whether there'll be anymore trouble from him."

"I have a hard time seeing Ernest with a soft spot," I said. "I hope you're right. I told you Saturday that I think there's more to your Dad's threats than concern about you. But if he really has strong feelings for family, maybe he won't do anything else. Right now Eddy is worried about trouble coming from another source."

Lisa looked alarmed. "What other trouble are you talking about?"

"Sam's exaggerating," Eddy said. "More people are learning about my power, and the more folks who know, the more likely there'll be trouble." I got the impression he was uncomfortable with the entire discussion.

I explained about Thurgood and his digging into the Eddy story and what it might mean.

"Eddy, I can't believe a newspaper article will make any difference," Lisa said. "Even if your story comes out, people will be grateful."

"That's exactly what we've been telling him," Mary said. She pushed back from the table. "I've been wasting time. I need to get this mess cleaned up."

"Here, let me help," Lisa offered, beginning to gather the dirty dishes.

"I won't hear of it," Mary said.

"No, really, I'd love to help," Lisa insisted.

"It is a beautiful evening. You and Eddy go out in the yard and visit. Maybe you can convince him to stay in Cranston the rest of his lie. Sam can make himself useful and help me do these dishes."

"Mary's right," I said. "You kids go out and sit in the sunshine. I enjoy helping in the kitchen, and it gives me an excuse to spend time with Mary."

Lisa had made her token offer, but was more than willing to accept Mary's invitation and visit alone with Eddy. So the youngsters went out in the yard with Mica, and I helped Mary clean up.

By the time we had finished dishes, it was beginning to get dark. There was a beautiful sunset and we all sat and watched until it was gone. Then Lisa stood.

"I really have to be going," she said. "I have the morning shift at the hospital. Thank you for inviting me. You know, I don't believe I've ever been to someone's house for dinner just because they wanted my company. The Bennetts haven't been very sociable."

"We loved having you, and hope you'll come again," Mary said. She gave Lisa a hug. Then Lisa and Eddy walked over to her Lexus. They talked for a moment before Eddy briefly hugged her. After she got in the car and started the engine, Mary and I walked over and waved as she backed out of the driveway and quickly disappeared down Oak Street.

"I know you did the dinner for me," Eddy said. "I really appreciate it. It was a great meal and wonderful day."

"Thank you," Mary said. "I love to have company and it was a good excuse. Lisa is such a sweet young lady."

With the sun gone there was a slight chill in the air. "I think we should go inside," I suggested. "I'm getting a little cold."

We were heading back into the house when we heard the sound of shattering glass.

Twenty-Two

I pushed past Mary and ran through the kitchen. The living room was dark, the windows leaking soft starlight into the area. As I crossed the room I noticed the window nearest the door, because the right side of the rod holding Mary's lace curtains had been dislodged on one end and was draped at an awkward angle across the recliner. The curtains moved slightly in a breeze wafting through the shattered window.

Without turning on the lights, I pulled open the front door and stepped onto the porch. The moon hadn't risen and the yard was shrouded in heavy shadows. The street was empty in both directions—no cars, no people. I didn't hear anyone running, but if they avoided the road's gravel shoulder and moved through the yards, there would be little or no sound. A row of lilac bushes marked the Abernathy's property line, and half a dozen men could have crouched in the shadows, invisible from the porch. A dog's bark came from up the block, but it was a single bark, not the wild yammering that would have signaled an intruder.

Suddenly Mica pushed past and scared me out of a year's growth. The living room lights came on, the sudden wash of brightness ruining my night vision. I turned and went back into the house, holding the storm door for Mica, before firmly closing the inner door.

"Whoever it was is long gone," I said.

Eddy had followed me into the living room, turning on the big overhead light, which we seldom used. Although it seemed like I had been on the porch a long time, it must have only been a few seconds, because he was still standing in the doorway, his hand on the switch.

Mica was sniffing around the room, a low growl rumbling in his throat. He nosed the brick lying in the center of the room, half under the coffee table, and looked back at Eddy, his tail waging.

After coming through the window and knocking loose the curtains, the brick had apparently hit the recliner and bounced because it lay at an awkward angle from the window. Shards of glass were scattered in a wide pattern across the recliner and the floor, a lot more pieces then I would have expected from just the bottom half of the window.

"Sam, what is it?" Mary had come into the living room and stood behind Eddy like he was a shield. She had one hand to her reddened cheek and I could tell she was frightened, on the verge of panic.

"Some asshole tossed a brick through our window," I said, bending over to pick it up. I was angry and just a bit scared myself. If the culprits had been within reach I would gladly have split a head or two.

It was a used brick like might have been found in a vacant lot, reddish brown with a trace of grayish mortar along one edge. Gobs of soil embedded in the porous surface were still moist. A dirty piece of paper was secured to the brick by a bit of string.

I snapped the string with a twist of my fingers, set the brick on the coffee table, and unfolded the paper. The words were printed in pencil and looked like a right-handed person had written with his left hand.

'What's it say?" Eddy asked. He didn't reach for the note, just stood in the doorway waiting for me to read it.

"Mary, call the Sheriff," I snarled, the anger evident in my voice.

Mary knew there was a time for questions and a time for action. Without comment she returned to the kitchen to use the wall phone.

"What does the note say, Sam?" Eddy asked again.

"It isn't important," I snapped "Just some stupid asshole with shit for brains."

"What does it say?" he asked again, his voice indicating he already knew the gist of the message.

"Get rid of the fucking witch or we'll do it for you," I read, wishing it were some other hate message.

Eddy didn't say anything, just gave me that 'I told you so' look.

"The Sheriff is sending someone," Mary said, coming back into the living room. She started to pickup the shards of glass, a pained look on her face.

"You'd better leave the glass where it is until the sheriff gets here," I said. "It might be evidence or something."

"Oh." Mary straightened up, letting the couple pieces she'd collected fall from her hand. "Why would any one do this?"

I put my arms around Mary and held her as she began to cry. "Probably some kids wanting to cause mischief," I suggested. "We'll let the Sheriff sort it out."

We waited in the kitchen, nobody saying much. I put the note on the table and Mary read it, but Eddy just sat quietly, stroking Mica's head.

Deputy Jim Alshard arrived in about fifteen minutes. He had either been on patrol nearby or had sped like crazy, because the drive from Elliott normally took closer to half an hour. He parked in the driveway and came to the back door.

Alshard was good looking, in his late twenties, about six feet tall, with enormous hands and the build of a weight lifter. He had short brown hair and pale hazel eyes. He took off his cowboy style hat when he entered the house, something Sheriff Simpson would never have done.

He had on a short-sleeved tan shirt and razor creased trousers. A silver badge was pinned to his breast pocket. A shinny black belt sagged from the weight of a service revolver and ten pounds of assorted police equipment.

After reading the note, he examined the brick although he obviously realized there was no chance of tracing it. Then he looked at the living room, spending a moment examining the broken window, like he was checking the trajectory of the missile. Next he went into the front yard, and using a long, wide-beam flashlight, traversed back and forth looking for footprints. He checked carefully close to the house, but moved as far as the road and along the property borders. The broken window wasn't very large and whoever threw the brick would have been close or had a damn accurate arm. We hadn't had rain for more than a week, and the clay soil hardened quickly, not a good surface for anything less than elephant tracks. I knew Alshard wouldn't find anything.

After maybe fifteen minutes of fruitless searching, he came back in and sat with us at the kitchen table. He took a small black notebook from his shirt pocket and began asking questions. As far as he was concerned it was a simple case of vandalism, but he treated the matter like it was an armed robbery and I appreciated his thoroughness.

"Where were each of you when the brick was tossed?" he asked.

"We were all in the back yard—actually on the back porch."

"Did you see anything?"

"As soon as we heard the glass break I ran through the house and out on the front porch. It couldn't have been more than a few seconds, but I didn't see anyone. They might have been hiding behind Abernathy's lilacs, but I figure they threw the brick and ran like hell."

"How about before the window broke?" Alshard asked. "Did you hear anything? People talking, cars on the road, anything like that?"

"No," I said. "Nothing unusual." Mary and Eddy shook their heads.

"Did your dog notice anything? Maybe bark or act nervous?"

"No, sir," Eddy said. "We were playing with Mica, so he was sort of distracted."

"Mr. Johnson, do you know of anyone who might've had a reason to break your window? Maybe some kids you chased away earlier or someone who didn't like your car repairs or gas prices?"

"Nope." Considering the message on the note, I was pretty certain the brick didn't have anything to do with Mary or me.

"Anyone else have any thoughts?"

Mary and Eddy shook their heads. It wasn't natural for Mary not to speak up like she usually did. Maybe she still wasn't all that strong after her illness, or was in shock.

Deputy Alshard made a notation in his notebook. "Okay let's try a different approach. Who is the witch the note refers to?" He looked at Mary when he asked the question. Because of stereotypes, everyone thinks of witches as female.

Mary, Eddy and I all looked back and forth at each other, not knowing how to answer that question. Finally it was Eddy who spoke.

"They probably meant me."

Alshard raised one eyebrow in a gesture of surprise. "Why would anyone consider you a witch?"

"Is your report going to be released to the press?" Eddy asked.

"I don't know," Alshard said, his tone patient, although he obviously didn't appreciate having a question answered with a question. "Probably not. Vandalism isn't a high priority crime and reporters aren't likely to be interested. If some reporter wants to follow up, it would be the Sheriff's decision whether we released details."

"What about the note? Does it have to be made public?"

Alshard shrugged. "Same answer. What difference does it make anyway?"

"If I tell you why someone might think I'm a witch, and it gets released to the press, there could be more trouble. Couldn't you ask the Sheriff to keep it confidential?"

"I can't answer that until I know what you're talking about," Alshard said. "But if I agree it would cause unnecessary trouble, I'll ask the Sheriff to keep a lid on it."

"Okay, I guess that's fair," Eddy said. Then he told Deputy Alshard about Mary and Johnny and little Ruth Goldstein and his own troubles before coming to Cranston.

Alshard was a good listener, nodding at the appropriate places and not taking notes while Eddy talked. He had read the newspaper story about the cures, so that wasn't news. He did raise an eyebrow when Eddy mentioned healing people just by touching them. I give Alshard credit for not interrupting or smiling. The story was a bit hard to swallow the first time around, but maybe cops hear a lot of weird tales and he was used to it.

"It doesn't make any difference whether you believe the story," Eddy said. "The point is, if this gets into the press, there are people who will believe."

"Yeah, I see your point. Obviously there are some folks out there who already think it's true." Alshard stood, closing his notebook and putting it back in his uniform pocket. He may have been skeptical and there were probably questions he'd have liked to ask, but they had nothing to do with vandalism, and he was responding to a vandalism call. "I can't make any guarantees, but I'll give Sheriff Simpson the facts and suggest he keep details about the note from the press. But it isn't likely reporters will be interested in some kid throwing a brick through your window."

"They might be if they see my address in the report," I said.

Alshard shrugged. "I can't do anything about that. I'll be as vague as possible, but I have to make a report."

"What about catching the bastards who did this?" I asked. "Aren't you even going to take the note and check for fingerprints?"

"The Sheriff's Department will make every effort to apprehend the vandals," Alshard said. We both knew the punks weren't going to be caught—no more than the thugs who had beaten Eddy had been identified and arrested. "I'll take the note and check for fingerprints, but truthfully, like I said before, vandalism isn't a high priority crime. No one is going to spend much time or taxpayer's money on it. I'll interview your neighbors to see if they saw anything, but chances are they would've been on the streets already if they knew your window had been broken. Without a witness, it isn't likely we'll catch anyone."

I was tempted to mention the previous attack on Eddy and my suspicions concerning Ernest Bennett, but I kept my mouth shut. There wasn't so much crime in our county that Alshard wouldn't be aware of the beating. Maybe someone had made a connection from the newspaper story or they had heard rumors. If Thurgood had learned about Eddy from kid's stories, others might have. But I didn't believe it. It might not have been logical, but I was certain Bennett's thugs had thrown the brick. Was it a warning before Ernest followed up on his threat?

Alshard turned to leave. "If you have any more trouble, be sure to call us."

"We will," Mary said. "Thank you for coming."

I walked Alshard to his squad car and watched him drive away. I noticed that after hearing Eddy's story he didn't offer to shake hands with any of us.

Eddy went to his room after helping Mary and me clean up the shards of glass and cover the broken window with a piece of cardboard. He didn't say anything but I could tell from the slump of his shoulders he knew there would be more trouble.

I took my pump shotgun out of the hall closet; rummaged around on the shelf until I found the box of shells, and began loading it.

"What are you doing?" Mary asked, sounding alarmed.

"I'm going to be ready if those bastards come back."

"No, you aren't," Mary said quietly in a voice that told me there wasn't room for argument. "I won't have a loaded gun in the house."

When I hesitated, Mary had her hand on my arm. "Please, Sam, put the gun away. You're frightening me."

"Okay," I said, unloading the shotgun and stuffing the shells back into the box. "But I'm going to keep it in the bedroom where it'll be handy, just incase."

"Hold me, Sam. I'm afraid."

"Me too." I wrapped my arms around Mary and we took comfort from each other.

Twenty-Three

Neither Mary nor Eddy mentioned the brick incident Monday morning, but it had been gnawing at me all night. The more I thought about it, the angrier I became. I considered myself an easy going guy, but an attack on the sanctuary of our home was intolerable. Mary had been endangered and it was time to fight back.

I wanted to believe Ernest Bennett was responsible for both Eddy's beating and the brick because that would have given my anger a single focus. However, in the back of my mind I knew there were other possibilities. What if Eddy had touched someone else who had hidden demons? So many people had events in their past they were ashamed of and were afraid of having revealed.

That line of reasoning quickly led to an endless list of suspects. There was Sheriff Simpson, customers at the service station, the cop who had fingerprinted Eddy, Doctor Calvin, personnel at Memorial Hospital, and dozens more. It appeared as though whoever had thrown the brick had waited until Lisa left, but that could have been a coincidence, and didn't prove Ernest had hired thugs to do it. The Herald reporter, Jess Thurgood, crossed my mind, but throwing bricks didn't seem like his style. Even if Thurgood had dark secrets, he was a reporter and would likely strike at Eddy on the front page of the newspaper.

By the time the Monday morning rush had slowed at the station, I had convinced myself that Ernest Bennett was the only logical suspect. A lot of folks in Henderson County were afraid to face up to Boss Bennett, but I wasn't one of them. I told Eddy I was leaving for my normal midday visit with Mary. Then I took off looking for Ernest.

I was prepared to drive to Elliott if necessary, but was lucky enough to spot Ernest's BMW parked behind Bennett's Hardware. There aren't many secrets in a small town and I knew he frequently visited the hardware store on Monday mornings to go over the books. It was common knowledge his managers worked for starvation wages, and he was paranoid that they might be ripping him off.

The only clerk was busy helping a customer in the paint department, so no one tried to intercept me as I strode briskly toward the rear of the store.

Without bothering to knock, I pushed open the door marked 'Office' and barged into the small room. Ernest was sitting behind the desk. His manager, Fred Sipple, had pulled up a chair beside him and they appeared to be studying a ledger. They both seemed startled by my interruption. I don't imagine many customers burst into the office.

"Can I help you?" Sipple asked, rising from his chair.

I ignored Fred and directed my comments toward Ernest, not even attempting to keep the anger out of my voice. "Someone threw a brick through my living room window last night."

"What's that got to do with me?" Ernest sneered. "If you want a replacement, see my clerk. That's what I pay him for."

Ernest looked like he didn't care about the window, and for an instant I had doubts concerning his guilt. But his expression of smug superiority pushed my blood pressure up a notch.

"You may think your money gives you a license to push people around, but you went too far this time. If anything else happens to endanger my wife, I'm personally going to come after you."

"Who do you think you are, barging into my office and threatening me?" Ernest's temper flared and I halfway hoped he would come around the desk so I could punch him in the nose.

"It isn't a threat," I snarled. "I'm stating a fact, and you'd be smart to pay attention."

Ernest pointed at Fred who looked like he would rather be somewhere else. "I've got a witness that you threatened me. I could sue you for everything you own, including your pitiful little gas station."

"I'm not afraid of you or your lawyers. When you threw that brick you made this personal."

"Throwing bricks isn't my style," Ernest said.

"No, you wouldn't get your hands dirty. But you wouldn't hesitate to hire someone, just like you hired the thugs who beat up Eddy Foster."

"Now I've got you for slander." Ernest leaned back in his chair, a smug expression on his face. "You've opened yourself to a world of legal trouble. If you don't get the hell out of here right now I'll tear you apart in court."

I had a nearly overpowering urge to reach across the desk and strangle Ernest with his own necktie. "Just remember, if there's any more trouble I'll be coming after you."

Ernest turned to Fred. "If this madman doesn't leave immediately, throw him out."

Fred hesitated, his eyes pleading with me to leave voluntarily. I didn't have anything against Fred and was sorry he'd been caught in the middle. He worked hard to support his wife and three children and couldn't afford to lose his job. We both knew Ernest would fire him in a heartbeat if he didn't do as ordered.

"It's all right, Fred. I'm going." I pointed a finger at Ernest. "You just remember that you've been warned."

I drove out to Lipton Lake and parked at the bluff until I cooled off. It wasn't likely that confronting Ernest had accomplished anything except to take the edge off my anger. I still wasn't certain he was guilty of anything more than being a first class bastard. I would have felt more comfortable about the confrontation if I could have been absolutely confident the beating and the brick were related and that Ernest was responsible for both.

* * *

The Elliott Herald delivery truck was pulling out when I returned to the station. Eddy was working on an oil change, so I grabbed the bundle of papers to take them into the office. The blaring headline immediately caught my attention.

DO YOU BELIEVE IN ANGELS?

I hadn't been too impressed with Thurgood the couple of times I had met him, which probably showed what a poor judge of character I was. He had done a lot of digging and had come up with the answer, but his story eliminated him from my mental list of suspects.

The feature wasn't written in great depth, but then, newspaper stories seldom are. The article's angel hook had obviously come from Ruth Goldstein's believing an angel had healed her. There was some stuff about faith healers and miraculous cures, but he didn't mention Eddy by name. He chronicled a peculiar string of healings throughout the country during the last five years, giving dates and the names of people who had been cured in some mysterious manner. Obviously he had researched databases that would have at least provided hints about Eddy. I wondered whether he avoided Eddy's name because he was afraid of a lawsuit if he couldn't prove his claims. But somehow I didn't think the fear of legal actions would deter a newspaper reporter. I know touching Eddy had interesting effects on people. I wanted to believe the warm, happy feeling, or maybe some sort of bonding, or who knows what, had convinced Thurgood to keep the knowledge about Eddy to himself. Perhaps appeasing his curiosity had satisfied Thurgood and there wouldn't be any need to worry about further newspaper exposure.

He ended the story with a question for the readers. "Do you believe an angel has been wandering around the country strengthening our faith by curing people? Is it possible an angel is living in Henderson County at this very moment?"

Eddy and I had read the article at the station when our papers were delivered. On top of the brick incident I figured the front page story would push Eddy to move on. However, he didn't even comment on the article and I wasn't going to bring it up. Maybe he realized Thurgood was no longer a threat. After all, he had seen into the reporter's soul and knew him better than I ever would.

Mary and I discussed the article during my afternoon visit. As I had expected, her first sentiment was alarm, and she was concerned about Eddy's reaction. After explaining my reasoning about Thurgood, I suggested we avoid discussing the story with Eddy so we wouldn't give it more importance than it warranted. I'm not certain she completely agreed with my theories, but she obviously realized there was no harm in pretending like the article had never been written.

Thurgood obviously knew who the story's 'angel' was. I just hoped no one else would do his own research and make the proper connection. I should have known better.

On Tuesday evening, we had finished supper and I was drying the dishes when the front door bell rang. Mary answered the summons, and after a moment, called from the living room.

"Sam and Eddy, would you please come in here?" Her voice was perfectly normal, so I wasn't worried the visitor might be trouble. I figured it was just someone we didn't know well—front room company rather than kitchen company.

When I entered the living room I saw three visitor—two adults and a child. The man, sporting a small mustache and wire rim glasses, was dressed in an expensive suit. I guessed he was probably in his early thirties and already tending toward excess weight. The woman was a few years younger and very pretty, with a slim figure and long dark hair. The child was a little girl wearing a curly blond wig, evidently intended to hide a bald head. I didn't have to be introduced to know they were the Goldsteins.

As soon as Eddy stepped into the room the little girl's face brightened. "Look, Mommy, it's my angel!" she shrieked. Ruth ran to Eddy and wrapped her arms around his neck as he scooped her into his arms.

The Goldsteins didn't seem surprised by Ruth's reaction. The man stepped forward and extended his hand. "I'm Aaron Goldstein. This is my wife, Helen, and that beautiful bundle of energy is our daughter, Ruth."

We shook hands all around. Ruth was light enough and was clinging to Eddy's neck so tightly he was able to support her with his left arm as he extended his right hand. When Aaron touched Eddy he almost jerked away, but caught himself and gave a hearty handshake. I was getting used to seeing people's reaction to the warm, happy feeling—the Eddy effect.

Helen Goldstein went directly to Eddy and shook his hand with both of hers. She held his hand longer than normal, as if she didn't want to let go. "I hope we're not intruding, but we had to thank you for saving our daughter." Her voice choked up and I was afraid she would burst into tears.

I could see Eddy was uncomfortable with the situation and would gladly have been somewhere else. Frankly, I felt a little uneasy myself. As usual, Mary saved the moment.

"Please have a seat," she said, indicating the sofa. "May we offer you some coffee?"

"No thank you," Aaron said. "We must be interrupting your dinner."

"Not at all. We've already eaten, or I would invite you share our meal. I'm afraid there are only leftovers. I can't even offer you dessert."

"Please don't trouble yourself," Helen said. "We've already eaten."

The Goldstein's sat nervously on the edge of the sofa. My living room isn't crammed with furniture, but there were enough other seats for Mary, Eddy and me. Ruth was content to remain on Eddy's lap.

"Where is the pretty lady angel?" Ruth asked, completely at ease snuggled in Eddy's arms.

"Her name is Lisa, and she isn't here right now," Eddy said. "But I know she'll be happy to hear you came to visit me."

As usual, Mica had followed Eddy and taken up a position at his side. He sniffed at Ruth and she reached out a tentative hand to pet him. "I didn't know angels had dogs," she said. "I wish I had a doggie like that."

"Maybe some day you will," Eddy said.

All in all it was a pretty uncomfortable gathering. Although I could appreciate how they felt about Ruth's recovery, I wished they hadn't come. More exposure wasn't going to help our efforts to keep Eddy in Cranston.

I don't believe the Goldsteins had considered what they were going to do or say once they arrived and confirmed their suspicions. I figured it said something positive about their devotion to Ruth for them to even make the effort.

"How did you find me?" Eddy asked, breaking the uneasy silence.

Aaron Goldstein jumped at the opportunity to answer the question, as if he were proud of his deductions. "It was yesterday's newspaper article. It didn't mention your name, but I asked around the hospital and learned you lived with the Johnsons and that you had been Johnny Winthrop's roommate. I know it was a stretch, but something told me you were one of the angels Ruth had seen. Of course we couldn't be certain, and I was a bit nervous about coming here tonight, but Helen insisted. Then when Ruth saw you, we knew."

"Ruth is our only child and I can't begin to tell you how happy we are that she was cured," Helen Goldstein said. "We were preparing ourselves for losing her, if you can ever be prepared for something like that. To be perfectly honest, we had given up hope. Then suddenly the tumor was gone. She told us an angel had taken away the pain. Of course we had been praying for a miracle, but even so, we couldn't believe Ruth had seen an actual angel. There didn't seem to be any other explanation until we saw the newspaper article and Aaron investigated and here we are." She began crying softly, but they obviously were happy tears.

Aaron put his arm around his wife's shoulders and comforted her.

I could feel tears coming to my own eyes. Mary and I knew better than most what it meant to lose a child. It was like part of you had died and could never be replaced. Even the possibility of losing a child was almost more than anyone could bear. Parents expect their offspring to comfort them in their old age and to be at their side when they die. It isn't natural to bury someone who had been the fruit of your love and had completed your life. God, it hurt more than anything else in the world. The pain, the emptiness, found a spot in the back of your heart but never left. It haunted you the rest of your life. I thought of all the years, the sorrows and the joys that Mary and I had lost when Albert died. Yet we had shared nineteen years with Albert. Ruth would have been with her parents for only four years.

Because of Eddy the Goldsteins had been spared the pain Mary and I would always live with. I felt compassion, but there was also a tinge of guilt because I was jealous of the happiness they would have and that Mary and I would never experience.

"I understand," Mary agreed. Tears were streaming down her cheeks. I could see the pain in her eyes as she also thought of our son. "It's hard to believe in miracles until they happen."

"I'm extremely pleased my conclusions were accurate," Aaron said. "It means a great deal for us to be able to express our gratitude."

"I'm very happy for both of you and your daughter" I said. I knew that if someone had saved Albert, I would have crossed oceans to express my appreciation. "But I almost wish you hadn't discovered the truth."

"I don't understand," Aaron said.

Eddy gave a big sigh. "Since you read the newspaper article you know there have been cures in a number of cities. It should give you an idea of how much traveling I've done." He gave a brief synopsis of his life before Cranston. "When people begin to find out I'm responsible they become frightened. It isn't long before there's trouble and I have to move along. I really like it here in Cranston, and wish I didn't have to leave."

"Oh, no," Helen said. "You won't ever have to leave Cranston if you don't want to. Isn't that right, Aaron? We won't tell anyone who you are. But we just had to thank you for giving us back our daughter."

"Any rational person would think it impossible for anyone to be afraid of you, Eddy," Aaron said. "But I understand about frightened people. My grandparents died in the Auschwitz Concentration Camp. Our people have been faced with fear and superstition for hundreds of years."

"Maybe if you don't tell anyone about Eddy and just stick to Ruth's story about an angel, no one else will learn how she was really cured," Mary suggested.

"Eddy is an angel," Helen said.

Eddy blushed. I knew he was uncomfortable being called an angel.

"If you want us to keep the secret, we will," Aaron said. "Eddy, we owe you more than we can ever repay. Everything we have is yours if you want it. Money, a home, whatever you want."

"You don't owe me anything," Eddy said. "I did it for Ruth." He kissed Ruth on the cheek. The little girl positively glowed with happiness. "Such a pretty little girl needs to grow into a beautiful woman."

"I don't want to believe there will be trouble," Aaron said. "But I promise you this—if there is ever any difficulty, or if you need help of any kind, you can count on me and my family." He handed Eddy a business card. "I'm an attorney and a pretty good one, if I say so myself. I'm at your service if you ever need me."

"Thank you. I appreciate that," Eddy said, slipping the card into his shirt pocket.

"I realize it isn't much after what Eddy did for us," Helen said. "But we would love to have all you to our home for dinner one day soon."

I looked at Mary and saw she was pleased with the invitation. "Thank you, we'd love that," I said. "It's been a long time since Mary has had an opportunity to visit anyone."

"I understand." Helen was beaming like she had just made a good friend. There was healing power in doing any little thing to express gratitude for a gift that could never be adequately repaid. "We didn't socialize much when Ruth was dying. It's impossible to put on a happy face when you have to endure such a tragedy. Now that our prayers have been answered, we want to celebrate. Would Sunday be convenient?"

"That would be perfect," Mary said.

We talked for another half hour before the Goldsteins all gave Eddy a hug and left. Little Ruth didn't want to let go of her angel, but allowed herself to be carried away when Eddy promised to see her again.

I hadn't believed Eddy when he had said the secret would get out and then spread. I had thought if Mary and I never said anything, the cures would remain a mystery. Once more Eddy had proven to be prophetic.

Even as the Goldsteins were visiting I realized everything was spinning out of control. I just didn't know when something else would happen. Even if I had been able to see into the future I don't know whether I could have done anything to change events.

Twenty-Four

Wednesday morning, after the early commuters had been serviced, I settled in the office to take care of neglected paperwork. Eddy was busy in the far service bay, working on an oil change for John Taylor.

A battered, extended cab pickup, obviously in need of a new muffler, pulled into the station and parked in front of the service bays.

"I'll get it," I called to Eddy. I wasn't in a big hurry to take care of the potential customer. Because they hadn't parked at the pumps, I figured they didn't need gas—maybe a muffler or engine work. Or they could have been tourists late following up on the newspaper article. However, for no reason I could define, I felt apprehensive, like I sensed the pickup wasn't there for any good purpose.

Before I even stepped out of the office, the driver and passenger had both climbed from the truck. Since I didn't recognize either one, I knew they weren't from Cranston and hadn't ever been to my station before.

They looked to be in their early twenties. The driver was huge, over six feet, bulky enough to have been a pro line backer, and was wearing a sleeveless T-shirt that showed off his muscular arms. His head was shaved and he had a hoop earring in his right ear. He didn't look like the sort of person I would want to have for an enemy, but it was his passenger who convinced me they were here to cause trouble.

The passenger wasn't nearly as large a man, maybe five seven or eight and a hundred and eighty pounds. A baseball cap covered his shaved head and his greasy jean jacket had some sort of patch on the sleeve that looked like a gang emblem. What really got my attention was the tire iron he held in his right hand and was slapping threateningly into the palm of his left hand.

For the first time since I'd owned the service station, I wished I kept a shotgun in the office. As the next best thing I reached down and grabbed the baseball bat I kept beside my desk.

"What can I do for you boys?" I called, staying close to the office so I could quickly retreat into its relative safety.

Eddy and Mica must have sensed something because they began moving toward me through the service bays. The hackles on Mica's neck were raised and he was growling softly. I may be paranoid, but I wondered if the dog recognized them as having been involved with Eddy's beating.

Before the two goons could say anything, I heard another vehicle pull into the station from the opposite direction. I didn't want to take my attention off the first threat, so I glanced out the corner of my eye to determine if the arrival was reinforcements for the two thugs.

I couldn't have seen a more welcome sight. The vehicle stopping at the pumps was a county sheriff's cruiser. If there had ever been a time for a cop to visit my station, this was it.

Like a switch being turned off, both goons suddenly assumed a benign demeanor. The passenger stopped slapping the tire iron in his hand and let it drop so that it hung beside his leg.

"We were wondering if you could tell us how to get to Lipton Lake," the driver called.

I didn't think these two wanted to go to Lipton Lake any more than they wanted to go to the moon. Without a doubt they had come to rob the station or to beat up Eddy. I think the timely arrival of the deputy was the only thing that prevented a serious incident.

Deputy Alshard stepped from his cruiser and settled his hat on his head. Apparently he had heard the question because he gave the thugs directions to Lipton Lake. If he had observed their threatening attitude as he drove up, he didn't give any indication.

"Thank you, Officer," the driver said. Both men hastily jumped into the pickup and slowly drove away in the direction of the lake.

Suddenly my knees went weak from the release of nervous tension and I had to lean against the station doorway to keep from collapsing.

"What's the matter, Mr. Johnson?" Deputy Alshard asked. "You look a little pale."

"No, I'm fine," I lied. Since nothing had happened, I couldn't very well tell Alshard I suspected the two goons had evil intentions, but they had scared me within an inch of my life. "Must be a touch of indigestion or something."

"Maybe you ought to sit down and stay out of the sun," he suggested.

"That's a great idea." I flopped down on the desk chair.

"Hope I didn't interrupt anything," Alshard said. "I just stopped by to let you know Sheriff Simpson agreed not to release information on the brick incident."

I didn't care if he had come to serve legal papers because I figured his arrival had saved me from a lot of pain. "No, you weren't an interruption," I said. "Far from it. We're always glad to see officers of the law. I really appreciate you driving over here to let me know."

"Actually I was cruising this way," Alshard said, "so it wasn't far off my route." A crackle of static came over his radio, and after he answered the call, he climbed back into his vehicle. "Gotta run. Have a good day."

If I were a drinking man I would have had a double when he pulled out of the station. As it was I could have used a couple of beers to take the edge off my nerves.

My heart beat still hadn't returned to normal when Eddy stepped into the office.

"Sam, can we talk a minute?"

I pushed back from the desk, but remained seated. "Sure. What's on your mind?"

"We both know those thugs weren't here to ask for directions. If the deputy hadn't stopped when he did, we'd probably be dead or badly beaten right now."

I held up my hand. "Wait a minute. I know what you're gong to say. You think the trouble's gotten serious and it's time for you to leave."

"Just hear me out," Eddy said. He had taken a seat on the extra folding chair and Mica lay at his side. "You believe I'm a coward to always run away, but I understand what's going to happen. We were lucky this time. You nearly got beaten up because of me. The next time it could be you and

Mary. I won't have that on my conscience. If I leave now the danger goes with me."

"And how do you know that? You always run away and as far as you're aware there could be all sorts of violence after you've disappeared. You weren't there when your family's house burned."

"That isn't fair." Eddy protested. "What happened to my family was different and you know it. The violence is directed at me, and if I'm not around there isn't any reason for you and Mary to be involved."

"That's a load of bullshit. Don't you think you're being more than a little selfish, only considering yourself? How do you know the violence isn't turned against the people you cured after you leave?" I didn't believe for one minute that Eddy was selfish, but I figured maybe I could shame him into staying.

"I'm not being selfish," Eddy insisted. "I'm thinking of you and Mary. Believe me Sam; it'll be better for everyone concerned if I go."

I would have liked to argue that he couldn't afford to take off, but I knew he had enough money put away to comfortably get a good start down the road. In addition to providing room and board, I paid Eddy for his work at the station. I had never formally listed him as an employee, so I paid his wages in cash, keeping them off the books. Depending upon business, I gave him between a hundred and a hundred fifty a week. He never complained except one week when I handed him two hundred. He returned fifty and just shook his head, like I'd made a stupid mistake. Even during the short time he had been in Cranston, he must have accumulated a nice nest egg because he never spent money. Maybe ten or fifteen bucks on toothpaste and such, and he insisted on providing Mica's dog food. Eddy didn't drink or socialize, so he never dropped his pay in the taverns like a lot of young people did.

"What about the Goldsteins?" I asked. "They've invited you for dinner Sunday to celebrate Ruth's recovery. You'll be taking away a big piece of her happiness."

"They'll understand. It'll be better for them when I'm far away from here."

"Tell that to Ruth. She thinks you're an angel."

"She'll get over it. You can tell her I've retuned to heaven or something like that. I've made up my mind, Sam."

"You know Mary and I won't let you go. You're like family, and family sticks together." More than anything, I wanted Eddy to remain in Cranston. Having him around the house was like having Albert back again. I hadn't realized how much I had missed my son until Eddy had entered my life.

"Do you think I want to go? This has been like a home for me. If there were any other choice I'd stay."

"There's always another choice, and you know it. Stay here and we can ride this out together. You've got friends who will stick by you no matter what happens. I still don't think it's going to be as bad as you suspect. We've already talked about this, and we both realize any problems we're having are because Ernest Bennett wants to scare you off. Why don't you just go over, shake hands with Ernest and cure whatever is inside him?"

"I wish I could, but it wouldn't make any difference. Believe me, Sam, if it wasn't Ernest Bennett, sooner or later it would be someone else."

"Damnit, Eddy, you aren't being fair. You have to give your friends a chance."

Eddy shook his head. "No, Sam, I've thought it over and there just isn't any other choice. I have to tell Johnny and Lisa, so I'll finish out the week, but I'll be leaving Sunday morning."

"You know Mary is going to fight you on this."

"Yeah, I know." Eddy sounded despondent. He must have figured facing Mary would be tougher than telling any of the rest of his friends.

When Johnny came after school there weren't any cars to be worked on. I knew Eddy wanted some privacy to tell the boy he would be leaving Cranston, so I took a folding chair and sat outside.

I sat far enough away so I couldn't hear what they were saying because I really didn't want to listen. Although the words were too muffled to understand, a couple of times I heard Johnny's voice raised in protest. It couldn't have been more than ten minutes before the youngster came out of the office. I saw that he wanted to cry but was manfully attempting to hold back the tears.

"Mr. Johnson, I'm going home," he said.

"I suppose Eddy can watch the station while I give you a ride." I didn't feel comfortable leaving Eddy alone after those two goons had stopped at the station, but the drive to Sal's Diner and back would only take a few minutes.

"No thank you. I want to walk."

"Are you sure you'll be all right?"

"Yes, sir," he said, a catch in his voice. "It isn't far."

I watched Johnny walking away and could see his shoulders shaking. Apparently the tears had finally broken free. I felt a bit guilty, but it really wasn't far to Sal's Diner and I realized there are times when even a youngster has to be alone with his pain.

I picked up my chair and turned back toward the office. Eddy was standing in the doorway watching Johnny leave.

"Guess you told him." I said.

"Yeah."

"How'd he take it?" I asked. It seemed like a dumb question since I'd already seen that Johnny had been devastated by the bad news.

"I feel terrible," Eddy said. "Telling Johnny was the hardest thing I've done in a long time. He just didn't understand."

"I can believe that," I said, "because I don't understand either. I think you're jumping the gun. You don't have to leave, and deep down in your heart, I think you know it as well as I do."

"You're wrong, Sam. I do have to go. I wish you would try to accept my decision. I have to move on to protect all of us—you, me, Mary, Johnny—all my friends here."

"Believe me, I've tried to understand. But it just doesn't make any sense."

"One day you'll realize I'm right," Eddy said, but his tone suggested if I didn't understand now, I never would.

During supper Eddy told Mary. She listened calmly, surprising me when she didn't make a major fuss. But she was like that sometimes. When something really important was happening she took her time thinking over the situation and preparing her arguments. I knew she had begun thinking of Eddy as the son we'd lost, and I didn't believe she was going to give up easily, but even after all our years together there were times when I couldn't begin to comprehend what was going on in her mind.

* * *

Lisa hadn't been at the station for several days because she was on the late afternoon shift at the hospital. Eddy was determined not to disappear without telling her, so he phoned her apartment to make a date for Friday night. I suspected she would do whatever necessary to arrange her work schedule to be with Eddy. At any rate she agreed to the date.

Friday evening Eddy dashed out of the house as soon as the Lexus stopped in the driveway. They were only gone for a couple of hours before Lisa dropped him off and immediately drove away.

When Eddy came in he was quieter than normal. Whatever had happened between him and Lisa had hurt deeply.

"I don't imagine Lisa was very happy with the news," I said.

"She'll get over it and realize she's better off." There was pain and resignation in his voice.

"None of us will ever get over it," Mary said. She reached over and took his hand in both of hers. "We all love you and want you to stay. No one ever gets over losing a loved one. I know."

"Please don't make this any harder than it already is," Eddy said. He gave Mary a hug. "I'm really tired. I'm going to bed."

When he climbed the stairs to his room, followed by Mica, Mary sat at the kitchen table crying softly.

Since I'm a meddlesome cuss, I decided to put my nose where it didn't belong and make one last attempt to resolve the situation. I was certain Lisa hadn't been able to change his mind because Eddy could be as pig headed as me. But, maybe if I talked with her again and told her abut the goons who had stopped at the station, she would confront her father. It was the only thing I could think of doing.

I figured Lisa had enough time to get back to her apartment, so I dialed her new phone number. There was no answer. I tried several more times over the next hour, but although I let the phone ring forever, there was no response. I will always wonder whether it would have changed anything if I had been able to reach her.

Twenty-Five

Saturday mornings were generally busy, with a lot of customers packed into a short day. With oil changes and minor engine repairs scheduled by folks who worked during the week, I was seldom able to close on time. It surprised me when we only had two oil changes and no repairs. Even the traffic at the pumps was only a trickle, as if most of my customers sensed trouble and were staying away from the station. More likely, it was my paranoia getting the best of me.

About ten-thirty Johnny rode up on his bicycle. Although he looked sad, I noticed again how much the boy had changed during the last few weeks. He was gaining weight and his hair was long enough that pretty soon he'd need a barber.

"Hi, Johnny." Eddy sounded friendly, but I could tell he wasn't looking forward to another confrontation with the boy. "How's my favorite mechanic doing today?"

Johnny leaned his bike against the garage wall and slipped a plastic bag off the handle bars. His face reflected my melancholy mood. "Hi, Mr. Johnson. Eddy."

"I just finished the last car in the service bay," Eddy said, wiping his hands on an oily rag. "Unless someone comes in, it doesn't look like we'll have anything to work on this morning."

"That's okay," Johnny said. "I can only stay a few minutes. Mom's got a bunch of chores for me. I brought this for you." He handed the plastic bag to Eddy. "I wasn't sure what you might like, but I figured you could use a new hat."

Eddy opened the sack and tenderly lifted out a green and gold baseball cap with a Green Bay Packer emblem on the front. "Hey, it's beautiful, but you didn't have to give me anything. Just being my friend is enough." He adjusted the plastic strip in the back of the hat, tossed his old one in the wastebasket, and settled the new cap on his head. "It's a perfect fit."

"I don't know if you like football," Johnny said, like his gift wasn't good enough.

"I love football, and this is perfect. I've been a fan all my life and always wanted a Packer hat." Eddy looked embarrassed. "I don't have anything to give you."

Johnny finally broke down and began sobbing. He ran to Eddy and wrapped his arms around Eddy's waist. "Please don't go."

Eddy returned the hug, holding the boy until the sobs receded. "Just because I'll be gone doesn't mean I'll forget you. As long as we think about each other, we'll be together. And I have your address. I'll write if you promise to answer."

Johnny pushed away and ran to his bike. "I have to go. My Mom's waiting." He swung his leg over the bike and wiped the tears from his cheeks. "Goodbye, Eddy. I love you."

"I love you too Johnny." Eddy watched the boy cycle away, his eyes as sad as I'd ever seen.

"You're breaking Johnny's heart," I scolded.

Eddy looked like maybe his heart was also broken. "I know," he said, "but he'll get over it."

"Damnit, Eddy, can't you see he isn't going to get over it. After what you've done for him and Mary and Ruth, none of us will get over it."

"No matter what you think, everyone will be better off without me around," he said. "Now, I'd appreciate it if you'd leave me alone. I don't want to talk about it any more."

I wasn't ready to drop the conversation, but Eddy turned his back and walked away. I bit my tongue and figured I'd wait until we were home and I could enlist Mary's aid in arguing with him.

For the rest of the morning I watched the pumps while Eddy swept out the service bays and restocked the inventory from the storage area in the back. He took his time, like busy work would keep his mind occupied.

We closed the station at one o'clock and headed home. Mary had fixed a late lunch of tuna salad sandwiches. No one makes better tuna salad than Mary but none of us had the appetite to appreciate it. As we ate and made uncomfortable small talk, I couldn't help but think if Eddy left in the morning we would never see him again. It was Albert's last day all over again.

I had been proud and happy the morning Albert left for boot camp. His high school grades had been excellent and he could have gone to college to avoid the draft, but I'd done my hitch in the Marines and felt humble thinking he wanted to follow in my footsteps. I'd always considered the military a great way for a young man to cut the apron strings and learn independence. The discipline turned boys into men, and it was possible Albert would receive valuable training for civilian life. With his background he might even have been assigned to the motor pool where he'd sharpen his mechanical skills.

With the Vietnam War heating up there was always the chance he would be sent over there but I guess I just never allowed myself to believe he'd end up in Vietnam. Lots of military men never served in a combat zone.

Of course Mary was against it from the start, but women are always hesitant to see their children move out into the world. She had wanted him to go to college and get his degree before he made any decisions about the military. I'm pretty certain she hoped he would become an engineer or choose some other safe civilian occupation.

I'll always feel guilty because I didn't side with her and insist that Albert go on to school although in my heart I knew it was a decision Albert had to make for himself. There comes a time when you have to let your son take control of his own life.

Eddy had to make his own decisions also, but I still prayed we would find a way to change his mind. I needed Mary's support and she still hadn't spoken up.

We were almost finished eating when she finally confronted Eddy. Most likely she had waited this long because she was marshaling her arguments.

"I realize you haven't lived with us very long," she said, "but Sam and I feel as if you've become our own son"

Eddy held up his hand in protest like he was attempting to forestall what he realized was coming. "Mary, I know you're going to say something to try to convince me to stay. I can't. Don't make this any harder than it already is."

"Please, let me finish," Mary insisted. "When I was dying my greatest sadness was knowing Sam would be left alone to bear the pain and emptiness. But I had come to terms with my death. In my heart I felt a special comfort because I was going to be with Albert again. You've seen into my soul and must have some idea of the guilt and pain that has scared my heart for so many years. But even you can't truly understand how horrible it is for a mother to lose the child she grew in her womb and would always be part of her. It's like tearing out her heart."

Mary had begun crying. "Albert's death was cruel and unnatural. A mother understands her son will grow to manhood, leave home, and begin his own life, but in her heart she will always think of him as a little boy who needs comfort and support. For him to be ripped away before he's had a chance to really live is more than anyone should have to endure."

She had to pause a moment to control her tears before continuing. "I argued against Albert joining the Marines, but he was a grown man. It was his decision and I couldn't make it for him. I'll always feel there must have been something I could have done to keep him safe. Please don't take away my last chance to make up for losing Albert."

"I understand your pain," Eddy said. His voice was soft and I thought I could see tears in his eyes. "If I could touch you and Sam and take away your pain and guilt, I would, but my power doesn't work that way. Maybe we all must endure bitter sorrow in order to be human. Maybe it's the price God charges for our moments of joy and beauty."

"I know you would heal the scars in our hearts if you could," Mary said. "When we touched I believe I saw into your soul for an instant. Felt your pain and loneliness. There was a bond, as if we were kindred spirits. I knew then that you were sent here, not only to heal me and Johnny and Ruth, but also to share our lives. Perhaps you can't really be our son, but I firmly believe God meant for our home to be the end of your road."

"I feel closer to you and Sam than I have to anyone since my family died. Leaving here is the hardest decision I've ever made." Eddy took a deep breath. "Please try to understand that it's because I care for both of you, because of our bonds that I have to go. If I were responsible for another tragedy in your lives, I couldn't live with myself."

"Isn't there anything we can do to change your mind?" I asked, feeling completely helpless. "I agree with Mary. If not in our house, at least Cranston was meant to be the place where you could finally find peace and happiness."

"God, this is hard." Eddy's eyes reflected his agony. Mica reacted to his master's distress by placing a paw on Eddy's knee and laying his nose on his thigh.

"Someday you'll realize I didn't have any other choice," Eddy said. "Saying goodbye to both of you is like cutting off my arm. I've even been considering leaving this afternoon so we don't make this more painful."

"I won't hear of it," Mary insisted. She had dried her tears and tried to put on a brave front. "How far do you think you'd get before dark? And then you'd end up sleeping under a tree somewhere. I won't have you worrying me that way. Maybe we can't change your mind about leaving, but you're going to stay here tonight, and I won't take no for an answer."

For a moment we were all too emotionally drained to speak. I suppose Mary and I finally realized there was nothing more we could say or do.

"If you've absolutely made up your mind, we can't keep you here by force," I finally said. "At least let us help you. I've got a couple hundred dollars I want you to take. You're going to need it for food and lodging. Maybe I can drive you to Elliott tomorrow and you can catch a bus. It'd save some walking."

"Thanks, Sam, but I don't need your money. I've put away almost everything I've earned, and it'll tide me over until my next stop. The bus is a good idea, but they don't allow dogs, and there's no way Mica and I are going to be separated."

"We'll talk about it in the morning. Mary and I have agreed we'd like you to have the money. It'll give us comfort to know you and Mica won't have to starve or sleep in the rain."

"I really appreciate the offer, but I don't want something I haven't earned."

Mary reached over and touched Eddy's hand. "Don't talk to me about earning. You've given Sam and me back our lives. I'd say you've earned our love and gratitude and everything we own."

I could see Eddy didn't know how to respond, so I changed the subject. "Have you decided where you'll be going?" I tried to sound nonchalant, but don't believe I pulled it off very well. How can you sound unconcerned when your heart is bleeding?

"One place is as good as another. I thought I'd head toward the southwest. I haven't been there before." He pushed back from the table. "If you'll excuse me, I think I'll mow the lawn one last time."

"You don't have to do that. I can take care of it tomorrow."

"No, Sam, I'd really like to do it. Mowing the grass helps me keep my mind off things."

After Eddy and Mica went outside, Mary again began crying softly. They were the same tears of frustration and helplessness she'd shed when Albert had left for Vietnam. I wrapped her in my arms and we comforted each other.

Suddenly she pushed away and wiped the tears on her apron.

"Sam, I want you to take me into Elliott so I can do some shopping," she said. "I'm going to make a special dinner for Eddy tonight."

No one knew better than me how much strength it took for her to face this last evening with courage. If she couldn't change Eddy's mind, at least she wanted his final memories of us to be happy ones. As hard as we tried to make the evening pleasant, it didn't work.

Mary made fried chicken with mashed potatoes and chicken gravy. No one makes fried chicken like Mary and it was delicious, but the dinner wasn't much of a success. I had the feeling we were sharing the last meal with a condemned man. Obviously Mary and Eddy felt the same way because conversation was awkward and limited to completely neutral subjects. Its funny how, when someone is leaving, you have a million things you want to say, but can't think how to say them.

After dinner Eddy went outside to play with Mica while I helped Mary wash the dishes. Then we all watched TV for a couple of hours because the programs encouraged us to avoid talking. There just didn't seem to be anything we could say to each other. The evening was so awkward we finally gave up the effort and went to bed about ten.

In our individual ways we were all dreading the morning. I lay in bed for a long time wondering whether we would ever see Eddy again.

Twenty-Six

Because the prospect of Eddy leaving had upset me, I expected to spend a restless night. However, after barely sleeping at all Friday and the day's anxiety, I was exhausted. Instead of tossing and turning all night, I immediately fell into a deep sleep. I was dreaming about being adrift in a boat on an endless ocean, when a noise snapped me awake. For a moment I lay with my eyes closed, my heart pounding, uncertain whether the sound had been in my dream or in the house. Maybe I had awakened myself, crying out in my sleep. Over the years I had done that once or twice since Albert's death.

I turned my head and saw Mary lying on her side, her back toward me, her deep, steady breathing indicating she was still asleep. I obviously hadn't called out, because my yelling would have awakened her. Glancing at the luminous bedside clock, I saw it was a little past one thirty. It was too early to get up, but now that I was awake I became aware of an insistent pressure in my bladder. The bedroom window was open, a light breeze ruffling the curtains, and I hated the thought of crawling out of the warm bed and walking to the bathroom.

I had just about decided I wouldn't be able to drop off to sleep unless I made the trip, when the bedroom door opened with the soft squeak of a rusty hinge I was always intending to fix, but never had. A shadow slipped into the room and I could see from the size and shape that it was Eddy. The door opened further and I heard the click of Mica's toe nails on the floor.

"Sam, are you awake?" Eddy whispered, crouching beside the bed.

"Yeah," I said, automatically replying in a whisper.

"Keep your voice down and wake up Mary. Then both of you get dressed as quickly and quietly as you can."

I reached for the bedside lamp and Eddy stopped my hand. "No lights."

"What is it, Sam?" Mary mumbled, rolling over to face me.

"We don't have much time," Eddy said. "There are men outside and I think they're pouring gasoline around the house.

"Damnit, Eddy, you've been dreaming," I said, remembering the story about his family dying in the fire. "There isn't anyone outside."

"We don't have time to argue, Sam. I haven't been dreaming. We have to get out of the house."

Now that I was fully awake, I could hear the faint sounds of men moving in the yard, talking quietly. "What the hell is going on?" I asked. I inhaled deeply and detected the faint odor of gasoline fumes coming through the open window. Eddy hadn't been dreaming. ""How many are there?"

"I don't know," Eddy whispered. "I saw four, but there could be more. It doesn't make any difference how many there are. If they light the gas, we'll be trapped in the house."

I was already out of bed, pulling on my trousers. "Are you awake, Mary? Did you hear what Eddy said?"

"I'm frightened, Sam," Mary whispered, throwing back the covers, sitting up, and shuffling her feet searching for slippers.

I stepped around the bed and kissed her on the forehead. She wrapped her arms around my waist and held me tightly. "You get dressed as quickly as you can," I told her. "I'll call the sheriff. Then we're going to get out of here."

"I already tried to call the Sheriff," Eddy said. "The phone is dead. They must have cut the wires."

If the men outside had severed our link to the police they obviously intended something a lot more serious than just scaring us. I was frightened for Mary and Eddy, but the fear was quickly overwhelmed by an intense anger. If the Sheriff couldn't help, I sure as hell would protect my own family and property. I went to the closet and grabbed my pump shotgun. I groped on the shelf, found the box of shells, and began loading the magazine.

"What are you doing, Sam?" Mary's voice was rising in fright.

"Keep your voice down, Mary," I hissed. "I'm loading my shotgun. I'll be damned if a bunch of drunken goons are going to attack me in my own house."

"Please, Sam, no guns," Mary pleaded. "You're scaring me."

"If those bastards are looking for trouble, I think the shotgun will make them think twice. I don't intend to shoot anyone unless I have to.

"Come on, both of you," Eddy whispered. "We don't have time for this. We have to get out of here, and we have to get out now."

"No one's driving me out of my home," I insisted.

"Damnit, Sam, think about Mary. You can't let her get caught in a burning building."

I knew Eddy was right. I grabbed Mary by the arm, clutching the shotgun in my other hand, and began directing her toward the stairs.

"Wait," Mary whispered urgently, pulling away and going back toward the bedroom.

"What is it?" I hissed.

"My album. I'm not leaving without my pictures of Albert."

"Damnit, hurry. We don't have time to fool around."

Mary was gone only a moment and returned carrying the large album that contained all of a mother's memories of her son.

It was a cloudy night, and the hallway was pitch black, but I knew the layout even in the dark, so I led the way. When we reached the kitchen Eddy moved to the window. Keeping his back to the wall, he lifted the curtain edge and looked out. Mica stood protectively at the back door, a low, throaty growl the only sound in the room.

"I can see one of them standing near the garage," Eddy whispered. "We're going to have to get the truck." He moved toward the door. "You two wait here. I'll get the pickup and drive it to the back porch. You both be ready to jump in."

"How the hell are you going to get the truck? You don't even drive."

"Just because I don't drive doesn't mean I don't know how." He reached for the doorknob and I put a restraining hand on his shoulder.

"Wait a second," I insisted. "You said you saw at least four of them. They'll be watching the doors. When you go out, they'll jump you. You'll never make it as far as the garage."

"Someone has to try. Do you have a better plan?"

"Yes. You and I'll go out together. Two of us will have a better chance."

In the darkness I saw Eddy shaking his head. "You can't leave Mary alone. If they jump us, she'll be helpless."

He was right. I couldn't leave Mary in the house and it didn't seem like a good idea to expose her to the danger of dashing for the truck. I made a decision quickly. "Okay, then we'll use plan B. You and I will go out together. I'll stay on the porch while you run for the garage. I'll fire the shotgun in the air to attract their attention and keep their heads down. That should give you the edge you need."

Eddy hesitated only a moment. "Alright, let's do it."

He pulled open the kitchen door and slipped outside. I was right behind, holding the shotgun muzzle up. Mica darted past my leg, scaring the hell out of me. The smell of gasoline was strong in the backyard.

I didn't see anyone in the yard, but with no moon, there were enough shadows to hide a dozen men.

Eddy ran in a low crouch and had almost reached the pickup when a man stepped from the shadows and grabbed for him. I fired the shotgun in the air at the same moment I saw Mica leaping at the man's throat. Dog and man went down in a heap. Eddy opened the driver's side door and dove into the truck.

"What are you bastards doing in my yard?" I yelled. "Get the hell out of here or I'll blow your balls off."

I heard a voice shout from the side of the house. "The sonofabitch has a shotgun."

"I'll fix that," someone answered from behind the garage.

The truck's starter was grinding and I knew from the sound that the spark plug wires had been pulled.

Suddenly there was a bright flash of light from the back of the garage. I heard the gunshot at the same instant I felt an impact against my side, like someone had hit me with a baseball bat. The force of the wallop must have driven me backward through the screen door, because I found myself lying on the kitchen floor.

Mary screamed and dropped beside me, cradling my head in her lap. I tried to brush her away and stand up, but didn't have any strength. I touched my side and the hand came away sticky with blood. I had never been shot before, and was surprised I didn't feel any pain.

"God, Sam, don't die." Mary was crying and rocking back and forth, stroking my head. "Please don't die."

I wanted to reassure her, but I didn't know whether I was dying or not. I was weak and there was a fuzziness in my head, like I had been drinking. I could feel my thoughts beginning to drift.

Through the haze I heard more gunshots and figured they were shooting at Eddy. He was any easy target in the truck because the thin metal body sure as hell wouldn't stop a bullet. I knew I should be moving, helping Mary out of the house, backing up Eddy with the shotgun but I couldn't even lift my head.

"Light the goddamn fire," A vaguely familiar voice yelled. I had heard that lisping voice before, but was too weary, too fuzzy to follow the thought.

With a whoosh, a wall of flames suddenly engulfed the house. The bastards must have circled the building with gasoline because everything was instantly on fire.

"Mary, get out of the house." I was shouting, but I could barely hear my own voice.

Mary was sobbing, holding my head. "I won't leave you, Sam. Not after all these years."

I knew Mary didn't have the strength to carry me and I couldn't help. "Please get out of here," I pleaded. "If you stay here you'll die."

"Then we'll die together," she said, holding me close and stroking my forehead.

A figure hurtled through the wall of flames engulfing the back porch. I thought the bastards were coming into the house and decided it was the stupidest move they could make. All they had to do was wait a few minutes and we'd burn to death.

Eddy knelt beside me. His face was soot streaked and there were wisps of smoke on his shirt where the flames had scorched it. His sleeve was blood soaked. I tried to smile at him, but couldn't even do that. He squeezed my shoulder.

Picking up the shotgun from where it had fallen on the kitchen floor, he took charge of the situation. "Mary, we have to get out of here." He was coughing so badly I could barely understand him. "Are you hurt? Can you walk?"

The smoke had thickened and was stinging my eyes, making me cough, but the air was still breathable near the floor. The paint on the cabinets began to blister from the intense heat. Even in my pain drugged mind I was amazed at how quickly my house was burning. In a moment walls and ceilings would begin falling.

"I won't leave Sam," Mary said, coughing and gagging in the thick smoke.

"We aren't going to leave Sam," Eddy said, sounding weak and tired. "I'm going to fire the shotgun into the yard to keep their heads down. Then I want you to run through the fire as quickly as you can. I'll carry Sam out."

Mary stood up and I felt Eddy's strong hands lifting me, setting me on a kitchen chair. "Hold him up for a minute," he said to Mary.

The smoke was thicker away from the floor and I began gasping for air. I leaned against Mary as she supported me with her free arm. I could feel her chest heaving as she tried to suck in air, but she still clung to her precious album.

Eddy emptied the pump shotgun blindly into the barrier of flames already eating through the kitchen walls. I heard the weapon clatter to the floor and Eddy pulled my arm behind his neck and jerked me to his shoulders in a fireman's lift. I felt him stagger under my weight and wondered if he could haul me as far as the back yard. I was a lot bigger than him.

"Go Mary!" he shouted and I felt myself being rushed through the flames, the heat scorching my legs and arms.

Then we were in the clean, cool night and I filled my lungs with the smoke free air. Eddy laid me on the ground and Mary threw herself on me. The numbness from my wound had worn off and pain racked my side. In the distance sirens screamed and I knew one of the neighbors must have called the fire department. They would be too late for the house, but maybe their arrival would save Eddy and Mary.

"Let's get the hell out of here," the tauntingly familiar voice lisped from near the driveway.

There was a last flurry of gunshots. I heard Mica yelp with pain. Eddy groaned and dropped to the ground beside me. Wet drops splattered my face and I thought it had begun to rain. But the drops were sticky and smelled vaguely like copper. Mary was screaming hysterically when a wave of blackness washed over me and I heard nothing more.

Twenty-Seven

"Are you awake, Sam?"

I knew it was Mary's voice, but it sounded dreamlike, as if it were filtered through a thick fog. A cool hand began stroking my forehead and I opened my eyes.

Still in a haze, I wondered why Mary's hair was frizzled on the ends and her face was red, as if she were sunburned. My mind groped for an answer, but I had difficulty focusing. Suddenly I remembered the fire and the gunshots and the fear. When I turned my head I saw the white, sterile walls of a hospital room. I tried to move, but had no strength and even the slight motion caused a sharp pain in my side.

"Don't try to get up." Mary kissed me on the forehead. "You're in the hospital, but you're going to be all right."

I reached out and touched her. "Are you okay? Were you hurt?" My voice was barely a whisper coming from a dry, sore throat.

"I'm fine." She held a glass of water so I could sip from the straw. The liquid felt wonderfully cool going down. "You and Eddy saved my life," Mary said. "I only have a few minor buns."

"Is Eddy okay?" I remembered the blood and the darkness and Eddy groaning as he fell beside me.

"Yes, he's recovering nicely." Mary had never been a good liar, and I could hear the fiction in her voice.

"Where is he?" I asked, afraid Eddy had died and Mary was trying to spare me.

"He's upstairs in intensive care but Doc Calvin says he'll pull through just fine. You rest now."

"Our house?" I mumbled. "The fire?"

"You rest now," Mary insisted, soothing my forehead with a cool, damp cloth. "We can talk later."

I didn't want to sleep, but I was so very tired. I drifted off even as Mary was speaking.

* * *

When I woke again, Doc Calvin was standing at the foot of the bed reading my chart.

"Good to see you back in the land of the living, Sam. How are you feeling?"

"I feel like hell, if you really want to know." Actually I felt much better than the last time I had awakened. At least my mind was clear.

A cute young nurse helped me drink. The water was deliciously cool as it soothed my sore throat.

"Where's Mary?" I asked, suddenly afraid I had only dreamed seeing her.

"Mary's fine. Only a few minor burns. I convinced her to take a break while I checked you out."

Just knowing Mary hadn't been a figment of my imagination, I felt some of the tension easing. "What are my damages?" I asked.

"Other than a few minor burns and a good deal of smoke in your lungs, you had a gunshot wound in your side. The bullet hit a rib and deflected away from any vital organs. You've got a broken rib and a nasty wound. You lost a lot of blood, but there isn't any permanent damage. However, I suspect you'll be my guest for a few days."

"What about Eddy?" I asked, desperately wanting Doc to confirm he was still alive.

"Well, he's in a somewhat more serious condition—but not critical. He had bullet wounds to his head, his arm, and his chest. The head wound was minor—the bullet glancing off his skull. Eddy's head must be as hard as yours. Another bullet went through his bicep and tore up the muscles. It'll take a while before he has full strength in the arm, but it should recover completely. The chest wound was the most serious. The bullet punctured a lung and lodged near his spine. An inch or so to the right and it might have been fatal. He had lost a great deal of blood and was very weak. It was touch and go for a while, but he's passed the crisis. If there aren't any complications, I'll be moving him into this room tomorrow. You won't mind having him as a roommate, will you?"

"That would be great." I remembered Eddy carrying me out of the house. Now I owed him both Mary's and my life.

"Sheriff Simpson is here," Doc said. "Do you feel up to talking with him?"

"Guess I'll have to sooner or later."

Simpson came into the room like he had been waiting in the hallway. He stepped aside to let Doc out, and then settled into the bedside chair. He was all business. Didn't even bother to ask how I was doing, but he never did have much of a bedside manner.

"Your wife gave me a pretty good picture of what happened Sunday morning. Your version can wait until later. Right now I want to know whether you saw anyone you recognized."

"It was too damned dark. All I saw were shadows and shapes." The memory of the last few moments came back to me and I recalled the lisping voice that had seemed familiar. "But I recognized one of voices. It was Joe Black."

"There was a lot of confusion Sunday morning. Are you certain it was Black's voice you heard?"

"Damn right I'm certain. Black is a regular customer at my station and I've talked with him several times at the lumberyard. He has a distinctive lisp I'd know anywhere. There's no doubt in my mind he was one of the hoodlums."

"Well, at least that gives me somewhere to start. Anything else you remember?"

I shook my head.

"If something comes to mind, give me a call." Simpson stood up to leave. "Doc said I could only stay a couple of minutes.

"Henry, you'll keep me up to date on what's happening, won't you?"

"Sure," Simpson agreed. "You've got a right to know."

When the Sheriff left, Mary came into the room looking like she hadn't had a good night's sleep in a while. She sat in the chair and held my hand. In response to my questioning, she told me it was Wednesday and then filled me in on everything that had happened since the early hours of Sunday morning.

Mica had also been shot and a Sheriff's deputy had taken him to a veterinarian in Elliott. Mary had just returned from checking on him and he was recovering nicely, but was heartbroken without Eddy. A bullet had gone through the fleshy part of one rear leg and he had bruises where he'd probably been kicked. I suppose if we had to have a fire and shootings, we were lucky no one had been killed.

Our house was a complete loss, burned to the ground, a smoldering pile of rubble. The adjuster had already assured Mary the insurance company would pay for all damages. All damages. What a misnomer. How could they pay for the laugher and tears and memorabilia that had gone up in smoke? How do you compensate for warmth and love and pain and memories?

"Damnit, Mary, I'm sorry," I said. "Everything we owned is gone. What are we going to do?"

"We're going to start over again. We have each other and I managed to save our album. None of the other things were important. We'll rebuild the house. It'll be just like when we were kids starting out. When you think about it, we're better off than we were in the beginning. We still have the service station. We'll be just fine."

"The service station won't be much good without someone to run it. By the time I'm able to work again, we'll have lost all of our customers."

"Don't worry about that. Young Billy Thornton and some of his friends are taking turns keeping it open."

All the medication must have made me more emotional than normal because tears began forming. I felt grateful beyond words that Billy was pitching in to keep the service station going. It eased my concerns about our source of income, but money was only a part of the problem.

"We don't have a place to live," I said. "Where are you staying?"

"Sunday night I stayed with Sally and Johnny. Lisa offered to share her apartment, but it really is quite tiny. Then Aaron and Helen Goldstein insisted I stay with them. They have a lovely guest room. When you and Eddy get out of the hospital we can all stay there until we find a place to live. So don't worry about any of that. You just concentrate on getting better."

It was such a relief knowing we had good friends who were taking care of things that I drifted off to sleep again.

Sheriff Simpson stopped by Thursday morning and told me Joe Black had disappeared, but one of his drinking buddies, Willy Jacobs, had been apprehended when he approached a doctor for treatment of dog bites on his wrist and hand. I figured Mica had gotten hold of him when Eddy had run to the truck. As soon as Willy was questioned he implicated Joe Black and two other men, Roger Tortino and Jim Bilhof. Willy also admitted they had been the ones who had beaten Eddy on May first.

I knew Willy slightly because his Dad and I had occasionally fished together. I'd always thought he was a nice kid, but a little wild, like a lot of youngsters are. I assumed Tortino and Bilhof were from Elliott or one of the other little towns in the area, and wondered if they were the two thugs Deputy Alshard had scared away from my station.

Sheriff Simpson said Jacobs, Tortino, and Bilhof had already been arrested and charged with attempted murder, assault to commit bodily harm, conspiracy, and arson. They were facing a long stretch in prison. A warrant had been issued for Joe Black who would confront the same charges when he was caught.

Only hours after the three were behind bars, a high priced lawyer, Sidney Westlake, had appeared to represent them. Simpson told me none of the men had the kind of money it would take to afford Westlake. That made me wonder if someone with deep pockets, like Ernest Bennett, was footing the bill. Westlake hadn't been Bennett's attorney at Eddy's hearing, but that didn't mean anything. Ernest could have hired a lawyer from out of the area.

On orders from their expensive counsel, all three men refused to give further statements. It didn't really make a great deal of difference. Sheriff Simpson had already gotten search warrants and found their rifles concealed under some boxes in Tortino's garage. He figured ballistics at the State Capitol would be able to match slugs recovered at our house. He had also located the convenience station where the four men had purchased enough gasoline to fill three five gallon cans. The attendant on duty Saturday night was willing and able to identify them. Simpson figured he had enough evidence to convict the bastards no matter who their attorney was.

As Doc Calvin had promised, early Thursday afternoon Eddy was moved into my semi-private room and settled in the bed closest to the window. He was wrapped in bandages and looked like he had come very close to dying.

"I'm not going to be able to cure you for a while," was the first thing he said when the nurse and orderly left. "I just don't have the strength."

"Don't worry about it." I said. "Maybe I need to recuperate on my own to pay for my sins."

Eddy smiled. "You may be right about that."

"Sam may be right about what?" Mary asked as she returned from lunching in the hospital cafeteria.

"He's giving me a hard time because I'm not going to cure him for a few days," Eddy said.

"After risking your life to carry him out of our burning house, he shouldn't tease you about anything," Mary scolded as she leaned over Eddy and kissed him on the forehead. Eddy's touch visibly eased the strain and tension of the last several days. Maybe he didn't have enough strength to cure my injuries, but obviously he still had the power to comfort Mary.

"I don't know if it's a good idea having you two in the same room, but it'll certainly make life easier for me." Mary looked refreshed as she settled in her bedside chair. "Now I won't have to chase back and forth between floors."

"Hi, everyone." Lisa swept into the room. Her bright smile encompassed us all, but was obviously directed at Eddy. There were fatigue lines around her eyes, like she hadn't been sleeping well. "I can only stay a few minutes," she said. "I'm on duty and you aren't supposed to have visitors yet. When I heard Eddy had been moved from ICU, I begged the head nurse to let me sneak up here so I could see my two heroes."

"I don't feel much like a hero," I complained. "Seems more like I came in second best." Lisa's concern was gratifying even though I knew she'd really come to see Eddy.

"You won't get into trouble for visiting, will you?" Mary asked. "They won't fire you or anything like that, will they?"

"Of course not," Lisa said, smiling brightly. "Volunteers aren't paid so we get away with a lot. Besides, if anyone sees me they'll think I'm working."

Lisa leaned over and kissed me on the forehead. "I'm happy you're all right, Sam."

"Not half as happy as I am to still be alive. I've had enough excitement to last the rest of my life."

Lisa acknowledged my lame humor with a tired smile before she turned to Eddy and kissed him on the forehead. "I was frightened you were going to die."

"I'm too tough to let a few bullets kill me." Eddy took her hand and I could see Lisa's tension ease as the warm, happy sensation swept through her.

"I feel absolutely terrible about those hoodlums burning your house and shooting you," she said, addressing both of us. "It just doesn't seem possible anything like that could happen in Cranston."

"If the Sheriff does his job, maybe it won't happen again," I said.

Before we could settle into aimless chatter, another unauthorized visitor burst into the room. I was pretty certain Ernest Bennett wasn't there to offer condolences. He looked like a man with an urgent mission. His hair was imperfectly combed, his silk necktie looked like it had been hurriedly knotted, and he hadn't bothered to shave this morning.

"Daddy, what are you dong here?" Lisa seemed startled by his sudden appearance.

He glanced around the room, quickly dismissing the rest of us as unimportant before concentrating on Lisa. "I'm taking you with me on a business trip and we have to leave right now." He sounded frantic and unsure of himself.

"What are you talking about?" Lisa seemed genuinely mystified. "You never take me on business trips."

"We don't have time to argue about this. We've got a plane to catch." Ernest stepped past my bed, grabbed Lisa's arm and began pulling her toward the doorway.

She spun loose and retreated around Eddy's bed. "What's wrong with you, Daddy? You're acting crazy." His aggressive attitude was obviously frightening her. "I'm not going anywhere with you while you're behaving like this."

Eddy was struggling to reach across his body for something on the far side of the bed. Even if there was some object he could use as a weapon, I didn't believe he had the strength to protect Lisa.

"It isn't open for discussion," Ernest snarled. There was a wild look in his eyes and he seemed on the verge of doing something desperate. "You're coming with me whether you like it or not."

"Damnit, Ernest, Lisa said she doesn't want to go with you," I shouted.

Ernest looked at me with pure hatred in his eyes. "None of this concerns you," he growled. "If you know what's good for you, you'll mind your own business."

"And what will happen if I don't?" I demanded, attempting to distract him. "Will you have someone burn down my house?"

Ernest ignored my comments, apparently dismissing me as a threat. He focused on Lisa, like she was the only person in the room. When he took a menacing step toward her, Mary moved between them.

"Ernest, please calm down," she said in a soothing voice. "You're frightening Lisa."

"Stay the hell out of my way." He swept Mary aside, nearly knocking her down.

Pushing Mary was more than I could tolerate. "You bastard," I said, attempting to sit up. The pain took away my breath and I realized I was helpless. Fortunately Eddy had finally reached the object he'd been fumbling for and repeatedly pushed the call button.

"If I have to drag you out of here, I will," Ernest threatened Lisa.

I doubt whether she had ever seen her father so out of control. She looked like a frightened little girl as she grabbed a small plastic tray from Eddy's bedside table and held it up like a weapon. "If you come any closer I'll hit you," she warned.

It seemed an eternity since Eddy had pushed the call button, but it couldn't have been more than a few seconds.

"What's going on in here?" The duty nurse stood in the doorway looking confused. Apparently an angry visitor was more than she was prepared to handle.

As usual, Mary was the only one thinking clearly. "Call security," she ordered.

The nurse hesitated long enough to realize she needed help. Then turned and ran toward the nursing station.

Ernest was so flushed with anger I don't believe he had even noticed the nurse. "Are you coming with me or do I have to drag you?" he hissed.

"I'm not going with you," Lisa was trembling and had shifted the tray so it was in front of her like a shield.

"If you have to catch a plane, you'd better go before hospital security gets here," Eddy said, attempting to sit up in spite of the pain.

Ernest turned on him furiously. "This is all your fault. I didn't give Lisa every possible luxury and send her to fancy schools so she could get involved with a freak like you."

"Lisa has a right to make her own decisions," Eddy said. "If you don't get out of here, you're going to say something you'll regret."

"Daddy, please go." Lisa moved closer to Eddy and reached for his hand. "I'm staying here with my friends."

Ernest was so furious I wouldn't have been surprised to see steam coming out of his ears. "Friends! These people are all freaks and losers. I thought I'd taught you to be a winner, but I should have known you'd be just as stupid and obstinate a bitch as your mother," he shouted.

"Don't you dare call Mom a bitch." Lisa might have been scared to death, but her temper suddenly flared. She took a step toward Ernest. "Mom was a sweet, loving person, and too good for you. If I'm stupid and obstinate it's your fault."

"Don't flatter yourself," Ernest snarled. "You aren't even my daughter. Your sweet, loving Mother was a tramp who slept with anyone wearing pants. Just like a street corner whore, she got herself knocked up in the back seat of Adam Fletcher's Chevy."

Lisa turned pale and her knees buckled, like she'd been struck a physical blow. I think she would have collapsed if she hadn't backed up to the wall. "That's a lie," she wailed. "My Mother wasn't a tramp. You're a hateful, bitter old man."

A heavyset security guard rushed into the room, followed closely by a younger companion. "What's going on in here?" he demanded.

Mary was still calm and in control as she pointed at Ernest. "That man has gone berserk. You'd better get him out of here before he hurts someone."

"Come along, sir." The heavyset guard took hold of Ernest's arm. "Let's not have any trouble."

Ernest shook free of the grip. "Keep your goddamned hands off me," he shouted. "Do you have any idea who you're dealing with?"

"I don't care who you are," the guard said. "You're causing a disturbance and you'll have to leave. Are you coming along peacefully or will we have to restrain you?"

For an instant it looked like Ernest was going to resist. Then the fury was suddenly gone as he must have realized he wasn't strong enough to overcome two big men. "Keep your hands off me. I'm leaving." He turned to Lisa as the security men escorted him from the room. "Adam Fletcher was a loser, and obviously being a loser is in your blood. You belong here with these other freaks and losers. You're a slut just like your Mother, and I'm better off without you."

"My mother wasn't a slut," Lisa moaned, almost to herself. She collapsed onto a chair and began sobbing violently. Mary went to her and wrapped the hysterical girl in a warm embrace.

I looked across at Eddy a question in my eyes. For a long moment there was no response, but finally, with a resigned look, Eddy gave a brief nod.

The tension eased as I lay back on my bed. It seemed anti-climatic to learn Ernest was so egotistical he had nearly killed three people simply because he didn't want anyone to know Lisa wasn't his daughter.

Twenty-Eight

When Lisa had cried herself dry, she used our bathroom to wash her face and fix her makeup.

"I have to get back to work before my supervisor wonders where I am," she said, although she didn't appear to be in any condition to continue working.

"Maybe you should take the rest of the day off," Eddy suggested.

"I'll be okay." Lisa attempted a reassuring smile. "I've only got another hour on my shift."

"What will you do then?" Mary asked, her motherly instincts aroused. "Where will you go? I don't think you should be alone right now. Maybe it would be better if you came back here and spent the evening with us." If our house hadn't been a pile of rubble, I'm sure my wife would have offered her a bed for the night.

Lisa hugged Mary and kissed her cheek. "Thank you for your concern, but I'll be alright. I need time by myself so I can sort all of this out in my mind." She leaned over Eddy so he could hug her with his good arm.

"It'll be okay," he said softly. His touch seemed to restore some of Lisa's strength.

As soon as she left, I turned to Eddy. "You could have told us Ernest's secret. We might have been able to figure out why he thought it was so important that he tried to kill us all."

Eddy shook his head. "It wouldn't have prevented any of this. I didn't want Lisa to know. You saw how much it hurt her."

"You may be right," I agreed. "I just don't understand how it could have been so important to Ernest that it justified all the harm he caused."

Mary patted my hand. "There's no way to justify what he did, but I think I can understand his motivation," she said. "Ernest is a perfect example of someone who acts superior and mean because he has low self esteem. He couldn't stand for people to believe he had normal human flaws. He must have realized no one really likes him but he could live with that as long as everyone respected him because of his money and power. It was all he had. I believe he was afraid he would lose that respect if folks knew his wife had rejected him for another man."

"It had to be something like that," Eddy agreed. "Like a lot of other people, he's hiding behind a mask. Inside he's a frightened, miserable man."

"Okay, I can accept that," I said. "But I still don't understand why he came to the hospital to get Lisa. It doesn't make any sense."

"Ernest had to always be on top, a winner," Eddy explained. "Since the fire everything has been falling apart for him. Maybe he was afraid if Lisa stayed around me she'd learn his secret. I believe he was trying to keep the truth from her because he really wanted Lisa to be his daughter."

"It still doesn't make any sense," I complained. "If he was so desperate to keep his secret, why did he blurt it out that way?"

Eddy shook his head. "Sam, there are lots of things that won't ever make sense. Ernest had lost control, and when people are angry or frustrated they say things they're immediately sorry for because they can't take them back."

"No matter why he came here, there's no excuse for blurting out his secret that way, making Lisa's mother sound like the villain," Mary said, tears filling her eyes. "Ernest may be a mean, selfish man, but he must have strong feelings for Lisa. In his own way he probably even loves her. I can't help feeling sorry for both of them."

"Maybe it's best for Lisa to know about her parents," Eddy said. "It will hurt for a little while, but in her heart she realizes her mother was a good person."

"Ernest might be insecure and scared, but he's still a bastard." I wasn't willing to forgive him or cut him any slack. "When she gets over the shock, Lisa will be grateful she didn't inherit any of Ernest's genes."

* * *

Apparently Eddy and I were recovering according to schedule, because on Friday Doc Calvin allowed visitors. He must have decided if we had survived Ernest Bennett we were strong enough to handle the company.

Lisa was our first official visitor, arriving about ten o'clock, bringing a large bouquet. She looked like she hadn't slept at all. After placing the flowers in a water pitcher, she sat in the chair between our beds. She looked so depressed Eddy reached out and took her hand. His touch must have gone a long way toward healing her pain because she attempted a tired smile.

"Thank you for the flowers," Mary said. She had quietly entered the room and taken her usual seat beside my bed. "They're beautiful, but you didn't need to bring anything."

"I know," Lisa said. "But I had to do something to make up for yesterday. I'm so ashamed of the way my father—I mean Ernest—behaved."

"It wasn't your fault." Eddy squeezed her hand. "I'm sorry you had to learn about your parents that way."

"It must have been a terrible shock," Mary agreed. "How are you holding up?"

"Better than I would have expected, considering my whole world has been turned upside down. I still can't get used to the idea the man I called Dad all my life isn't really my father. I suppose I should hate him, but I want to believe he was protecting me. He did take care of me after Mom died, when he could have just walked away."

Mary came around the bed and hugged Lisa. "Just remember it doesn't change who you are. Sam and Eddy and I will always be your friends."

"I appreciate that, but it's a huge adjustment to realize I'm an orphan now. I don't even know if my name should still be Lisa Bennett or something else."

"Of course you're still Lisa Bennett. Even if Ernest disowned you, that wouldn't change."

I suppose you're right." Lisa sighed. "The worst part is that I never really knew my actual father."

"Adam was a good man," I said. It had been years since Adam had been killed in a car accident, but I remembered him as a handsome, gentle man with the sort of charm that drew people to him. He had coached Albert's summer league baseball team and had always treated my son like a little brother. Now that I knew the truth, I could see a lot of his personality in Lisa. "You would have loved him, and been proud to call him Dad, just as he must have been proud of you."

"Thank you Sam, that's sweet. Maybe someday you'll tell me about him. I'd really like to know what sort of man my real father was."

"It'd be my pleasure," I said.

Eddy squeezed her hand. "Lisa, don't hold on to the pain. You have to let go of the past and move forward."

"I'm trying, but I'm so confused. I feel as if I'm to blame in some way. Maybe if I had listened to Sam I could have prevented all this."

"It probably wouldn't have made any difference," I said. "We still don't know for certain Ernest had anything to do with the fire."

"I hate to say this about my father." Lisa shook her head. "It's going to take a while before I can remember he isn't my father. Any way, I'm certain Ernest was behind everything. I believe when he heard the news reports about the arrest of the men responsible for the fire and shooting, it scared him. He's disappeared on that supposed business trip and no one knows where he went, but he took a lot of cash from his bank account. I'm pretty sure he hired Sidney Westlake to defend those thugs. Westlake is the head of the firm that handles most of his legal work." Lisa attempted another smile. "I'm so confused. I don't know whether I ever want to see him again."

Before we could continue the conversation and before I could make some acid comments, Johnny and Sally Winthrop dropped in bearing flowers.

Johnny went directly to Eddy and leaned over the bed to hug him. He began to cry. "I was afraid you were going to die," he sobbed.

Eddy stroked Johnny's head with his undamaged hand. The touch immediately quieted the boy. "Hey like I told Lisa, I'm too tough to let a few bullets slow me down."

Sally was looking pretty uncomfortable standing in the middle of the room with her arms full of flowers. Mary quickly accepted the bouquet and placed it in my water pitcher. "It was nice of you to come Sally," Mary said including her in the conversation.

"I didn't have any choice. Johnny would have run away from home if I didn't bring him over as soon as you both could have visitors."

"Who's watching the diner?" Mary asked.

"I closed for a couple of hours. We won't be able to stay very long."

Since it was nearly lunch time, closing the diner was a serious gesture on her part. But she owed Eddy nearly as much as I did.

"Johnny, I'm sorry," Eddy said. "I lost my Green Bay Packer hat in the fire."

"That's okay," the boy said, like the cap wasn't important compared to his hero being alive. "I'll get you another one."

At that moment Aaron and Helen Goldstein entered carrying a huge bouquet of flowers. The room was beginning to look and smell like a funeral parlor. They also brought a special guest.

Mica shot into the room, and when Aaron released his grip on the leash, the dog leapt onto Eddy's bed, frantically licking his master's face. I figured Aaron Goldstein must have been a big shot on the hospital board in order to get away with sneaking a dog into our room.

"Hey, Mica, take it easy, boy." The dog jumping on him must have been painful, but Eddy had a huge smile.

The fur on Mica's hind leg had been shaved off and there was a big white bandage over his wound. The injury didn't seem to slow him down one little bit.

"Thank you for bringing Mica. But I don't have the money to pay a veterinarian's bill," Eddy said. "I'm afraid all my cash went up in the fire."

"Don't worry about it," Aaron responded. "Doc Schuster is a friend of mine and didn't charge anything for the treatment. Helen and I have agreed that Mica can stay with us until you folks find a place to live. Ruth has fallen in love with him."

"Thank you. I appreciate that," Eddy said.

"It's our pleasure. Just remember, if you need a lawyer to handle any of this mess, I'm ready and willing to help." He turned to me. "If you need any assistance rebuilding, let me know. I've got a lot of contacts in the construction industry."

Sally and Johnny only stayed about half an hour, and the Goldsteins just a bit longer. Although Mica was reluctant to leave Eddy, Aaron dragged him out at the end of his leash. Lisa lingered until the volunteers began delivering the evening meal. She had been holding Eddy's hand and I was pleased to see the bond strengthening between them. Maybe my plans for Lisa and Eddy would work out after all.

Before Lisa left she leaned over and gave him a kiss on the lips that Eddy returned. I knew we would see Lisa again soon. If she was half as smart as I thought she was, she'd finagle a way to be assigned to our floor

Mary remained in the room after everyone was gone, waiting patiently while Eddy and I began eating.

"It's going to be a long time before you're strong enough to leave Cranston," she finally said to Eddy. "I think the worst that could happen is over. If Ernest Bennett has really left town, he won't be able to cause more problems. Now that his secret is out, there just isn't any reason for you to even consider going away."

"There could be more trouble" Eddy said. "Ernest Bennett isn't the only person with secrets. Look at all the problems I've already caused. Your house is burned down and you've lost everything you owned. On top of that Sam's been shot."

"We haven't lost everything," Mary said. "We have a future. We didn't have that before you came to Cranston."

"And it's probably a good thing the house burned down." I suggested. "It needed a lot of repairs. Now I won't have to worry about fixing up the place."

"It does look like I won't be going anywhere for a while, but the trouble could get worse. You both could get killed next time."

"Nothing else is going to happen," I argued. "Look at all the people who want you to stay. Sally and Johnny. Aaron and Helen and Ruth. Lisa. Mary. Me. Particularly Lisa. You've got friends here. This is your chance to settle down and finally have a home."

"I don't know," Eddy said. "I'll think about it."

"We're going to require a strong young man to help us rebuild," Mary suggested. "And Sam is going to need someone to help at the station."

"We'll see," Eddy said

I could tell from the tone of voice that we had finally won him over. By the time he recovered enough to travel, I was certain Lisa would have convinced him to settle down. Mary and I were going to have the son we had lost so many years ago. Life was looking good. I was beginning to believe it had been worth a gunshot wound.

* * *

That's the entire story, written down exactly as it happened. I suspect there are some people who won't believe a word of it, but everyone in Cranston knows it's the gospel truth.

The four thugs who burned the house and shot us were all convicted of the handful of charges against them. When they realized they were going to prison for a long time, they turned State's evidence for reduced sentences and implicated Ernest Bennett as the man who had hired them. A warrant was immediately issued for Ernest, but I doubt whether it will ever be served.

Ernest still hasn't returned to Cranston. The word is that he's living in Canada and isn't likely to come back until the statute of limitations has run out.

I hear Mary calling. We have to attend the christening of a bouncing baby boy. He's a very lucky child to have been born in Henderson County. It seems as if during the last year or so almost no one ever gets sick around here.

The baby is Eddy and Lisa's first child and they're going to name him Samuel. I don't know whether that makes him my namesake, but it certainly makes me proud and happy. They asked Mary and me to be the godparents. I hope they let me hold the baby during the ceremony. I get a warm, happy feeling every time I touch that little boy.

If you enjoyed this book, please consider posting a review on Amazon. Even if it's only a few sentences, it would be a huge help for other readers when they make a decision whether a book is worth reading. This link will take you directly to *The Vagabond Healer* Amazon book page: https://www.amazon.com/dp/0980071682

www.ingramcontent.com/pod-product-compliance
Lightning Source LLC
Chambersburg PA
CBHW022139240626
47153CB00007B/2419